TREADING

Water

Notes From The Deep End

DANIELLA BLUE

OLIVERHEBERBOOKS

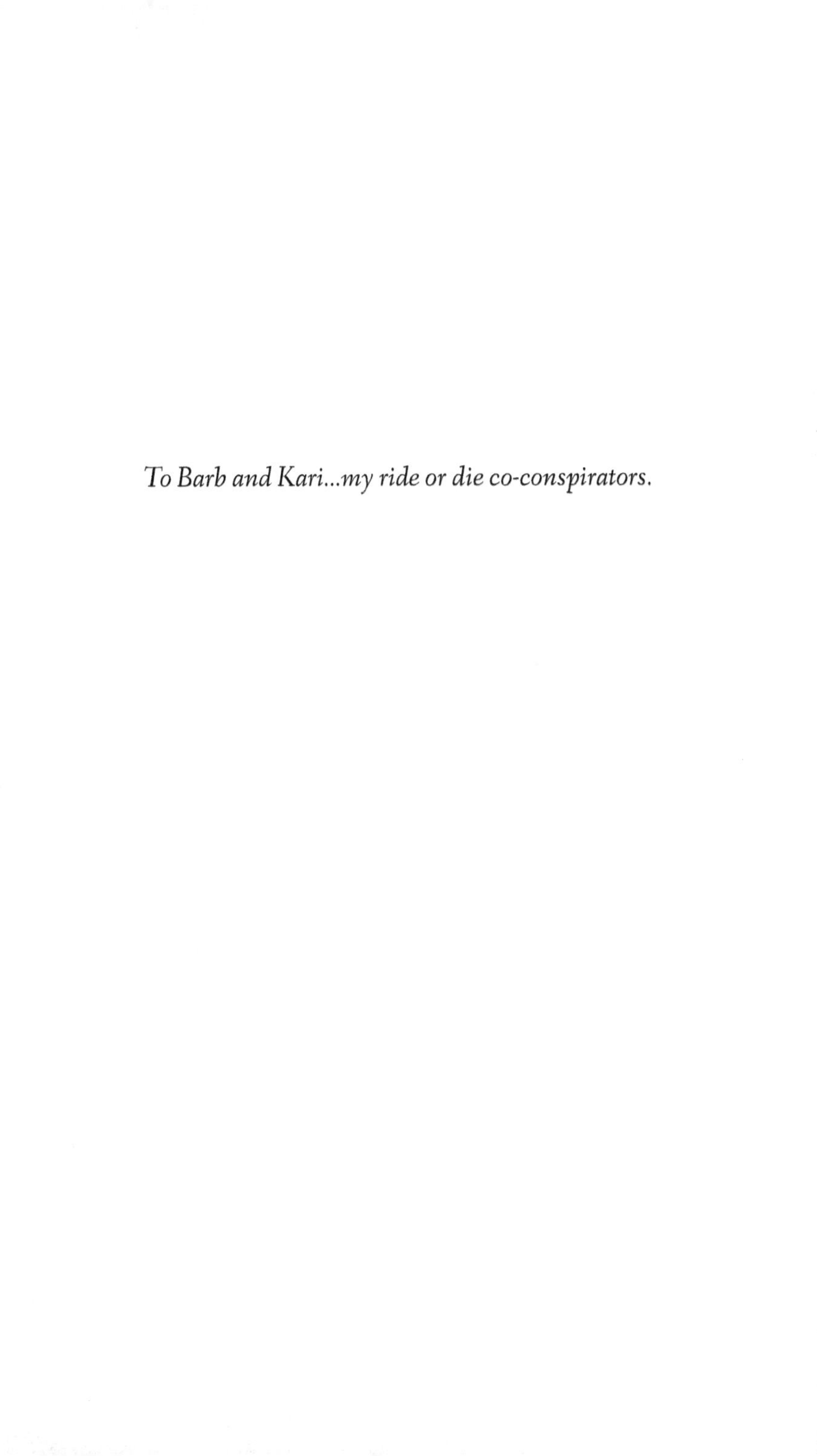

To Barb and Kari...my ride or die co-conspirators.

ONE

January 15, Sunday
Mood: Pissed

Dear Annie,

I hate airplanes. Never understood them. Like, how come I can't suspend myself in the air, but a ten-ton plane has no problem? If I tried to wrap my brain around that, I could really freak out. I'm already halfway there. My skin itches and I'm frozen, but my sweaty shirt is sticking to me like a fat man's at a barbeque. Holy crap, am I dying? Is this what it feels like to croak? It could be a stroke or a mild cardiac arrest.

What would happen to cabin air pressure if I spontaneously combusted?

I even took Valium before I boarded. Two pills. That's all my escort guy, Mitch, (who looks like Justin Bieber, by the way) would spot. I told him that was like giving Flintstone Vitamins to an elephant, and he told me I was funny. Right now, Mitch is beside me with earphones over his ears, leaning against the window like he's really not watching me. But he is. Anxiety overload aside, I can still tell when someone is staring.

So, I guess the wedding crashing fiasco pushed Dad over the edge. I must admit, the vandalism and the car theft were more Racer's ideas than mine. I thought it was immature, but Racer is close to forty and he thought it was brilliant. The cops, however, (who knows how old they were) did not share the sentiment because today at the ambush, someone mentioned charges being filed. I guess by hopping on this plane with The Biebs, I'll beat the rap. Although I can't see how rehab and prison are that much different.

Speaking of stoned, there's a guy kitty-corner from me sleeping way too soundly to have been brought on naturally. I'll have what he's having.

Anyway, this little girl across the aisle was playing with a Ballerina Barbie. Both her and Barbie's hair were fixed in pigtails.(BTW, do you think my hair is still blonde under the green Manic Panic I'm sporting now?) She smiled at me like she meant it and asked if I liked dolls. I couldn't remember the last time someone sincerely inquired about my about personal preferences. I told her I played with dolls all the time when we were little. Back when Mom still acknowledged my existence, Dad shared our address and you weren't...under the weather.

Circa normal.

I could tell that she could tell in her little elementary school way that I was some sort of fucked up. Her eyes were deep blue. Not the least bit bloodshot, and kind. She told me she liked my charm bracelet. You know, my purple "best friends" one that you have the other half to. I thanked her for the compliment, and suddenly I couldn't shut up.

I told her my name was Natalie and extended my hand to shake. Just when I thought she'd take it, her mom, some *dyed-e sweetheart in Liz Claiborne, whispered loud enough for me to hear, to not talk to me. The little girl asked why, and the mom shot me a death stare, mumbled something about me being "gross" and "scary" then flipped the magazine over in her lap making sure the front cover was down.*

Subtle. Like the whole plane didn't know who I was.

Mitch just slipped his earphones off and told me not to worry about it. I think he's reading this over my shoulder. Anyway, he flashed his rock star smile, handed me a bag of complemintary pretzels and launched into some hearts and flowers speech about how I should start believing that I was worthwhile. A "winner despite everything." Blah, blah, blah. Out of nowhere, he whipped out a yellow pad of paper and a pen with the airline logo on it. He said if I had something to say, I should write it down.

And now I've composed this pointless little note.

The little girl stroked her doll's hair with a tiny plastic brush, and in a weird way it soothed me as if the brush was pushing though my own. She bit her lip in deep concentration, and I did, too. The brush hit a snarl, but she muscled through it. I think we're heading down now. I know we're landing at LAX but after that, only Mitch knows where I'm going. I guess that was the point of yesterday's ambush. Give the cute guy a few hundred bucks and a set of one-way plane tickets to dispose of the trash. Mom was too preoccupied with media damage control to notice my departure, but Dad looked more than pleased when we pulled out of the driveway. Even Coach Simms looked relieved, and I never pegged him for betrayal. They should have left me on the bathroom floor where they found me.

———

LOS ANGELES. The land of sun and "special." Palm trees, sunshine and ninja paparazzi that would love to get a load of my trainwreck self, sporting a dirty t-shirt and jeans with a Buffalo Bills cap jammed on my greasy head. I stood under the airport "Arrivals" waiting for someone to point and laugh.

I didn't blend.

Neither did the Dodge Caravan that tried to parallel park itself at the curb. It looked out of place maneuvering between the Mercedes and Bentleys and the beautiful people milling about between them. Some brunette in a white, flimsy tube top strolled past, almost knocking me over with her Versace carry-on slung over her shoulder. Our eyes met and I braced myself for that stunned wide-eyed stare like she'd spotted a wild animal on safari. "What are you looking at?" I snapped feeling agitated and exposed. Thankfully, after a quick once over she scurried back into the terminal.

After six tries and a few bumps against the sidewalk, a skinny, seemingly petiole-soaked lady with a long grey braid and overly tanned skin jumped from the caravan's driver's side. She said her hellos then ushered me into the back seat. Mitch loaded up my one allowed duffle bag before hopping up front. The whole thing was so methodical and fast that I felt more like a Fed Ex package being prepared for delivery than a person.

We lumbered along the crowded freeways while I cursed my existence. The duo up front chatted about record heat and Santa Ana winds. Apparently, not a good combination. I personally wouldn't have minded a little boost in temps because without a fix, I was freezing. They must have heard my teeth chattering because Mitch snapped on the heat.

"You like out West, Natalie?" he asked.

I stared out the van window at the mountains. The yellow sun made me squint. "I'm more of an East Coast person." I didn't know what I meant by that, but it seemed an answer that didn't invite more questions.

"Climate's more agreeable than Buffalo," Mitch said.

I rolled down the window and took a whiff of the air. It zinged up my nose in a warm rush. He was right. Nothing like the rotten egg stench of dying leaves back home. Not even a hint of diesel exhaust.

"Could be worse places to spend your time." He raised his brow like I was supposed to catch his drift. I thought he meant jail, and I considered the difference between here and there.

Sunshine. That's about it.

"You know, being here is an opportunity, not a punishment. It might surprise you, but over time you might actually start thinking of it that way."

Mitch's voice was deep and soft, but it knocked around my brain like a hammer. My eyes stung; my face felt like fire. The bottom of my feet itched, so I ripped off my sneakers and had at them. My jagged nails against the soles only made it worse. I pulled the bottled water out of my backpack and dumped what was left of it all over them.

I remembered my first trip out to California with my old swim team in middle school. We had bake sales to raise money for the Junior Championships in San Diego. Annie made brownies with chocolate chips and fudge frosting, and I made sugar cookies with M&M smiley faces. We sold enough for the trip. That was my first national title I ever won and Annie made a few of the finals. We celebrated by ordering chicken fingers from hotel room service and staying up all night telling ghost stories. Coach Simms could barely wake us up for the flight home the next day.

I reached for my cell phone, normally stowed in the back pocket of my jeans, but I realized that my phone and every other belonging of mine had been taken. If I remembered correctly, I wouldn't get to use a phone of any sort for as long as I stayed out here. No Internet or mail contact either. At least in jail you could mail a freaking letter.

"Being out of contact with family and friends can take a little getting used to," Mitch told me through the rear-view mirror. "Sometimes isolation is not so bad."

"Believe me, there's nothing to miss. At least about my family."

"You're talking about that Racer guy, huh?"

Was ole' Mitchie a mind reader? For a guy, he sure did like to talk. Or maybe that was just his thing. Get girls to buy into his bullshit and distract them from running the other direction. "That 'Racer guy' is my boyfriend," I told him, using air quotes to be extra.

"Oh yeah, it was his Wrangler you totaled and the cops pulled from the ditch, right? After you crashed your dad's wedding and passed out at the wheel."

Clearly, he'd read the tabloids. "Maybe, but I wasn't passed out," I quickly corrected. "I was just taking a breather before running home. I passed out there."

Mitch shared a look with the driver. One of those pursed-lipped head shakes that loosely translated to "darn those crazy kids" and turned back toward the windshield.

I leaned my head against the window. We had left the freeway long ago and were now somewhere in the desert. Palm trees had been replaced by what I took as cactus, (Racer watches Wile E. Coyote cartoons) and tumbleweeds that blew across us on the narrow road. Miles passed and we were the only car I saw. I wondered if my parents actually paid someone to human traffic me.

The thought of my picture attached to an Amber Alert was floating through my mind when we pulled up to a giant white gate. I half expected St. Peter to pop out from somewhere with a clip board. We passed through and at the end of the road was an equally cool estate that reminded me of a castle. "Holy shit," I mumbled to myself, and I guess Mitch heard me because I saw him crack a smile in the mirror.

Despite being in the desert, the place had a lawn. Perfectly green and mowed in intricate designs with ridiculously beautiful gardens and fountains around it. I stuck my nose out the cracked window to catch a whiff of the puffy white peonies, mine and Annie's mom's favorites. I closed my eyes when the breeze hit my face.

"Home sweet home," Mitch declared. It sounded like he thought I'd be relieved, but it sort of freaked me out. This place was too beautiful, too clean, too...*pristine*. The type of place my mother would never allow me to wear my sneakers past the front step. My heart raced. I wished I had a pill or two to chill me out. Again. My hand slipped around for my back pocket.

"The first few days will be a little hard," Mitch said as we pulled up next to the entrance. "But if you just accept that you're here because you need the help, it won't be so scary anymore."

My cheeks heated under the skin and my eyes blurred with tears. FYI, I do not cry. Babies cry. Wimps. People who can't handle shit. The type of individual my father and Coach Simms claimed to hate. "What happens when I go in there?" I asked with a quiver in my voice that even I could hear.

"You'll rest. You've had a long trip. The staff will make sure you're comfortable while you adjust."

"You mean I have to detox."

He nodded. "Does that freak you out?"

"No," I lied. "But then what? You guys pick my brain and tell me how screwed up I am?

"Is that so bad?"

"I'd rather land crotch first on a cactus." There. It felt good to lash out. Hold him back. It was a tactic I used at home that inspired my mother to refer to me as a "junkyard dog." If I bark loud and fuss enough, eventually the tormentor will just leave me alone.

Mitch stepped out of the van and slid the back door open. His eyes were fixed on mine, clear and coffee brown that somehow warmed me like the beverage would. He leaned in, smiled and said, "Look, Nat, from where I'm sitting, I see you have two choices. You could fight this tooth and nail with that green-haired, tough girl attitude of yours, or you could accept it."

"What for?"

"Because you don't have a choice."

"I got lots of choices."

"Which is more than you can say about your friend, Annie, now, isn't it?

If that was his version of a cheap shot, it landed where he intended it to, in the gut, and power-packed enough to free a tear or two. To his credit, he didn't concede success. He wasn't much older than me. College age maybe and the way he had the collar popped on his Tommy Hilfiger shirt, reminded me of the preppy boys my mom insisted I date, "to bolster a marketable image."

"Hand me your backpack, and I'll get your duffle," he offered. "I'll take it inside for you."

"Don't bother. I can do it myself."

He shook his head and walked around to the trunk. "When people offer help, take it. First rule of this place."

I watched him sling my pink Speedo bag over his shoulder and head to the front door. Taking a deep breath, I slid from my seat and followed.

Like I really had a choice.

TWO

January 17, Tuesday Morning (I think)...
Mood: Too early to tell

Dear Annie,
I'm at The Dunes. At least that's what my white robe says. That's all I've been allowed to wear since they stripped me, hosed me down like lawn furniture and brought me to my "suite."

"Closet" or "cell" would have been a more accurate description.

Tillie greeted me when I got here. I think she's a nurse or something. She's a fifty-ish, curly short brown-haired woman who weighs about three hundred pounds, with a smile about as wide as she is. Very Grandma-ish. She ran her hand through my now blonde again hair, like a sincere person might, and even copped a hug. A one-armed one, the kind one gives when they feel like it's a good gesture but don't want to commit to the full-on invasion of personal space. I appreciated her perception but probably wouldn't have minded had she risked the whole-body bear variety.

She told me I should feel safe and that she understood that I might not feel well for a day or two. A tall blond man in a white coat with obscenely bleached teeth told me we could "work out" something to manage detox. Dr. Blaine, as he introduced himself, reminded me of a Ken Doll personified, and I resisted the urge to thank him for taking time out from riding shotgun in Barbie's dream car to spot me. But instead, I just said "great" and informed them that I was fresh out of chill pills from the plane trip. They laughed.

Apparently, I'm funny.

So here I am in my little prison cell, staring out through the pinhole-sized window at the mountains. All I hear right now is quiet. I'm used to more noise back home. Mom screaming at me, my brother's stereo, the planes landing at the airport next to Racer's trailer. Always something a little louder than the voices in my head. Not that I hear talking in a creepy way, just me talking to myself.

The room smells like ammonia and the bed looks hard. The mattress is as stark white as the walls. In fact, everything around here is white. Blank. The paint, the furniture, the rugs. Must be on purpose. Maybe they were trying for a hospital motif. Really, it's more like living among nothing. A cloud. A haze. I can't explain it.

Anyway, Tillie and Dr. Blaine went through my bags and informed me I'd get my street clothes and such back when "the time came." So here I am in my robe and slippers, padding around like Heff did at the Playboy Mansion. No belts or shoelaces (the robe has a zipper) allowed. I told them they didn't need to worry because I was too whipped to hang myself with a shoelace anyway. They also took my purple bracelet. I know we promised never to take them off, and I even tried to explain the whole matching-best-friend-charm thing, but they didn't buy it. So much for compassion.

This morning I woke up even more tired than before I fell asleep. The nurse who came in to take my blood pressure told me it was noon and I'd been out for almost a full thirty-six hours. My legs ached like it had been too long since I'd used them, and my throat hurt like hell. She told me that I was screaming in my sleep. Could be, but that's hard to believe because I'm not a dreamer, figuratively or literally. Nor do I scream, unless I am pissed or on fire. So, I played it off like my nocturnal tantrum was totally planned. She nodded and congratulated me on my first night of sobriety.

Man could I use a...something.

Tillie told me I had appointments today with doctors and counselors, but I wouldn't be introduced to the community until tomorrow. Until then, I'm stuck here. She offered me food, but I told her I didn't want it. When she brought me a turkey sandwich, I nibbled on the crusts and poked holes in the bread like I thought a disturbed girl would. Maybe give Dr. Blaine something to work with.

Tomorrow after my meet and greet with the other freaks, I'm supposed to get more information about my stay here. She also said something about a roommate. I've never shared a room, except when we traveled for swim meets. I'm not sure it's something I could do long term. Sharing swim lanes with people in training even made me feel claustrophobic sometimes.

Unless it was with you, of course.

———

"SO, your admittance information revealed quite a few things about you. Aside the fact that you smelled like bourbon, we found all sorts of drugs in your system. Marijuana and cocaine and of course the sedatives we allowed to get you here in the first place."

"Well, you know, I do enjoy a good buffet."

"Natalie, why don't you sit down? It's just talking."

Dr. Blaine, who I now refer to as Dr. Teeth and highly dislike, sat in my room desk chair with elbows on his thighs and that parental look that meant he wanted to "get real." Suddenly, I reverted back to my distant youth remembering when my brother, Jake, drowned Dr. Teeth's Ken Doll likeness in my Barbie Dream House pool. Ah, the good old days.

"Come on, Natalie, I'm not that scary, am I?"

I paced the tiny room that was about the size of my closet at home. Was it possible I was claustrophobic because there was no other reason for my shaking? I considered opening the peep hole window for air but, shocker, it was nailed shut.

"I know it's only been a few days, but I think you'll find the sooner you embrace this, the easier recovery will be."

"Why does everyone keep telling me that?"

"Because it's the truth." He flipped through the papers attached to his little white clip board. The wrinkles on his tan forehead told me he was looking for something particular, so I sat down on the bed and prepared myself. "I had the opportunity to read the letters your family wrote you as part of the intervention. You have an awful lot of people who care about you."

The image of the ambush a few days ago bloomed in my brain. My high-speed getaway from my dad's wedding ended with Racer's car totaled in a ditch. Then I ran home. Nothing sobers you up more than the sound of sirens and red lights flashing in your rear view, especially when you have a baggie of cocaine in your back pocket. I had a feeling the Buffalo police were waiting for an opportunity to nab me for something. Watching the news lately, it was hard to believe the whole world didn't have it in for me. Somehow, I got to my mother's house before the cops and had time to flush the coke before I collapsed. I'm convinced it was not the police on her doorstep threatening my arrest, but the crime of puking all over her fancy bath mats that was her last straw.

Two days later my mother, father, brother (who they somehow managed to wrestle away from his oh-so-important studies at Princeton), Annie, Coach Simms, some intervention counselor my dad found online or some shit and Mitch all sat with folded hands at my mother's dining room table like it was fucking Thanksgiving. The only person who would even look at me was Annie.

"Your intervention had been in the works for a while, and they're all praying very hard you'll recover," Blaine said.

"Most of them are just worried about losing their cash cow. And, I'm not sick. Sick people recover."

"Well then you're suffering. How about that?"

"Does it matter?"

"It will when you realize where you'll end up if you don't at least try."

What was that? A fucking riddle? Dr. Teeth crossed his legs at his penny loafers and raised a brow like he was really smart and knew it. "Would Annie want you to be here?"

Annie. He said her name like the word carried extra weight than the rest of them in the sentence. I pretended to yawn to fight off the threatening tears.

"Feeling things is scary sometimes, isn't it?"

"I don't know." I laid down on the bed and stared up at the textured ceiling. My vision seemed better than usual. I figured I needed contacts. Or at least the chlorine was eating away my pupils. Improved vision aside, I now had a killer headache, but I tried not to show it. For no reason, other than it was a good feeling to know something he didn't. Like the withheld information of a stupid headache gave me some form of control.

"Well, happy about it or not, you're stuck here. This is a drug rehabilitation center, but we like to think we focus on the whole person. Mental health is a big priority here.

"So, like drug rehab but also looney bin," I said. "I guess that fits because according to the press, I'm both burned out and crazy."

"You'll be here at least three months, probably more. You'll continue your schoolwork like any other high school senior, but like any other addict you will also be responsible for your recovery. You'll be assigned your own counselor and required to go to group therapy. Plus, there are extra-curricular activities. Each week you will be evaluated by our board. There are more than a few people on the board. Nurses, therapists, even random staff members who might observe you in the day room or in the cafeteria during the course of the day.

"That's creepy."

"Depending on your performance, you will be awarded movement to levels. Right now, you are on Level One."

"At which level do I get to dress myself?"

"Is dressing yourself important to you?"

I rolled my eyes. "You answer all my questions with a question. Is that on purpose?"

He chuckled and tapped his pen on the chicken-scratch-filled paper in front of him. "A Level One wears The Dunes standard issue jump suit with a zipper. Your shoes are white and of course for a Level One, they have no laces. Twos, Threes, and Fours wear the uniform of khaki pants or shorts and a white shirt. Only a Level Five gets to wear street clothes and dress how they choose. Does that inspire you at all?

"You did it again. The answering questions with questions thing."

"Maybe I keep asking questions because you are avoiding

them. From what I've heard, that's the method of your madness. Avoidance."

I cursed and swung my legs to the floor, wishing I could up the dramatics with a stomp, but my socked feet wouldn't allow it. "I just want a straight answer. Why is that bad?"

"Right. Straight answers. Just like your mother wanted when she caught you stealing her pills from the medicine cabinet."

"She wasn't using them."

"Just like your father wanted when you showed up trashed at his wedding and destroyed a fifty-thousand-dollar limousine."

"Believe me, he and Cruella had it coming."

"And what about Annie your best friend? How do you think she feels being put through all this? And what do you think brought on that meltdown at the Olympic press conference?"

I shook my head, trying to trick the words from finding my ears. His yammering was like being stabbed in the eyes with needles. I meant to tell him so, but I got distracted by his jack-o-lantern-smile.

"Your swim career is not a main focus at this point, but we will address your apparent problems with male attention," he added. "Your family believes a man named Racer is a bad influence."

"Is this going to be another math lesson about how much older he is than me? Because if it is, then I'm not interested."

"The age doesn't bother me, but the nature of the relationship does. Why don't you tell me about him, Natalie?"

The inflection of his voice sounded like a dare, like eating worms. Something only a seven-year-old would be dumb enough to take. I padded over to the window and fixed my gaze on the mountains.

"If you are uncomfortable talking about him or anything else we've touched on, maybe Tillie will be easier to talk to. She's been assigned to you as your one-on-one counselor. You'll meet with her tomorrow afternoon."

It didn't matter who I was talking to but what was said that irked me. Defending my relationship with Racer was something I'd done for months, and I was sick of it. Yes, I was sleeping with him, and forgive me, but I liked it. He didn't judge and was generally around when I needed him to be. Why the hell was that so bad? "No comment," I mumbled.

"Fair enough, but that may change once you get your feet wet. You don't strike me as someone who can keep your mouth shut for long."

"Now that might be the smartest thing you've said all day." I turned to him and conceded a smile.

Later in the afternoon Tillie and Dr. Teeth informed me that it was time to "insert" me into The Community. Insert. Was I a bomb or something? Would I get tossed into a group of poor unsuspecting kids and blow up?

Tillie lumbered beside me down the long hallways, giving little puffs of breath every few steps. I didn't mind the snail pace because it gave me a chance to scope the place out. It reminded me of my brother's dorm at Princeton. Doors with dry erase boards, for posting messages, and faded construction paper decorations from the recently passed holiday season. Toward the end of the corridor, a few doors were open so nosey people like myself could see right in. One girl actually had bedding with *color* and, don't quote me, a *flowery pattern*. A definite departure from the stark white "Dunes Issue" décor. There were also cork boards with snapshots on the walls, and vases (plastic, of course, glass equals weapons) holding beautiful arrangements of flowers.

"That's Fiona," Tillie told me. "She's going home next week. You work hard, that could be you in a few months."

It was tempting to laugh in her face, but somehow, I held it in. It wasn't the leaving part that was funny, but the implication that my experience would inspire an interest in interior design or move anyone at home enough to send me flowers. Maybe Annie, but she was more of a chocolate or Bear-a-Gram kind of gal.

"I think you'll find that this place isn't so bad. The boys are in a separate dormitory, and your paths don't cross except during academic instruction and dinner if you choose."

"So, you mean I won't be distracted." I laughed because the notion really was funny. "You think I'm here to get a boyfriend? Figures. I was already told I had guy issues."

"Of course not. I'm just giving you the lay of the land." She squeezed my shoulder and winked. "Anyway, smarty, there are currently sixteen high school girls here at all stages of recovery. You'll attend class and group therapy with them. And you're encouraged to try to establish friendships."

"Really? I thought you would discourage that."

"To make friends? Why?"

"Doesn't that mean you're..." I flipped my wrists and hunted around my brain for the right word. "Co-dependent?"

"It beats the people you've been hanging around with at home."

The smile in her voice told me she was kidding around, and I was almost flattered that she thought I could take it. Tillie was cool. I couldn't remember the last time I could take a joke at my expense.

We turned a corner near the front door where all the personnel hung out behind a long counter. On the other side were their offices and the admittance room where I'd spent so much time a few nights before. A guy, who I thought was a counselor by the blue tag around his neck, offered a wave. "Hey, Natalie."

"Hey." I waved back. The rest of the staff at the counter said "hi" as I walked by, too. I felt like I was on parade, like I needed to hurl a handful of candy at them or something. This was something I was used to though. People knowing me without really "knowing" me. It was one of the things that stressed me out sometimes. Like I always had to be ready to make a positive impression.

"There are always doctors and nurses on premises if needed. Counselors. People like that. There is a full kitchen and grounds staff. Clint, you'll see milling around. He's the maintenance manager in charge of all that."

Beyond the offices at the end of the hall was an atrium with the sign "Day Room" written in calligraphy next to the door. Although there wasn't really a door. Just this huge, pillared entry way that led you into a place that seemed more suited for wearing formal dresses than somewhere you'd play Scrabble. It was huge, about half the size of my high school gym, and completely encased with glass, unbreakable I assumed.

Of course, everything inside the room was white. The leather couches, the carpets, the chairs and tables. The only hint of color was what the outside provided. The blue sky, the grey peaks of the mountains and the killer gardens between here and there. A few girls milled around. Some with books, others had laptop computers. I noticed that some kids even had shoelaces on their sneakers.

Something to aspire to.

Tillie paused before we went in and looked around before lowering her voice. "I know you're kind of in a unique position. People know who you are. Even if they don't have access to the outside world, they can guess why you're here."

"Yeah."

"Try to forget all that. Just be you."

So, I walked myself in and plopped down on one of the oversized leather couches. I felt like a worm on a hook waiting for someone to take a nibble. On the wall was an enormous TV with the volume so loud, I couldn't believe no one tried to turn the thing down. I felt around the cushions in search of a remote.

"You like Family Feud?"

A mousy blonde girl with a really bad complexion sat down beside me, but she didn't take her eyes from the TV screen. I noticed she had a death grip around a remote, but it looked too big, beat up and old to belong to the flat screen on the wall. "This is Family Feud, but I like all the game shows. I like reality TV, too. At home, I usually watch The Voice and all the talent shows because of the singing and dancing. I don't mind the classics like ICarly and Full House, but right now I'm really into the reality dating shows. Do you watch The Bachelor?"

Her eyes still fixed on the television, she tucked her legs under herself like she would wait as long as she had to for an answer. I was still trying to process the twenty questions and oddity that I knew this girl's entertainment preferences and not her name. But who was I to judge, right? She wore not only shoelaces, but uniform shorts and top. Me in my jumpsuit, she was my superior.

"The Bachelor?" was the first thing that came out of my mouth.

"You know, the reality dating show where one guy picks a wife from a bunch of girls that wear bikinis and cry a lot? That show. I've seen every season. I have every episode memorized."

"I've never seen it."

"You should watch it," she looked at me finally with an eager smile. "It's really romantic. But also pathetic in some ways. But awesome."

She pressed a few buttons on the weird remote but nothing happened. Still the same Family Feud contestant lady sweating the fast money round with Steve Harvey. It seemed more urgent to pay attention to that than finishing the conversation. "I'm

Cassidy,' she finally said when a laxative commercial came on. "You're new, huh?"

"Yeah, two days ago."

"How do you like it so far?"

She asked like we were at summer camp or something. Did people actually enjoy incarcerations like this? I ran a hand through my newly rediscovered blonde hair and sighed. "I don't know. I could have passed on the plane ride out here."

"It will get better. I've been here three weeks."

Was there a protocol to conversation around here? A right way to break the ice? I really wanted to ask what she was in for, what she did, what her intervention was like. But even if it was acceptable to ask, it wasn't my business, anyway. Besides, she seemed more like the type who if she wanted me to know something, her filter might be more like a sieve.

"I'm a Meth addict. I'm from Kansas. It's pretty big there."

It came out like declarations. Like in her three weeks here, she'd practiced saying the words but wasn't sure yet what emotion to attach to them. The thought of spilling my guts to total strangers like that was something I could not fathom. But those sorts of abilities were probably what earned you shoelaces and belts in this place. "I'm sorry," I said, for lack of anything else.

"That's why it looks like I have bad acne. Meth messes up your skin."

If I was staring at her face I didn't mean to, but I'd never seen such horribly purple zits. If that was what crystal meth did to someone's complexion, I couldn't imagine any girl bothering with the shit.

"Wanna see my remote?"

"You're what?"

"My remote." She rested it on her two open palms like a

most precious gift and held it in front of me. "It's special. It doesn't work on just the TV, but real-life people too."

Since she offered, I looked at the thing more closely. The "power" and "volume up" buttons were missing, and I could tell by the remnants of scotch tape that there had been numerous attempts to close the now missing battery compartment cover. "Does it work at all?" I asked.

She batted her glazed eyes and smiled. "It works for me."

"Hey, Road Kill, who's your new friend?"

Cassidy spun around. A girl with a long black ponytail and a faded full sleeve rose tattoo on her left arm peered down at both of us. She was in standard white shirt khaki short uniform, but with a few stains here and there. She must have been here for a while. At least longer than poor Cassidy, and I was curious as hell to know what for.

Cassidy cleared her throat and tensed up. She seemed afraid, but not totally distracted by it, because one eye was still fixed on the Stayfree commercial. "I don't know her name," Cassidy mumbled. "We just met."

"I'm Natalie." I extended my hand because it felt necessary. "Nat."

"Nat?" Mean Girl scoffed. "What the hell kind of name is that? "

"I think its short for Natalie," Cassidy told her in monotone. "A nickname."

"A gnat is a fucking insect. Why would you want to be called an insect?"

"Actually," Cassidy said, "A gnat is spelled with a 'G' and her name is spelled with an 'N'..."

"Just watch the TV, Freak show."

Cassidy turned back to the screen like she didn't mind the suggestion. I, on the other hand, was pissed. I hated bullies. In fact, in second grade, my dumping glue on a bully's head in

Annie's defense was how I met her in the first place. Even 'till this day, she'd jokingly call me her "hero." Funny, but me in my white jump suit, I didn't feel that heroic.

What I was, was hugely annoyed.

"So, what's your name," I asked, trying like hell to smile through my clenched teeth.

"Missy."

"You're making fun of my name and your name is Missy?"

A small group of girls gathered around us giggled. These must have been her minions. Girls too scared not to support her in her obvious "head bitch" role. Missy flashed a crooked smile to her five or six wing girls before putting her hands on her hips and looking down to where I still sat on the couch. "What's wrong with my name, Nat?" she taunted.

"Was your mother a hamster? People don't have names like Missy. Animals have names like that. Cats, rodents..."

"Well, you know rodents eat insects for lunch, don't you?"

The wing girls giggled again with her but quieted when I stood and walked around the couch. I had been dealing with an older brother and a smart ass like Racer for months. I was the queen of comebacks. It wasn't even a fair matchup.

"Actually, my old dog's name was Missy," I said, waxing wistful. "We had to put her down because she ate her own shit."

My spit from the "t" sound that she wiped from her cheek was totally unplanned, but I can't say I was sorry it happened. I was also surprised it didn't earn me a punch in the face. Instead, she just stood there with a smirk, dramatically wiping her index finger where my warning shot landed. Like she was trying to save face in front of her minions.

I'm not a fighter. Don't get me wrong, I could land a mean right hook if I had to, but I was more of a hugger, or at least a fist-pump type. It's just there hadn't been many opportunities for either lately. A punch never came, though. In fact, no one moved, breathed or spoke except for Cassidy, who pointed the remote at us, furiously pushing the "stop" button.

"You think you're the new big deal, don't ya?" Missy sneered. "I suggest you watch your step."

I shrugged. "That's probably good advice. I wouldn't want your next meal stuck to the bottom of my shoe."

Finally, I pushed between all of them and headed back to my room. This was probably not what Tillie pictured in my first experience with others in the community, but there it was.

Consider me inserted.

THREE

January 18, Wednesday Morning
Mood: Hungry as hell

Dear Annie,

I'm in the mood for eggs. I wonder if this place has them.

When the hell did I start liking eggs again? You'd think with all the protein loading forced on us in season, my consuming-eggs-as-a-preference days would be over.

Anyway, apparently, I passed the socializing test yesterday because today I am going to be formally intro-duced to "the group." So, from what I gather, it will go some-thing like this. I'm led around on a short leash like a Pomeranian at a dog show. The others will sniff me out, and we all hang out together and then amuse each other with our shitty lives.

I can't wait.

I have to say, forced imprisonment aside, I am dying to see what these other people are like here. If they are as bitchy as Missy or whacked out as Cassidy then it might be sort of entertaining. Dr. Teeth told me that when the staff (him, Tillie and a few people I haven't met yet) feel I am "ready" they will "allow me" visits with my family. Lucky me. Lucky them, if the staff can pull it off. Getting Mom on a plane for a reason that isn't business related is like moving a mountain, and prying Dad, Jill and the Chipmunks from their "family" honeymoon love fest in Cancun would be a downright miracle. That's cool with me. They can all stay where they are. If this place is supposed to inspire me to feel better, no point in pouring salt in the wound.

There are a few people I wouldn't mind talking to. Racer for one. He wasn't there at the ambush, probably because my parents wouldn't allow it. Also, because it was early morning, and he doesn't get up for anything before noon. But I wonder if he misses me. Like, really misses me. I think about him a lot. Not sexy stuff or anything, but stupid boyfriend/ girlfriend things we used to do. Like when I cooked for him.

Sometimes I would make him grilled cheese and cut the crusts off just like he told me to. One day, he had me remake it about three different times and then broke the frying pan handle when he got mad that all the bread was gone. He's crazy sometimes, but that's just his personality, and I do stupid things that rile him up. He cares about me, though. And he needs me. I can tell, and that's cool because I like to be needed.

Anyway, breakfast is in a half hour, and Tillie said she'd walk me down to the commissary. I can't remember the last time I was actually hungry for a meal and not jonesing for munchies. I wonder if they have Eggs Benedict. Nice and runny on crunchy toast with a tall glass of OJ.

Wow. I forgot I even liked orange juice.

———

"GROUP SUCKS," Cassidy grumbled from her chair beside me. "I hope we get out of here fast today. There's a Full House Disney Channel marathon. I've never seen the first season."

It was now obvious to me that not only was Cassidy a crystal meth addict, but she also had a serious problem with bad television. Clearly, her brain was more than a little charbroiled. Not that I'm that perceptive, but the broken remote and fifteen-year-old TV Guide (do they still print those?) she carried around was a tip-off. I also noticed a lot of the staff looked at her with this weird glassy-eyed half-smile that if it was directed at me, I would read as pity. I sort of shared the sentiment.

Tillie sat me next to Cass for group (I think because she saw us interact yesterday) and while we waited for Dr. Teeth to bless us with his presence, Cass lectured me about why Sabrina the Teenage Witch totally blew away the classic sitcom I Dream of Jeannie. I'd never seen either but didn't have the heart to tell her. Kind of for the same reasons you don't tell a mother her kid is ugly. There's no point, and she'd be hurt to the core.

"John Stamos, he plays Uncle Jessie on Full House, has been in a few movies and things. But personally, I think he can't break away from the Uncle Jessie roll." Cassidy shook her head as if she were discussing an unfortunate relative. "It's a shame. He's a good actor, but once you're type cast...curtains."

"Full House," I repeated. "That's the show they rebooted with the whole cast older, right?"

"Yup, you watch it?"

"No."

"Well, then, you'll start today, right after group." She glanced at the clock above the door, the only wall that wasn't a window. "I wish Dr. Blaine would hurry up."

Me, I was in no rush. Revealing my problems to a roomful of

head cases wasn't something I had the urge to do. The tutorial on "The Life and Times of John Stamos" interested me more than that. There were fifteen other girls in the room, and all but two had shoelaces, but I was the only one still in my white space suit. Of course, I was the newbie. New meat. The person everyone was curious about, waiting to hear how messed up I was and measure themselves against it.

We sat in a circle, like demented Duck Duck Goose, in a smaller version of the day room. Lots of sunlight, a view of the mountains, and a sick display of shrubbery my mom would pay the landscaper good money for at home. Missy sat across from us book-ended by two bleach blonde girls who were built like bikini models. They both sported this blank stare that I could only describe as perpetual confusion. "Hey, Pizza Face," Missy called to Cassidy. "Tell your friend we're just dying to hear all about her."

"Natalie, Missy says..."

"I heard her," I said before she finished the sentence. "Tell her to fuck off."

Cass bit her chapped lip like the direction confused her. "Do you mean I should tell them you said to fuck off, or I should tell them to fuck off?"

"Fuck off," I blurted, evidently loud enough for the rest of the room to hear, but only the Level Fours and below reacted. The Fives must have missed it, being so far away in their "better place" and all.

A girl a few seats down with spiked red hair and an armful of healed track marks stared hard at Missy and her constituents. "Girls, do you think you could save your games for recess. I have a GED test to study for, and I want to get out of here on time. You were new once. Have a heart and cut the bullshit."

Missy rolled her eyes. "Really, Staci, a GED? Are you sure you're not just studying Mitch?"

"Shut up," Staci grumbled.

"I bet you'll do really well on the English part," Missy taunted. "You write such beautiful love poetry."

"Don't tangle with me, Street Trash," Staci spat. "You talk a big game but you can't back it up."

The rest of the room glared at each other like this Staci girl had poked the Devil with his own pitchfork. Did Missy mean Mitch, the preppy, blonde-haired Justin Bieber looking guy who flew me out here? What the hell did this girl have to do with him?

And why did I care if she did?

"I'm street trash?" Missy laughed." I wasn't the one selling sucks for a hit."

Staci cocked her fist and was half-way out of her seat when Dr. Blaine opened the door. He greeted everyone with his blinding smile and urged us to be inspired by the healing heat of the sun outside and have a good day.

I must ask what he's been on.

Tillie waddled in behind him holding a folder with my name on it. While Blaine rambled, she stood by my chair and offered a shoulder squeeze for support. I think she sensed I was tense.

"So, let's get down to business," Blaine declared when he sat down. "As you can see, we have a new friend here with us today. "

"Everyone, this is Natalie," Tillie announced. "She's come a long way from Buffalo, New York. Let's all make her feel welcome."

"Hello, Natalie," the circle chanted like a bunch of robots. I gave a weird little wave-nod combination and settled on "Hi" for my first word.

"Natalie came to us because she's like all of you," Tillie said. "She's struggling with addiction and wants to heal. Of course, when she's ready, she'll volunteer her feelings and what circumstances brought her here. But until then, it's your job as the community to get to know her and embrace her, just as you were when you first arrived."

"You're that swimmer, right?" A girl with a long, blonde ponytail and street clothes smiled at me from over in the corner. The name Fiona was scribbled on her "Hello, My Name Is" sticker on her chest. "I'm actually a big fan of yours," she said. "I was sorry to hear you hit a rough patch."

I scanned the crowd for a reaction. Nothing, which was nice, but not really surprising because this crowd didn't strike me as hardcore fans of competitive swimming. People don't usually follow the sport unless it's an Olympic year, and eight months had gone by since that debacle. Of course, man, was I front page news then.

"You swim, like laps in a pool?" Cassidy asked.

"Yeah," I replied and smiled back at Fiona. "That's me."

A few smiles erupted in the circle. 4's and 5's with clear complexions and adjusted attitudes. Missy and the Bikini Twins scowled. I expected more from their Level Three statuses.

"I'm sure living your life with that much pressure and the world watching can be stressful. Does it freak you out sometimes?" Fiona asked.

Wow, no one had asked me that pointblank before. Coach Simms always said "only the weak felt pressure" so to even think about it seemed like a personal failure. "Um, maybe. I don't know."

"So, why are you here?" Cassidy asked. "What happened?"

All eyes locked on me. The room was silent until Dr. Blaine pulled from the depths of his doctor wisdom, "It's good to talk so we can all know things. Go ahead, Natalie"

Go ahead? Where the hell did I begin? Besides, there truly wasn't anything significant I could think of to say. It was like a press conference when obnoxious interviewers baited you for juicy sound bites. Coach Simms hated how I would mull over every word and literally sweat over getting up in front of people to speak. I liked to think I did my talking in the pool, anyway. Who cared what I thought just because I could backstroke the fastest from point A to B?

For whatever reason, Fiona did. I recognized her as the girl whose room I had peeked in on. With the pretty comforter and flowers. Answering her questions might help her cause, and she did say she was a fan and all.

"I got tired," I said simply. "I just wanted to be done."

"The press wasn't kind to you," Fiona said. "A mental breakdown is one thing, but the world watching you do it must be terrible."

It was, I thought to myself, but there was no way I would show any weak spot in front of these vultures. They wouldn't understand where I was coming from anyway. Like truly. Five a.m. swim practices during Buffalo winters, school all day then the weight room at night. Traveling to random countries where the language is foreign and the food barely edible. The nasty coaches. The injuries. The feeling of being surrounded by people, but you never felt seen or heard. The weird flip-flop feeling of your family treating you like a business investment, and strangers professing their loyalty and love. Thank God I always had Annie. We'd soldiered through together.

Until we didn't.

"I heard before you got here, you were fucking some old guy and were just arrested for stealing a limo."

"Missy," Blaine snapped. "How many times have we talked about respecting community members?"

"I was just prompting the conversation." She turned back at me and leveled her dark beady eyes at mine. "So, what are you, a prostitute now or something?

If her intention was to embarrass me, it didn't work. I was numb to it all now. Can't think of anything more mortifying than showing up at the Olympic Games, where the world expects you to take home six gold medals and leaving with nothing except a bad case of swimmer's ear and prescription for Valium. Embarrassment would also require a sincere interest in what these people thought of me. I couldn't care less.

"I'm not a prostitute." I informed her. "I live in suburban Buffalo. My parents are divorced and my dad just married my stepmother, Jill, and they have twin three-year-olds, Chip and Dale."

Staci laughed. "You mean your stepbrothers are named after Disney Chipmunks."

"Or dancing naked men," Cassidy mumbled.

I was about to wax fancy about my new family, when the door creaked open. Mitch stepped inside with his aviator sunglasses still pulled over his eyes. He lifted his hand to Blaine to signal an apology and sat down in an empty chair in the corner.

"I'm sorry, Natalie," Blaine said, "Continue. We're listening."

"Yeah, I'm enthralled," Missy teased. "And I'm sure Staci is, too, despite the distraction of Lover Boy joining us. And speaking of boys, tell us more about this pedophile boyfriend of yours."

I cringed and waited for Blaine, or Tillie, or someone to step up and gag the bitch. No luck. Of course, maybe this was how it was supposed to go. Shame the new girl into sobriety. Interesting tactic.

"So, like, was he your pimp who led you from this apparent stardom as a swimmer, or whatever, to a life of crime?" Missy prodded. "We're dying to hear about this guy, and I bet Staci can relate."

I glanced at the Staci girl who was now red faced, probably mortified by both Mitch showing up and Missy's antics. Poor girl. Distracting everyone with my sob story didn't bother me if it helped the girl out.

"Racer was my boyfriend," I told them. "He is almost forty and not my pimp. Also, I did not steal the limo. I merely defaced it."

"Deface?" Missy repeated. "What the fuck does that mean?"

I took a deep breath. This girl talked a big game, but truly, I had never met such an easy target. The eager eyes of the circle stared back at me, and I considered taking the high road. But even the presence of Mr. Hilfiger Mysterious in the corner wasn't enough to convince me to do so.

"Deface is a verb, although in some special instances it can be used as a noun. Let me use it in a sentence." I put my finger to my cheek for drama's sake. "The smart and funny new girl was tempted to smack Missy, the stupid girl, in De face."

Evidently when you make Dr. Blaine laugh, group is automatically dismissed. I felt this was priceless knowledge that I could use at a later date.

———

That afternoon, a nurse escorted me to one of the courtyard patio tables. It was nice to be out in the fresh air among the flowers and fountains. A few girls met with some of the counselors at other tables. Out on the lawn, a small group of boys sat in a circle with whom I figured was the Dr. Teeth counterpart for the male patients. If I didn't know better, I would have thought I'd been beamed to my brother's über-perfect Ivy League campus. I laughed. People as fucked up as me probably had never heard of Princeton.

Tillie plopped down onto the chair across from me and set the folder on the table. It wasn't overly hot in the shade, but she was sweating enough that when she dragged her handkerchief across her forehead, her foundation went with it. A soggy lock of dark hair stuck in its wake. "So, this is our one-on-one time," she said. "You ready?"

She looked hopeful, her wide smile making her chubby cheeks look like big red buttons. I hated to disappoint. "I guess. I should warn you, though, I'm not a fan of talking about feelings and stuff."

Tillie patted my hand. "That's okay."

"Am I supposed to? I mean, talk."

"Do you think that's what we expect of you?" She leaned back in the cast iron chair and folded her arms against her huge chest. "Maybe we should discuss that, Nat. What you think people expect of you."

And here it was. THE TALK. The brain picking they show in the cheesy health class movies. I ran my hand through my ponytail and sighed. "I know what you're doing, trying to get me to 'open up.'" I quoted with my fingers. "I can tell."

"So, what if I am? You're here because people have a problem with your behavior."

"I don't see an issue."

"Then tell me why you don't think so. You've got nothing else to do."

I brought a shielding hand to my forehead and studied her face. Not like I'd be able to tell because I figured counselors like Tillie were trained in tricking patients, but there was nothing in her expression that told me she was bullshitting.

"Your parents think you need to be here, and you don't. Why is that?"

"It's my dad," I corrected. "Not my mom. Me being here

puts a serious strain on her cash flow. To her I'm a commodity, not a kid."

"So, you're saying she'd like it if you were still home stealing her Valium from the medicine cabinet."

"No...I mean yes." I shook my head. At home I was never speechless. Shit would spew from my mouth without even having to think about it. But maybe that was the problem. Now when my brain was involved, there were more words to trip over and push around. I licked my lips and cleared my throat. "Okay, so taking my mom's pills is bad. I get it. You're right. Bad Nat, I'll never do it again."

"Maybe you will, maybe you won't. But that's not what we are talking about now. I just want to know, if you were home right now, what would you be doing?"

A day in the life I thought to myself. That seemed harmless enough. "Well, it's afternoon, so I'm awake. No school, because I don't remember if that's something I actually do anymore. I'd probably go to Racer's."

"No swimming?"

"Nope. Retired."

Tillie scowled. "So, what did you do at Racer's?"

Had to think about it a minute. "I don't know. Hang out with friends."

"Your friends or his friends?"

"Both," I answered quickly. The truth was half the time I had no clue who was there. My recollection was just random faces lurking in the heavy smoke, all as stoned as I was. Some people would show up once and never be heard from again. There were times when I was so out of it, I barely remembered being there myself. One minute, it would be dinnertime and the TV would be blaring cartoons. Then it would be hours later, sometimes the morning after, and I would be in his bed or on the couch, having no idea how I got there.

"What are you thinking about Natalie?"

Racer's trailer wasn't Shangri La, but it beat the boredom at my mom's house and the lunacy at Dad's love bungalow with Jill and the Chipmunks. Finding a place on my own was a long shot considering I had no idea how to access the money I'd made. God knows if that money even still existed. And once Annie got sick, I didn't feel comfortable staying at the Madsen's.

"Natalie?"

"Huh?"

Tillie cocked her head and smiled. "What are you thinking about, Kiddo?"

Kiddo. No one had called me that since Annie's dad, Mr. Madsen, coached our first club swim team when I was eight. "I'm sorry," I stammered. "What were we talking about?"

"You were telling me about Racer, and the things you would do at his house."

"Right, well I guess I made food mostly."

"Interesting." Tillie scribbled something down on her pad. "You like to cook?"

"No, but Racer liked to eat." I explained. "If he was awake, I would make his bed and if he was sleeping, I'd get his pills and set out some clothes for him to wear."

"He expects you to do that?"

"No, I do it because I want to."

"So, if you weren't at Racers, where would you be?"

I shrugged. "I don't know. Home probably, hanging out by myself. My mom's been on the road doing "damage control," I used air quotes for drama's sake. "She was worried after the Olympics most of my sponsors would drop me. I'm sure when the world catches wind I'm in this place, she'll plan a nation-wide candlelight vigil. And you know about my dad already."

"It says on your sheet he's remarried to a therapist named Jill with two boys under five."

"She's a massage therapist," I said. "Evidently the life as a used car salesman is stressful enough to require four rubdowns a week. That's how they met. But now she is the shift manager at our local Hooters, since my dad got her new boobs. His idea of a business investment, I guess."

"You don't like her much, do you?"

"Geeze, how could you tell?"

Tillie laughed. "Blended families are hard."

"There was no attempt at blending, believe me. My brother can't stand our father either. They haven't even talked since Pete left for Princeton a few years ago."

"What about you? When does your dad speak to you?"

I thought about that because I really had to. "There was that one conversation when he was setting up direct deposits from my bank account to his. Other than that, crickets. He more yells or lectures. We don't really have much to talk about anyway now that I don't swim anymore."

"So, Racer is like a family to you, isn't he?"

I'd never really thought about it in that way before. Certainly, I liked him more than either of my parents, and for all intents and purposes, I lived at his trailer. "I guess you could say that."

Out on the lawn, the circle of boys was breaking up and I wouldn't have minded calling it quits myself. To Tillie's credit, she picked up on it and put her papers to the side. I was ready to claim victory before she leaned across the table, removed her glasses and looked me straight in the eyes.

"How about we get to the heart of the matter, shall we?"

"What's that," I asked.

"How long has Annie been sick?"

FOUR

January 18, *Wednesday after group*
Mood: Surprisingly amused

Dear Annie,

Today I was tempted to entertain my group therapy session with tales about Dad and Mommy New Boobs, but I didn't. It just didn't feel right. To tell these people all my problems would be like giving them ammunition to use against me. Granted, there were a few girls that seemed very nice. A few Threes, (minus Missy and the Bikinis) most of The Fours and all The Fives made a point to introduce themselves. But I'm still not on board with this incarceration yet. I'll let you know if and when my attitude changes.

I may or may not have mentioned the girl down the hall with flowers and colorful bedding. In my head I called her Martha Stewart, but I was introduced to her today and her name is Fiona Tannenbaum. She's from Alabama and an ex-swimmer like us. We ended up having lunch together in the commissary, and now we're heading to the gym together.

Fiona says she's a fan of mine. Like, she knew all about

me and followed my career. It kind of sketched me out how she knew the names of my dogs and my favorite kind of protein smoothie, but I played it off with a smile and a thank you, just like we were taught. Fangirling is weird. Don't get me wrong, it's very flattering. Fiona seems real nice, but total strangers knowing personal stuff about me creeps me out and it's straight fucked up when someone says to you "Hey, you remember that time when you said..." and you have no idea who the hell the person is or what the fuck they are talking about.

I'm not saying fame and fortune is all bad, but anonymity in a place like this has its advantages. If no one knew me, I could reinvent myself. I wouldn't have to cover tracks or give explanations about that thing I was quoted about in the news. It's like playing an open hand of poker. It's pointless to bluff because all your cards are already laying out on the table.

Fiona was pretty honest about herself in group. That must be a quality of Level Fivers. She sounded like she accepted her life and the different things that would happen once she got out of here. Before, she was living on the streets with two drunk guys, eating hotdogs and popcorn from a dumpster outside a Birmingham movie theater. She drank two bottles of vodka a day. Her parents kicked her out after she withdrew thousands from their bank accounts. After that, she was arrested for shoplifting wine from a convenience store, and they had to bail her out. They sent her here six months ago, and next week she's leaving.

I can't imagine living on the streets. Although if I was honest, in the weeks before this West Coast jaunt, I wouldn't have known the difference. And six months? That poor girl has been here for six months? Maybe that's just for *real bad cases like her. The ones near hopeless. The terminal cases.*

I hate that you can relate to that. So this will be the first time I've actually worked out in a while. I know, right? Maybe a little physical activity will burn off some anxiety. And Fiona seems a nice enough workout buddy. I'd much rather it be you.

———

MAKING friends in this joint was not at all a priority but I felt like if Fiona was making an effort to connect, I should at least reciprocate. Otherwise, these people were the types of folks you met on vacation. Ones you share a few laughs with, a meal or two, and then hop flights back to wherever it was you came from. I felt like, though, if I'd met Fiona on the outside, I might actually be her friend. Or, if I did meet her on a vacation, I might actually keep in touch and not just through SnapChat or whatever. Which was why when she asked me to head to the gym after our lunch the day before, I agreed to.

Her long blonde ponytail swept across the lower back of her sunshine yellow Nike track suit as she led me down a flight of stairs to the field house. I noticed she kind of walked with a bounce. A sort of confidence I wondered if all Dunes graduates earned. People waved with wide smiles when she passed, like subjects acknowledging their queen. I felt like I was being sucked into her vortex of positivity. It was too bad our time spent together wouldn't be long. "I'm so happy you came with me today," she said to me over her shoulder. "It helps to have a workout buddy. Keeps you motivated."

I thought about Annie and our contests of how many laps we could swim in a month. The loser had to buy the winner strawberry shortcake at the Erie Bakery. The memory put an ache in my chest. "I haven't worked out in a while," I said, stretching my arms in the air. "I probably won't make the best company."

The gym was another massive, beautiful glass enclosure with every healthful machine or tool one could imagine. I followed her past rows of treadmills and ellipticals to the corner with the fancy bikes. We got ones next to each other. I could tell by the way she placed her towel and water bottle and punched the buttons that this was a serious habit. Me, I put my feet on the pedals and half-assed pushed. If I had shoes with laces, I might have upped the effort. "I'm not sure I'm dressed to do much," I said.

"Yeah, those jump suits aren't high fashion." I made sure I brought as many work-out clothes as I could pack. It's kind of my other addiction. That and hair products. I have a thing about my hair."

She shook her head like a girl on a shampoo commercial waving her long ponytail in the sunlight. My hair was now blonde again but it didn't looks shiny and beautiful like hers. Between the chlorine and basic neglect, my hair was pretty gross and forever in a long stringy ponytail. I yanked on it to tighten the elastic. A funny fidget I had when I was nervous or focused.

We pedaled a few moments in silence, before she took a swig of water from her bottle. "That Racer guy?" she said in a pant. "He get you into it?"

The change in subject startled me. "Into what, working out?"

"No, I mean. Did he get you into the life? The drugs and stuff."

The lack of segue confused the hell out of me. What exactly was "the life?" Was there something I missed? She looked at me now with a different intensity, like any prior conversations between us were just a means to an end.

"No judgment," she added quickly. She brushed her hand on my arm as she pedaled away. "Believe me, I get it. Some older dude acts like he loves you, and fucks you like he loves you, and then you end up a drug addict whore. It's okay to be mad at him."

Clearly, she was talking from experience, but I didn't know the "rules" enough to feel okay to ask her about it. Was it prying or cathartic to want follow-up information? So, I responded with on a non-committal, "Yeah," and let her keep talking.

"Are you mad at him?"

I shrugged. "Mad that part of the reason I'm here is because of him, yes."

"No. Mad that it feels like he doesn't give a shit about you. Mad that you trusted him with your body, and he used you."

"You don't know him." I told her. "It's not like he was out to get me or anything."

"Are you sure?"

Again, she caught me off guard. I turned to her in what I'm sure was a glare.

She laughed. "I told you no judgment. I'm just observing that our stories are kind of similar. My Julian is older and an asshole, same as yours. But I love him just the same."

She peddled harder, like she was vindicated that her point was made. "Here's the thing. A lot of us have Racers in our lives. Most of them truly are pieces of shit who couldn't care less if we were found in a ditch somewhere, but sometimes true love really is involved. That's definitely how it is with my Julian, and maybe that's how it is with your Racer."

In my mind's eye, when I pictured Racer and me, it wasn't like some romcom movie montage of us walking through the park or sharing an ice cream cone or laughing at, well, anything.

I just imagined him "there." Like when I needed someone to be. Was that love?

I was beginning to wonder if Fiona was the best person to ask.

"So, you still love Julian?" I asked.

"Hell, yeah. Just because I'm in here doesn't mean I'm just going to abandon him." She stabbed the pause button on the bike, yanked the towel from the handle and dragged it across her head. Obviously, I'd struck a nerve and I couldn't decide if she was perspiring from the bike or because she was agitated. "I won't be in this place much longer and I'd like to think I won't be back. But the reality is when I leave here, I won't be running back to the drugs, but I will be running back to him."

Even to me, someone in a jump suit only hours with a clear head, that sounded like a bad idea. "You really think Julian is what's best for you?"

"In here, they'll preach to you about choosing new friends and turning your back on people who hurt you in the past. But I'm a Christian and I believe in forgiveness. We can cut people out of our lives, or we can forgive them for the bad stuff and give them second chances. Isn't a second chance what we're all after in here? Seems hypocritical if we don't reciprocate with the ones we love."

This was not at all the calm, centered girl who bared her soul the day before in group and shared chicken nuggets with me at the commissary. She almost sounded bitter. Calculating. When she jumped off the bike, she scanned the immediate area before leaning in close to me as if sharing a secret. "Don't get me wrong," she said. "These people are wonderful and absolutely spot on about so many things. But when it comes to true love, they don't get it. They don't understand that you can't help who you fall in love with. Even if logic says it's wrong to be with someone, the heart wants what it wants."

The way she looked at me told me she expected a response, but I didn't trust myself with what I'd say. So, I just stopped myself on the bike and took a gulp from my bottle. Even with my Level One reasoning, this sounded like the opposite advice I'd expect to be getting from someone about to be let loose back into the wild.

"Don't you believe in fate? Destiny?" she asked. "Like the Lord was looking down on you the moment you two met and you were meant to be together, despite anything bad?"

Her dark brown eyes locked hard on mine, and I could tell she felt deeply about every word she said. I didn't have the heart to tell her that I didn't think God would be quick to bless a union that started in a dirty stall in a Buffalo mall men's room. "I'm not sure I believe in that stuff like you do."

"But you must love him deeply for him to have this much control over your life, right?"

I shrugged. "He took care of me when I needed him."

"Right," she said. "So did Julian. That's why when I leave here, I owe it to myself to rekindle our love. If we can get through this, we can get through anything. He's my real addiction."

There was a part of me that wanted to stand up and applaud her. But there was another one that wanted to scream for help or tether her to one of the heavy free weights so she couldn't leave the place. "Fiona, this guy you love. When you see him again, do you think he'll make you relapse?"

"He won't make me do anything," she said, simply. "And if he makes me want to, the fates will take care of me."

With a flip of her long blonde ponytail, she slung her towel over her shoulder. "I'm glad we met, Natalie. I feel like we vibe."

I was a little nervous she was right. On the way back the rooms, she yammered on about the legend of Julian. The candlelight dinners she planned and romantic poetry she'd written. Julian appreciated her brain, she said, and I wondered if Racer had even cared if I had one. I made a mental note to consider it all later, so long as the thought was still accessible after my head exploded.

———

Since Fiona was heading home, there was a whole rooming shake up. When the dust settled, it ended up that Cassidy was my new roommate. I asked Dr. Teeth if the maneuver was planned, but all he would cop to was "the chemistry of friendship is definitely a factor in successful recovery."

And I thought I was a bullshit artist.

So right after dinner, (Fiona's last) Clint, the maintenance guy, some of the girls and I helped Cassidy move her stuff in with mine. I was hoping Cass would score some of Fiona's shwag, like her flower vases or picture frames, but then I remembered she was only a Level Two. Cass was lucky just to have shoelaces, much less ambiance. I was almost flattered the staff thought I was stable enough to be in the same room as shoelaces. Even if I couldn't wear them myself, it was progress. What Tillie called "Baby Steps."

Some of the girls stayed in our room for a while to chat, help make our beds and rearrange furniture. All under supervision, of course. Tillie and a few of the nurses made brownies for the occasion. Someone commented that they couldn't remember the last time they had one that was pot free, and the rest of us laughed. Dr. Teeth probably wouldn't have had he been there. Or at least he would have asked her to elaborate on how eating drug-free brownies made her feel.

I didn't think it was possible, but for a moment I felt normal. Like I was a kid at summer camp eating baked goods in our bunks, laughing and telling jokes with girls I had just met. Some of the girls asked me about being famous and if I knew any movie stars. I recited a short list, and they seemed impressed. People weren't stiff like in group. It was cool, and for the first time I was actually okay to be where I was.

I sat on my bed against the wall with Cassidy. Two Three's, the unfairly gorgeous Hispanic BF's Ari and Tia, were across from us on the other bed. Staci, the girl who Missy teased about Mitch in group, sat on the floor between us. Staci didn't open her mouth once. I wasn't sure if it was shyness or having nothing to add to the conversation, but she just sat there with her red bangs hanging in her eyes, studying the chocolate that stuck to her fingers.

"Hey, Staci, you okay?" Ari asked. "You look kind of down."

Staci looked up like she just realized there were other people in the room. "What?"

"You look sad," Tia, said. "Missy really hurt your feelings this morning in group, didn't she?"

The girls all looked up when Fiona came into the room with a plastic pitcher of milk and cups. She sat down at the desk and poured Staci some. "I was hoping you were going to lay into her," Fiona grumbled.

"Right, so I can further embarrass myself? Forget it. I've had enough with public ridicule."

"Come on, Mitch was flattered," Tia said. "At least, I don't think he was offended."

Tia took the cup that Fiona offered and sat down on the floor next to Staci. "Come on, you were being honest about your feelings. Isn't that what we're supposed to be learning here?"

"Yeah, brutal honesty without the help of Jack Daniels." Ari raised her cup of milk in a toast.

"And let's face it." Tia smirked. "Mitch is pretty good looking for a white guy."

"He'd be gorgeous if he were purple with pink hair," Staci agreed. "I just wish the whole world didn't know I felt that way."

So, it wasn't only me who was curious about Mitch. "What's with that guy, anyway?" I piped in. "He works here, but he's too young to be a doctor or anything."

Ari sighed. "Mitch escorts some of the kids here after intervention. Staci's got a crush on him, and one day she left a poem she wrote about him in the day room by mistake. Missy found it and read it in front of everybody in weekly assembly."

"Wow," I said. "What did Mitch say?"

"He was cool about it." Staci wiped her hands with her napkin. "But the things I said in it were really embarrassing."

"She wrote about them having sex," Cassidy blurted with a mouthful of brownie. "Lots of it."

"Wait, you had sex with him?" I asked.

"Of course not. First of all, he's not a douche bag. Second, we barely even see the guy because he's always hopping a flight somewhere. And believe me, I'm sure he wouldn't be interested anyway. He's probably got a gorgeous model girlfriend he lives with in L.A. or something. I doubt I'd ever be on his radar screen."

"I hope not," Fiona said. "What are you, eighteen? He's like twenty-three."

Staci shrugged. "That's not much. It's legal."

"He works here. And we're residents," Fiona declared. "Either way, it's totally inappropriate, and Mitch doesn't strike me as a perv." Spoken like Level Five Gospel. Fiona brought her cup of milk to her lips as if to signify her point was made.

I took a gulp myself when the image of Racer flashed in my brain. Lots of people made a big deal about Racer's age. Truly, I didn't see much difference. On the few occasions we'd actually been out in public together, we'd get weird looks, but I figured that was more because of his piercings or people trying to place me. The only time anyone got in my face about it was Annie when she brought me to the doctor for what turned out to be a syphilis infection. It was her first day home from a lengthy hospital stay. She may have been weak, but she managed to wrestle me from Racer's trailer, call him a slimeball and lecture me the whole way to a free clinic about "getting my shit together." I gave them a fake name, they gave me a shot of penicillin, and I miraculously walked away with a prescription of Vicodin for the pain. Racer and I went through 30 pills in three days.

"If you like someone, age shouldn't matter," I said, although I meant it more to myself than to say it out loud.

Ari looked at me with a smirk. "It should matter if it's a felony."

The girls all stared at me, and I realized I'd struck a nerve. I didn't know whose or what about, but if the dagger eyes Ari shot at me were an indication, my guess it was her. "You tell that to my baby's daddy that age doesn't matter."

I held up my hand to show no offense. "All I'm saying is that my boyfriend Racer is not that bad."

Ari slid off the bed and glared at me with dark eyes. Pretty, but intimidating. The scar on her cheek led me to believe confrontation didn't bother her. The girl was scrawny, but the scrappy kind with long dark hair in a neat braid. I could see her veins pop on her arms when she crossed them against her. "Listen, Little Miss Special. You think you're different than everyone else here? We all had the boyfriends who we thought gave a shit. What did he do? Teach you how to roll a joint? Cut a line? He got you high, right? But then what? One day you had to pay for it and couldn't. Then what did you do?"

I gulped. The first day I met Racer we smoked a bowl in the mall bathroom with some friends. A week later I was practically living with him playing games like "Boobs for Blow" where I had to flash him and his friends for a bump. But I didn't care. I just liked that I was with someone and somewhere that Natalie Collins, World Champion, didn't exist. Nat, the stoned girl, was a more relatable incarnation, and I didn't mind the stuff that came along with it. "Racer cares about me. I know he does."

Ari chuckled. "Believe me, Buffalo, he's screwing you in more ways than one."

If I offended someone I didn't intend to, but I didn't think anyone would believe me if I told them so. So, I opted for a lame, "I'm sorry."

Ari stormed out of the room, and I just sat there with my jaw in my lap. The girls looked at each other before Fiona smiled and said, "I know you're new and all, but one day you're going to realize that for some of us, apologies are nothing but sugar-coated insults."

Huh?

"Ari is sensitive about boyfriend shit," Tia said, peering over the rim of her milk glass. "She's got a two-year-old son that was taken from her because of her, 'boyfriend.'" She quoted with her fingers. "He's thirty-seven, and she was thirteen when he started shooting her up with heroine and sending her out to hook for drugs."

Fiona shook her head. "She's not too fond of any guy right now. I don't blame her."

Evidently there was a language that only the higher levels were fluent in, because the room cleared out before I could blink. Except for Cassidy, of course, who still sat across from me with her head buried in a TV Guide.

"Do you know what I said that was so bad?"

"It's not so much what you said, but how you said it. Your attitude."

"What's wrong with my attitude?

Cass slammed the magazine shut and chucked it aside.

"Okay, it's like on the Bachelor when a girl steps out of the limo and says before even meeting the guy how she's the woman of his dreams. She can't *know* that," she explained. "You can't just act like you know everything when you know nothing at all."

Cassidy had a language all her own on a planet all her own. If I wanted her insight, I'd have to pay a visit. "So, what you mean is that girls on the Bachelor should take the time to get to know the Bachelor before having an opinion about anything. But, Cass, I wasn't telling the girls what to do."

"Just be considerate of feelings. No one likes a Know-It-All!" She took a deep breath. "Sincerity gets you roses, Natalie."

I still didn't know what I did wrong, but Cass acted like she'd brought peace to the Middle East. She slid off the bed and returned her TV Guide to the stack on her newly-moved-in desk.

We both got dressed in our white Dunes PJ's (t-shirt and elastic pants) and climbed into our beds. Cass tucked in her remote control beside her and I waited for her to snap off the lights, but she didn't. Now that I was all paranoid about my alleged attitude problem, I made sure I was extra polite. "Would you like to go to sleep now?" I asked.

"I'm not tired yet. I mean, my body is, but my brain isn't. There's a difference you know."

"Sure."

"Sometimes when people fall asleep, they think about what they did that day and the things they'll do the next, and that makes them fall asleep. That doesn't work for me."

I rolled over and propped my head in my hand. "Then what does work for you?"

"I think about TV. Sometimes I make up shows in my head. I think about setting and dialog and camera angles. I can create my own characters. Cool right?"

Her singsong voice sounded like a child's, and it was hard

not to answer her like she was one. I overheard from some of the nurses that Cassidy was "Tagged ED." ED stood for "emotionally disturbed" and from what I understood from her brief chats in group, it was more than the drugs that made her that way.

"Wanna see what's in my box?" Throwing off the covers, she reached under her bed. She pulled out a beat up FootJoy shoe box and climbed back between the sheets. "I don't show many people. But it's really fun."

I sat up in my own bed, watching her rub the thing like Aladdin's lamp. "You're allowed to have personal stuff?"

"They let me have this." She opened it up and pulled out a blue pencil with a yellow crescent moon eraser. Underneath were four or five old TV Guides, the kind that looked like the small magazines you could buy in the grocery checkout lines back in the day. She laid them on the white comforter and stared at them. "Aren't they awesome? I look at them all the time."

Curiosity got the best of me, so I went over to get a closer look. The things were beat up, glass ring stains, fraying spines and the mailing strips hastily rubbed off. I noticed that they were all from the month of March, fifteen years earlier.

Cassidy just stared at them with that faraway smile that was neither comforting nor inspiring. The kind that was too blatant to be natural. Her eyes moved across the pages, her fingers tightly gripping the sides. Totally engrossed. Mesmerized. Suddenly, I realized I was too. Not in the TV Guide, but in Cassidy's attachment to them. Earlier, before my scene with Ari, I probably would have just blown her off, not knowing or caring where the poor girl was coming from. But maybe everyone had a point about understanding other's perspectives. Cassidy's, Ari's, my family's.

Annie's.

"So, what exactly do you like about watching TV?" I asked. "You want to be an actress or something?"

She cocked her head, like the question never occurred to her. "No," she finally said. "But I would like to be 'in' the TV."

"I don't get it."

"Inside the TV," she repeated. "Like on Full House, I could be the Olsen Twins older sister, or on Friends, the girl who lives next door. It would be fun. Everyone is always laughing."

"And your problems are solved in a half-hour."

"Twenty-two minutes without the commercials. Forty-four if it's an hour drama."

"So, what is it about the Bachelor that you love so much?"

She held her hand over her heart like I asked her to tell me why she loved her own child. "When I was a kid, my mom would put on an episode and run to get groceries, and she'd say she'd be back by the time it was over."

"That's cool. Do you still watch it with her now?"

Her face clouded. The magazine shut, and she dropped it back in the box. "I want to. I hope we do, if she ever gets back from the store."

When I watched her pull the comforter back over her and turn towards the wall, I could tell the conversation was over. Gently, I closed the box and considered putting it back under the bed but instead, tucked the shoe box next to her pillow. "Sleep well, Cassidy."

"You too, Nat," she mumbled. "Tomorrow is another day of regularly scheduled programming."

"Can't wait," I replied and was almost asleep before my head hit the pillow.

FIVE

January 22, Sunday
Mood: Confused

Dear Annie,

So I've been mulling some things over. Incarceration is making me thoughtful but also slightly paranoid. I had no idea how easy it was to offend or piss people off in a place like this.

So, I have a weird question. Promise you won't laugh at me when I ask it. Could it be that I'm lucky? Or, could it be that luck is just relative. Confusing right? Okay, let me try to give you an example.

What if you were watching the news and the reporter said, "A man was run over repeatedly by a train but is lucky to have survived." You could look at the statement two ways. This person was totally unlucky to be run over in the first place, and even more unlucky that it happened over and over again. But how lucky was this person, that after repeated railway assaults, to still be alive? One could then make a case that luck is relative.

Wow, this seems like a conversation I would have if I were stoned.

What I'm getting at is that I'm beginning to think maybe my life is not so bad. I mean, my mom may be a cold opportunist, and my dad a thief who's totally mid-life crazy, but at least I wasn't sold for sex by a guy who drugged me and got me pregnant when I was a young teen. And unlike my roommate, I also have enough gray matter still intact that I can tell the difference between reality and a very special episode of The Real Housewives of Orange County.

People used to call me lucky all the time. Lucky I can buy nice cars, fly on private jets, stay in penthouse suites. But I worked for that shit! It's not like I won some lottery that awarded me athletic ability and some sort of member-ship card to "celebrity." I dedicated my existence to mastering a skill and arguably I succeeded. But so what? Where did it get me? Am I lucky or an idiot who pissed it all away?

But then I think about you. Talk about unlucky. You swam as many laps as I did and traveled to all the same meets, but you got sick. At least the rest of us had choices. Tia chose to let her baby's daddy into her life, Cassidy chose to do Meth, and I chose to quit swimming and deal with shit the way I have. But why? Am I a wimp like my father thinks, or stupid because I'm not my brother at Princeton, or not good enough because I couldn't beat the world record in the 500 meter freestyle?

Am I lucky to be alive instead of OD-ing next to my mother's toilet?

The last few days I've been finding myself comparing everything—my life, being here at the Dunes—to one big swim meet. Not even an entire meet really, but a race. This is definitely like a distance event, not a sprint, and that

*seems fitting right? I mean, I'm the endurance swimmer
and you're the speed queen who anchors our relay. Anyway,
showing up here was like diving in. Or more so like being
shoved in off the blocks into super cold water. It's a shock to
the system. I feel like I just broke the surface and now I
gotta swim. Ready...set...go!*

But it feels like I'm just treading water.

*It could be considered unlucky that I ended up here at
The Dunes, but could it be that in a weird way I might be
lucky? Maybe that's the difference between looking at things
with the glass half-full or half-empty. Maybe addicts are just
pessimists. I'm not sure. But that could be a Level One
thing. Pose some big complex questions, and once you jump
a few Levels you gain perspective. Something I realized here
is that without chemical enhancement, I'm really not the
belligerent type. But I am a sucker for competition and if
these people claim they have all the answers, I challenge
them to give them to me.*

*Swimmers, take your mark! (Dare I attempt cliché and
say, "I'm feeling lucky.")*

———

A FEW DAYS later I walked out of my first evaluation with Tillie and staff and, congratulations to me, I'm a Level Two. The kicker? Basically, all you have to do is survive the first two weeks, and you are automatically promoted.

The whole meeting lasted about five minutes. The other fifty-five minutes of the hour was spent with Tillie in the courtyard discussing Cassidy and things I had to "be aware of" as her roommate.

And I thought the "mom-not-coming-home-before-the-show-ended" story was sad...

Turns out, after her mom "went to the store" (read: crack house), Cass lived in a condemned apartment for three weeks before the police found her mother's body in the garage, apparently a suicide from drinking Clorox. Cassidy had been in and out of an alternate reality ever since.

At the time of her death, her mother was estranged from her rich family, and when Cassidy was found, her grandmother took custody of her. As she got older, Cassidy headed down a bad path. Drugs, booze, all sorts of stuff but it was the meth that really fried her brain. When her grandmother suffered a recent stroke, Cassidy was sent to treatment. The consolation was she would inherit her family's fortune. When the time was right, that would all be explained to her.

But in Cassidy's world, no one wore a watch.

Tillie and I then worked out a whole Level Two checklist of things to see, experience and accomplish before my next promotion. It read as follows.

1. Start academic tutoring program. Peer tutor assigned. (Done and on my way.)
2. Make necessary advances in personal recovery. This includes group and individual therapy. (Yeah, yeah, yeah.)
3. Further assimilate into the community. (If I must.)

Tillie also told me that taking part in physical activities scored brownie points. Disclaimer: I AM NOT A KISS ASS and brownie points don't really interest me. However, physical activity was kind of my jam, and I figured it didn't hurt to play to my strengths in this situation.

Level Two through Fives could come and go to activities as they pleased, but ones and below had to adhere to the "buddy system." We had to have either a higher-level patient or a counselor supervising us. I'd scoped out the pool a few days before with Cass, but I figured hanging there was a ways off. I wasn't sure I even wanted to. Right now, I was more concerned with getting to my tutoring session on time. Thank God I had my shoelaces back. There was no safe way to run in slip-ons.

So, armed with my To Do List, I headed out to my tutor meeting but realized I had no supplies. This being like my first day of school, I felt like at least I should come prepared, so I swung by the front offices to get some pens and pencils and maybe a notebook or two. Things that gave the impression of "studious."

I hadn't been to the front offices since the day I arrived. The actual living quarters of the Dunes residents was kind of isolated, on the opposite end of the complex away from the detox center and main entry. There was a big open reception area in front of the main glass doors and a long white desk with smiling people on phones and reading files. It amazed me none looked stressed or put out. Like they actually enjoyed their 9 to 5 life.

"Can I help you, Sweetie?"

An older brunette lady in a Dune's blue blouse leaned over the desk. She had her hand covering the receiver of a phone, but her gaze told me she'd wait all day for me if she had to.

"I'm just looking for some school supplies," I said. "I thought I could score some from up here."

"You bet," she said, pointing over her shoulder. "Down the hall behind me and on the left. The supply closet has everything you could need. You can look yourself."

I thanked the woman then headed down the hall. When I came to the door with the sign "supplies" written in calligraphy, I went in.

The light snapped on automatically revealing rows of shelves neatly filled with files and boxes. There were random things stashed in there, too. Holiday decorations, table linens, old magazines. I spied a box on a far shelf with "school supplies" scribbled on it in sharpie. I grabbed a step stool and dragged it to the back shelf.

All the plastic bins on the top were tightly sealed except this one. Its lid was ajar and I figured some ill prepared kid like myself just didn't put it back on. I flipped it open all the way, expecting notebooks and ballpoint pens.

What found was piles of money.

It wasn't like in the movies where there were neat stacks tethered together according to denominations. These were literally piles, scattered about like someone had thrown them all in. The bills were mostly twenties, some torn with frayed edges. I noticed some were rolled up as if someone used them to snort lines.

At first, I wondered if it was fake. Like this could have been some old collection of board game money and I was just hypersensitive thinking a rolled-up bill automatically meant bad news. But it looked real, and it smelled real. I reached in and scoped up a handful. It felt real, too.

"Hey Natalie, need some help?"

I almost fell off the step stool when I heard the deep voice. Standing in the doorway was Clint the janitor, looking at me wide-eyed as if he'd located a fugitive on the loose. "What are you looking for? Maybe I can help?"

"I had to get some schools supplies. The lady up front told me to come in here."

We stared at each other a moment before he suddenly broke into a smile. Clint was a bulky ex-military guy with a sandy blond crew cut, beefy muscles and an efficient way about him. If you saw him in the street, his mass and dark eyes might be intimidating, but I'd seen him around and he seemed nice enough, joking and kidding around with the residents. He liked to show off his enormous tattoo on his neck of a scorpion eating a cow.

"I'm sorry," he shook his head and held up his hand in apology. "I didn't mean to snap at you. I'm just not used to seeing anyone in here other than me."

"I'm not really sure I'm in the right place."

He gently closed the door behind him and stowed his mop and bucket. "You're looking for school supplies you say?"

"Yeah, like notebooks and pens...."

"Well, of course, my friend, we have some right here." He grabbed a box out from a shelf next to him and pulled out a few notebooks and packages of pens. "What else do you need? Markers or colored pencils? We even have crayons..."

"That's okay," I said, stepping down from my perch. "Just the pens and notebooks are fine. Thank you."

He pulled out a piece of gum from his pocket and popped it in his mouth. He chewed slowly, like a cow would eat cud, and I could tell he was watching me intently as I tried to slip my way around him. "You're that swimmer girl, aren't you?"

"Yeah."

He nodded, folding his arms against himself, giving me a glimpse of the scorpion cow image in full flex on his neck and disappearing under the shoulder of his blue t-shirt. "So, you'll probably be using the pool now and then, huh?"

"Maybe down the road," I said. "You know, right now I have other stuff I have to get straight."

Again there was an awkward silence. He still stood between me and the door and I could feel his gaze move over me. Tillie told me Clint was a little "off" but he was a good guy. A Gulf War vet who had PTSD addiction but got straight and worked at the Dunes. I heard kids say they felt comfortable around him because he was one of them.

I wasn't sure if I shared the sentiment.

"Petty cash."

I shook my head, confused by what he said. "Excuse me?"

"Petty cash," he repeated. "That box up there. That's where the front office people keep the petty cash."

He nodded his head, like a period at the end of a sentence. This whole scene felt off. Like I had the sense his words were more of a warning than a statement of information. I glanced back up at the box. Its top was still ajar with a twenty hanging out the side. Like a conspicuous something that should not be acknowledged. "I gotta get to a meeting," I said, and I attempted a tone that oozed oblivion. On the inside, though, I felt like I'd walked in on some public service announcement about stranger danger and "if you see something say something."

Mercifully, the same brunette woman who had been at the front desk stuck her head in the door and smiled. "Clint, have you seen the accounting files we were looking for earlier?"

"I was just gonna pull them from the shelf for you."

"Thank you." She then turned toward me, nodding to the notebooks now under by arm and the pens clutched in my hand. "Clint find you everything you need?"

"He did," I said and thanked them both. I tried to follow the woman out but Clint discretely blocked me, holding the door half closed above me.

"If you need anything else, Natalie. You let me know. I know how hard it can be to adapt here. And I'll take extra good care of the pool for you, too. Physical activity is good for recovery."

He gave me a wink then released his grip on the door. I made my way through and didn't look back. It felt like I'd made some great escape from somewhere, or that the front desk had interrupted "just in time." Whatever it was, I just knew I wanted to get back to the residence halls. And maybe send the front desk ladies some flowers.

———

My first "class" turned out to be postponed for a day because of a few unplanned parent visits. That was fine because it allowed extra time for my high school transcripts to arrive. Without them I could have been sent to any old class group, but if I remembered correctly, I was smart. Like, I hadn't been to school in a while but when I last attended, I was near an "A" student. Maybe there was a benefit to blowing academics off completely. You can't fail a class if you hadn't taken it at all.

So finally, I found myself heading for the big circular "school day" table positioned dead center on the patio. There were six kids sitting there, all at various levels of concentration, with pencils in their hands. These were the students "preparing for high school graduation." That sounded about right because I didn't have a diploma, and at almost nineteen years old, I probably should.

Staci, the girl who wrote the love poetry about Mitch, was actually a decent person and rumor had it, an even more decent peer tutor. She sat with the group, her red hair shining pink in the sun, and about four different text books fanned out in front of her. Across from her was a boy with the same size book pile. Only instead of the pages, he seemed to be studying the trees behind him. His dark hair was freshly buzzed, and he was so pale that his lips looked like he'd smeared on lipstick. When I got closer to the table, he pulled his chair away like he was afraid of me, or something.

Sort of the same reaction people gave me before I got to this place.

"Hey," I said and dropped my shit on the table. "Sorry I'm late. Tillie and I were chatting."

"No problem," Staci chirped. "The empty seat is yours."

I followed her nod to the chair next to the boy. He stared at me with wide eyes and his bottom lip trembled like a scream was about to pass over it. When I actually sat down, he clutched his legs to his chest and buried his head in his lap. "Don't do it! Don't come closer!"

Normally I'm not one to take offense, but after my scene with Ari a few days ago, I was hypersensitive. So, I decided that my reaction was just not to have one, and let Staci handle it like I could tell she wanted to.

She closed her text book and reached across the table, patting him gently on his pasty knee."It's okay Kevin," she calmed. "This is Natalie. She's going to study America History with us."

"No, no, I don't like her!"

"You just met her."

He peeked at me between his knees. "She looks hungry. I don't like hungry people!"

"She's not hungry, Kevin, she just wants to study history."

"No, I can tell! She really wants to eat me."

I looked at Staci. She didn't seem alarmed so I figured I shouldn't be either. It took a lot to offend me these days anyway. Instead, she calmly brushed her red bangs aside, got up from the table and kneeled in front of him to meet his gaze. "Kevin, Natalie is very nice and she doesn't look hungry to me at all."

"I just ate," I chimed in. "Not even thirsty."

"Are you sure?" he asked.

Now I realize that most people would find this exchange odd, but here it wasn't. Everyone at the Dunes, including me, was whacked one way or another. Second, I lived with Cassidy. When you have to console a girl who cried every time a TV show ran closing credits, you get used to dealing with the bazaar.

"Kev, Natalie is here because she wants to graduate high school, too."

"You mean she won't eat me?"

I looked at Staci for some sort of direction, but all I got was an eye roll and a smile hidden behind her hand. "Natalie, Kevin is also a Level Two. He's sixteen, from Arizona and thinks he's an onion. He has a thing about people trying to peel him."

"What?"

"She looks hungry, Staci!" Kevin again cowered behind his knees, and I sat there biting a hole in my cheek to stop the laughter. None of the other kids seemed to share the sentiment because I had yet to see anyone even look up from what they were reading, much less react to what was going on.

"Kevin, I promise I don't like onions or any type of vegetables," I said. "And if it's okay, I would really like to study history with you."

Slowly he brought his feet to the ground. "Are you sure?"

"Positive."

He looked at me as if to mull the whole thing over, then got up and pulled his chair to the other side of the table. After I slid his books across, I took over the empty space next to Staci. "Are you sure you don't mind that I join you?" I whispered. "I mean, if it's going to flip Kevin out..."

"Please, he's fucked six ways to Sunday. Besides you can help me baby-sit him."

"Staci wants to go to RISDI," Kevin blurted. "She has this really cool service project all lined up."

"Kevin!"

"She's an artist, and she likes to paint sexy things. She tells everyone at Show and Tell!"

"I do not!"

Show and Tell? Now there was a term I hadn't heard since second grade. I'd been here only a few weeks, and I'd already gotten used to people knowing way more about my future plans than I did. But that didn't mean I wasn't curious. "What's Show and Tell?" I asked.

Staci smiled. "Never mind."

"Oranges have skin to peel, too!" Kevin declared. "But I'm not a fruit." He burst into a fit of laughter. "Get it, I'm not a fruit."

Staci shoved a pile of books in my face. "Listen, Nat, I'm only supposed to tutor schoolwork. Anything else, ask Tillie or Dr. Blaine."

"What's RISDI?"

Staci sighed. "Rhode Island School of Design. It's an art school where even clean kids with talent can't get in to. I'm a drug addict hack. Night school at the local rec center is probably where I'm headed. But Kevin's right. I do have a cool service project that might help me out a little."

Was it possible there was an orientation that I missed? I'd never heard of service projects until Staci just mentioned them. But maybe that was the point, 'one day at a time' being their motto.

"What's a service project?" I asked because I couldn't help my curiosity. "Like, what do you have to do? Pick up garbage on the highway or clean the pens at the zoo or something?"

"No. You aren't a fucking prisoner. It's like an internship." Staci set her notebook down beside her. "Okay, so we're all high school students and the goal is to get us to graduate or get our GED and be productive people again. The Dunes believes by getting us interested in a possible career, we can focus positively on our future."

"Makes sense."

"When you make Level Three, they ask you to fill out one of those bubble scantrons— What-I-Want-to-Be-When-I-Grow-Up questionnaires. Then they talk about your areas of strength and your interests in the future."

"Okay, so your interest is going to art school."

"Which probably won't happen. But I totally lucked out because I scored an internship with Lance Bates. He's an artist with a really successful pop art gallery in Los Angeles. He was a resident here, and every once in a while, he takes on a Dunes resident with an interest in art to help them out."

Staci smiled and pulled her notebook back in her lap. It was weird, but I realized this was the first time I ever saw Staci as a 'kid.' Her interactions seemed more mature and put together than everyone else's. Not that nineteen was a child, but I saw her as this older, more mature woman. Maybe because she had goals and was working toward something other than a clear head. She actually had a *plan*.

"Will I have to do a service project?" I asked.

"Everyone does. Bosses are called mentors. Some people work in clothing stores, or hospitality. If you like social work, they pair you with the group homes where you can work with kids or the homeless. All sorts of stuff."

"Well, well, well...Look who has some shoelaces."

Missy and her entourage strutted towards our table with shit-eating grins I read as a call to battle. They all had towels in their hands and wore red Dunes issued bathing suits. (The only clothing not white for safety reasons) Another testament to their Level Three-ness. Tan lines. I made a mental note to lie out in the sun during my next rec period.

"Congrats on the Level Two, Nat," Missy said. "You know, I thought it was the space suit that made you look fat. Turns out you look like just as much of a cow in the shorts and T-shirt."

Missy and the Bikinis laughed. Actually, I almost did myself. I admit, I have my body image issues, but if Missy wanted to one-up me on something, my looks was a poor choice. For one thing, I had about three inches on her five-two frame and I weighed about thirty pounds less. My teeth were also straight.

Let's not even talk about her lazy eye.

Or, let's.

So, I folded my hands in my lap and smiled up at her. "If you wanna body shame others, maybe you should check out yourself in the mirror first. Or is it too hard to see with that fucked up eye of yours?"

On the other side of the table, Kevin again burst into laughter of total inappropriate proportions. "Ha ha she burned you! It's funny because you're really the fat ugly one!" He threw his head back and held his stomach.

"Shut up, Onion Boy! I'm in the mood for a salad!"

And just like that, his mouth clamped shut and his pencil was poised at his notebook. The Bikinis smiled in awe at their leader. When Missy nodded toward the pool, the three turned and headed down the path.

"Ugh," Staci mumbled. "That girl is a waste of space. Her friends aren't that useful, either."

"Please, they're harmless."

"Hey, Natalie. Do you like apples?" Kevin was staring at me over the rim of his text book. His eyes shifted back between Staci and myself.

"They're okay," I said, not sure what answer was a safe one.

"If I was one, I would let you bite me."

"Excuse me?"

"I think he's hitting on you," Staci supplied. "Last week he told me that if he were an ear of corn, he'd want me to smear him with butter."

SIX

"ISN'T Onion Boy so cute! I met him yesterday in OccuTher. He asked me if I wanted to nibble on him. You didn't try to peel him, did you?"

I sat next to Cassidy in the day room waiting for one of the nurses to cue up her favorite season of The Bachelor. Over the past couple of weeks, Cass had become the staff favorite, and they would do anything for her, including indulge her TV obsession. I tried my best to support her habit, too. I'd already seen seven final rose ceremonies. According to Cassidy, confessions of love followed by devastating heartbreak are the main components of great television.

Evidently Onion Boy was highly entertaining, too.

"Yesterday, in class we were reading bus maps," Cass informed me. "We pretended our chairs were seats on the bus, and he let me sit next to him because I promised I wouldn't peel him."

"Wow," I said over the Bachelor host handicapping the contestants. "So, you guys like each other?"

"I'm not sure. The only vegetable I eat is broccoli."

"OccuTher" was Occupational Therapy. Somehow people

like Staci and I had managed to keep most of our brains from frying, but for those like Cassidy and Onion Boy who had not, regular school was morphed into OccuTher class. They learned "life skills." Stuff like doing laundry, paying bills, and riding the bus. There was also a unit on grocery shopping. God knows how Onion Boy would handle that.

"Next we're going to learn about reading the news," Cassidy said. "A big stack of magazines was brought in the classroom today." She scanned the room and then smiled at me like she had a secret. "I saw you on a cover of one of them."

I felt like a parent wanting to shield a child from sensitive material. "Was it at least a flattering picture?"

"It said you 'cracked under pressure.'" She shook her head. "That sounds like it must have hurt."

Cassidy's six-year-old literal interpretation of the headline made me smile. "No, that's not what they mean. I didn't actually crack open, Cassidy. You know, they meant I like cracked inside my head. A mental breakdown."

"Oh yeah," she said slowly, like she suddenly remembered the meaning. "That's not very nice of them to say. I'm sorry."

"Its fine. It's not like its isn't accurate, I guess."

"But I feel like the world should make you feel better and not worse." She paused the TV and looked at me, like what she was about to say was gospel. "Natalie, you are my friend and if you were sad about something, I would want to cheer you up. Why would I want to make you feel even worse about something you already feel so bad about that you screwed up your whole life and ended up here because of it?"

It amazed me how she could make complex things so simple.

"It's not like you're a bad person and trying to hurt people. You're a good person in a bad way. We should help people in a bad way. That's why we're here. So we can be helped."

"You're absolutely right." I told her.

She settled back against the couch and pushed 'play' on her remote. "There're way too many terrible people out there."

"True."

"Like Missy is the worst. I saw her at the pool today with the other mean girls. The mean girls swam, but Missy hid in the pool shed."

I leaned forward to look her in the eye. "Wait a minute, what were you doing by the pool?"

Cassidy shrugged. "I walked by it on my way to the courtyard for my one-on-one with Tillie. She got me new batteries for my remote." She held it up in the air. "See?"

"Did you tell Tillie?"

"Tell her what?"

"About Missy in the pool shed?"

"Why?"

Good point. What did we care? There was a lot to be said for minding your own business around here, but since getting the weird vibes from Clint the day in the supply closet, I couldn't help being a little more nosy. Also, I'm a passive aggressive type, a tactic I'd seen my mom use in my business dealings. While I couldn't imagine using Missy hiding in a shed as ammunition for anything, I thought the knowledge might come in handy for self-defense at a later date.

"And I found something else out today, too." Cass looked over her shoulder at the nurse's station before turning back to the TV. "Our parents are coming to visit."

She said it like demons were coming to claim us, and I realized I could relate. I also knew to tread lightly considering her bazaar family status. I ran my hand through my ponytail and prepared myself to ask the obvious question. "Whose parents, Cassidy?"

"Everyone's. I was in the office waiting for Tillie to get my batteries, and I heard two of the nurses talking about it. It's a Level Three thing. I saw Ari's mom come in today. She had a little kid with her. I think it was Ari's." She looked at me with a crooked smile. "I'm not so out of it that I don't know what I heard."

Okay, it made sense parents would want to visit kids here. But I couldn't imagine my dad caring enough to want to, and good luck getting my mom to fit a visit into her busy schedule. Of course, there was always the chance Cassidy's information was wrong. Like yesterday, when she told me that once she stayed awake to prove she could sleep with her eyes open, or last week when she swore she was sunburned from sitting directly under the fluorescent lights in the OccuTher class room. Sometimes though, Cassidy had moments of clarity. Maybe this was one of them.

"What do you think Kevin is wearing underneath?"

"What?"

"Onion Boy, he doesn't want anyone to peel him and I'm just wondering, if I did peel him, what he'd be wearing underneath."

"I can't imagine."

"Do you think I would cry?" Cass slumped in disappointment. "Maybe I need to get those onion goggle things, just in case. Would that hurt his feelings? I don't want to onion body shame him."

Cassidy's moments of clarity. Unfortunately, they didn't last very long.

———

At nine am, after an Onion Boy approved breakfast of French toast and coffee, the OccuTher class and I all headed out the front entrance to the drive-in loop. This was oddly exciting to me because I hadn't been outdoors, not fenced, for in three weeks. Not that I was a prisoner, per say, but leaving the premises would be considered an escape. Either way, it felt special, like a third grader with her friends on a field trip.

"Riding the bus is so easy, Nat," Onion Boy bragged. He stood on my left and Cassidy on my right as we waited at a makeshift 'bus stop,' which was the welcome sign at the front door loop. My job was to stand there with the dangerous duo while the OccuTher teacher observed them walking me through the process of using public transportation. Parked at the far end of the entrance was what looked like a Los Angeles city bus. It had a real authentic bus driver, too. Very legit.

"I'm really nervous," Cassidy said. "So many things can go wrong. You could get off at the wrong stop. The bus might break."

"Cass, what if the bus is magic!" Onion Boy looked around me to meet Cassidy's gaze. "Like the Magic School Bus on TV!"

"That would be awesome!" Cassidy replied, with equal amount of awe.

When we heard the start of the bus's engine, Onion Boy took a deep breath as if to get serious. "Okay, as long as we aren't going to a grocery store, I should be fine."

"We aren't really going anywhere, Kevin," Cassidy soothed. "It's just pretend. Don't freak out."

As if on cue, both took my hands on either side. I gave them each a supportive squeeze. Clearly this was a big moment. What they had trained for.

The teacher, who I'd only heard Cassidy refer to as Braid Lady and who ended up being the woman who had driven me to the Dunes, rattled off the rules. They were to board the bus safely using all their new skills they had learned, tell the driver where they wanted to go, ride the bus and then return to where they started. My job was for them to walk me through it. Like they were teaching me. So basically, we all get on the bus, make up a place to go, ride around the parking lot as if going to that place, and come back. Easy A for Cassidy. If that's how they graded this type of thing.

There were six other kids with a few other "helpers" like me, but we were first in line. I wasn't sure if there was a placement advantage for this kind of thing. Like if you went first, you were more or less likely to get a better grade. If this were a swim race, I'd make sure they were in the center lane. The fastest. So, I shoved the kid behind us ahead. That kid could go first, and we could draft off them.

Strategy.

The bus pulled up and opened its door. A young actor type looking guy with a wide toothy smile and dressed in full on bus driver garb, tipped his hat like he was greeting a bunch of preschoolers. The boy ahead of us, some really tall kid with a dark mullet, hopped on the front step but suddenly jumped back.

"I'm not ready," he said, panic stricken. "I forgot where I'm going!"

Kids gasped and looked at each other like the world might possibly end. No one said anything, so I didn't think it hurt if I did. I stepped up on the bus, stood in the aisle behind the driver and offered my hand. "Hey, kid, it's fine. This man will take you wherever you need to go. Think of anywhere."

"I can't!" He pressed his eyes shut. "I can't think of anywhere I need to go. I'm destinationless!"

"Oh, no," Kevin whined. "Natalie, he has to think of somewhere to go or he fails."

"Hey, I know who you are!"

Suddenly, the bus driver threw the bus in park and jumped from his seat. The next thing I knew, I was knocked on my ass with his phone shoved in my face.

"What the fuck is your problem?" I yelled, getting up from the floor.

"You're Natalie Collins, the swimmer, right? So, you ARE in rehab?"

I shook my head. This asshole clearly wasn't letting me off the bus until he got his pics, so I might as well bide my time with favorable conversation. "You think I'd be here by choice? So, this is a long way to come for paparazzi. You that desperate?"

"Everyone in LA is paparazzi, girl." He held the thing in my face and by the light I could tell he now was making a video. "How long are you here and when're you going back to swimming?"

"Swimming!" Some girl standing next to Braid Lady at the curb shrieked and burst into tears. "I don't want to go to a pool! I don't know how to swim!"

And then all hell broke loose. I'd never seen anything like it. Some kids laughed, a few cried, and one took off all his clothes and sprinted out across the lawn. Onion Boy and Cassidy just stood there while personnel filed out the front door to retrieve the wayward and console the upset. Meanwhile, I tried to push past the bus driver guy who still blocked my exit from the bus.

"So, Natalie, is it true you were prostituting yourself for drugs? And some forty-year-old guy was your pimp?"

"What? No! Of course not!"

"Are you at this place because you're having a nervous breakdown? How stoned were you at the Olympics? Did you fire your coach because he doped you?"

"Get the fuck out of my way!"

"How do you feel about your teammate Annie Madsen dying of cancer?"

And then, as if my right fist worked independently from my body, it unleashed its fury-filled blow to the asshole's chin. It had so much power behind it that he catapulted off the top bus step on to the pavement below in a limp heap. He landed at the feet of Cassidy and Onion Boy, the two lone calm people among the chaos.

"Oh my gosh, Natalie!" Cassidy yelled at me. "Why are you beating up the bus driver?"

I jumped off the bus and stood over him, waiting for him to get up so I could hit him again. I felt this white hot, almost electric surge shoot through me. Sharp and tense. Things I hadn't felt in a long time. A horseshoe of people now stood around me with slacked jaws and wide eyes. When I spotted his phone still clutched in his hand, I snatched it and slammed it against the ground.

The thing bounced off the curb and shattered in a million pieces. In that moment, Tillie appeared out of nowhere and grabbed my cocked shoulder. "Let me go, Tillie!" I told her. "This guy had it coming!"

"We know." Tillie replied calmly. "We're taking care of it."

"That bitch broke my phone." The bus driver crawled on the ground attempting to recover a few pieces. "The world is right! You are a crazy fucked up bitch!

"Wanna know how fucked up I am?" I taunted. "How about I break your face next?"

"Peel his face off, Natalie!" Onion Boy yelled. "Get him!"

When he staggered to his feet, he was bookended by two burly Dunes guards. He spewed off a bunch of "fuck you" laced insults at me, before they hauled him off toward the back of the building. "I'm suing you for breaking my phone, Natalie Collins," the bus driver screamed. "I'm taking this to court!"

"How about you go to hell and fuck yourself instead!"

"Ha ha!" Kevin laughed. "Yeah, go there, asshole!"

Tillie still had a death grip on my arm and having nowhere else to go to avoid the curious crowd, she hauled me back on the bus and shut the door. I sat down in the front seat looking out the window at the crowd. Tillie plopped down in the driver's seat and after a beat talked to me through the rearview mirror. "Well, that was quite a show," she said.

"I suppose I have to apologize now."

"He shouldn't have been here in the first place so in that sense, no apology necessary. But from a using-violence-to-manage-crisis standpoint. Not your best moment."

I glanced out at the curb. The OccuTher kids now mostly composed and collected, waited patiently on the sidewalk for instruction from Braid Lady. A group of Dunes security people huddled in the side parking lot with at least one talking urgently on a walkie talkie. I hated that this scene was all on my account. "Now the world is gonna know how fucked up I am," I said.

"Well, and also what a killer right hook you have."

I looked at Tillie, and she shrugged. "These news stories are all about the spin. You think you're the first famous person we've ever had here?"

Given the swankiness of this place, I figured I wasn't. But if that was the case, I felt like a system of vetting the hired help would have caught this douche bag before I had to clean his clock. "So, what do I have to do now? Add 'anger management' to my list of things to work on?"

"We can talk about that tomorrow in one on one. After your Show and Tell."

And the hits just kept coming. I couldn't help chuckling, both impressed and horrified by the bad timing.

"That's tomorrow?"

She bit her lip. "Today actually. We changed the schedule because so many of you were helping with the OccuTher kids today. I was coming to wait for you when this whole thing happened. You ready?"

"You can't be serious."

We were both startled by a knock at the window. The tall

kid with a mullet waved hysterically, smiling at us. Like he had to tell us something important. I knelt on the seat and lowered a window. "Hey, Natalie, you gave me an idea on where to go! I figured out my destination!" He looked back at Cassidy and Onion Boy before turning back with a shit-eating grin. "I wanna go to hell and fuck myself!"

He collapsed in a fit of laugher on the sidewalk. Braid Lady came over, retrieved him, Cassidy, and Kevin and offered an apologetic wave before heading inside.

———

February 19, Friday Night/Saturday Morning
Mood: Moody

Dear Annie,

I'm writing this by moonlight, well before sunrise. I feel it provides a dramatic ambiance for my personal tragedies. Also, I don't feel like getting shit from the night supervisors for having lights on when I'm not supposed to. But I couldn't sleep, and I have so much to report so I hope this note is coherent. I feel wrecked, but of course I'm totally straight.

Yesterday started when some dude with a camera, (Paparazzi in the desert, who knew?)broke into the Dunes. One thing led to another, but at the end of the day, I think all he got from me was a black eye, so I guess that's a win. The main event yesterday, though, was my Group Therapy Show and Tell. I'm sure that's not the clinical word for it, but it's what us Fuckups call it. Anyway, it can best be described as a violent case of verbal vomiting in front of an audience. What happens is you sit in a circle with fifteen other girls, then stand and tell your whole life story without interruption and elaborate on why your life sucks. It's not that I didn't have a lot to say, I just didn't know where to begin.

So, there I was, standing there, after just beating that paparazzi guy up, trying to wrap my head around bearing my soul when I now face possible assault charges from a guy who wanted to sell parts of it. Am I keeping things in or letting stuff go?

Pick a lane, Natalie!

Anyway. Show and Tell. It was like standing there right before a swim race, set in the blocks and staring down the still water, anticipating that micro-moment between a false start and the gun. Intense. So, after pleasantries and the obligatory whatever-is-said-stays-in-the-room and everyone-supports-you blah blah blah, I started with common knowledge. Name, age and then I held my breath, dove in and just kept going.

I started with the divorce. How I thought it was ridiculous to have a father named Jack married to a Hooters Employee of the Month named Jill. Of course, I talked about my swimming career and how I loved the sport but hated the bullshit that came along with it. The TV, the social media, people treating you like a paycheck and not a person. I told them about us swimming together. How you're my best friend and the best IM anchor in world history.

Then it got weird. It was as if the rest of the room disappeared, and I was just standing there talking to myself. Like with that little girl on the plane ride out here. Stuff started falling out of my mouth.

I heard myself babble on about Buffalo and about my house by the pond, and my spaniel Lollie that I couldn't remember if we still had. About my white paneled basement and the huge pink dollhouse Dad built. It fit all of my

Barbies along with some of the match box cars I stole from my brother. I talked about our swim meets my parents never came to, unless they knew the press would be there, and how much I wished your mom was mine. We always pretended we were sisters. It was my number one wish when I blew out the candles on my birthday cake each year. Usually, one your mom made because mine didn't bother.

I gushed about our matching bikes Coach Simms bought us one spring. We were nine, I think. I named mine Ms. Shiny, and you named yours Steve for no other reason than you said it "looked like a Steve." The princess phone I got in my room when I was ten, the first time I saw myself in a magazine or on TV. That crazy live interview during the Olympics when I burst into tears and told the world to "fuck off."

There was more. Shit I hadn't thought about in years. I didn't bother with Dad's wedding fiasco, or Racer, or all the other stuff with the Olympics. No one asked so I didn't elaborate. Maybe that's for some other day.

I also didn't mention that you had leukemia.

I just couldn't. I can barely write the word. It's like some mental hot potato I keep pushing around in my brain so it doesn't burn me. You have every right for hating me for being such a terrible friend. Landing myself here when you needed me most.

It's way past bedtime and I'm wiped out. Tomorrow I have "follow up" with Tillie when I suppose I'll have to dish some more. Just want you to know that I'm actually starting to swim a little here. Not just treading water.

SEVEN

TILLIE SAT BACK in her wrought iron patio chair. The half-sun reflected off her silver rimmed bifocals and sweat trickled down her chubby cheeks. I could sympathize. Heat and I didn't get along, and between yesterday's shitshow at OccuTher and my meltdown in group, I felt less prepared to tolerate it. So, I sat across from her, nursing my Evian, pitying the group of kids on the lawn behind Tillie having a study session in the hot sun.

"So, yesterday was a big day for you," she said.

"Yes, I'm now the official hero of the Occupational Therapy crowd."

"That guy was a jerk." Tillie took a swig of her water. "I'm sure he completely blindsided you."

I shrugged. "Well, at least I know what the press is reporting about me. It is kind of nice I don't have to deal with it right now while I'm in here.

Tillie eyed me a moment before patting my hand on the table. "The bus incident was one thing, but I'm more interested in talking about group yesterday. Sharing your struggles with people is a sign of openness and a willingness to move forward."

"I was told to do it."

"No one put a gun to your head. Anyway, by now I'm sure you've probably heard in the next few months you can expect visits from family members, a service project, and of course keeping up with your studies. Also, we are looking for progress in group therapy and one-on-one work as well."

I raised my water bottle in a sarcastic toast. "Great. Can't wait."

"There are however a few subjects I would like to broach right away."

"Like?"

She leaned forward, resting her chubby arms on the table. "Well, for one, what the hell happened at your father's wedding?"

I reached around to my ponytail and pulled it tighter, something Tillie called a "nervous habit" but what I considered something I did to draw focus.

Potato potahto.

"Okay, well, my dad was getting married to this crazy woman..."

"No, no, no." She waved her hand in the air. "I'm pretty clear about your relationship with your dad and stepmom, and what you did to their limousine, and the fire sprinklers at the reception and all. What I am more interested in is what motivated you to do what you did."

"My parents are now named Jack and Jill and my step monsters are Chip and Dale. They spend their time coordinating matching outfits and creating their own private language. Tell me how that doesn't make you want to set something on fire?"

"Okay, so maybe your parents are flakes. So what? But you should realize that your dad is angry because you won't try to see things his way. Just like you're mad because no one tries to see things your way. Like when you defend your relationship with Racer."

I saw her point. And I hated that I did. "Yeah, but Racer's just misunderstood."

"You are aware a forty-year-old man sleeping with a seventeen-year-old is a crime in some states."

"Not in New York. And I'm almost nineteen now, so it's a moot point."

Tillie sighed. "You don't like when people question your choices, do you?"

"Does anyone?"

"And I suspect that your father doesn't, either." She picked up her pencil and pointed the tip to the empty notebook page in front of her. "What was going through your head when you crashed your father's wedding?"

I'd been asked this before. At my ambush, and Mitch even tried to tease me about it on the plane. No one ever worded it in a way that made me stop and actually think about it. What *was* I thinking?

My first memory of the day was waking up at Racer's trailer, feeling like shit and having no recollection of the night before. Recently, I hadn't been coordinated enough in the mornings to do much at all, but that day I had a mission. I managed to get my ass to the hardware store, score some red spray paint and sneak into the party house parking lot where the limo was idling. For days, I had this graffiti thing planned, but I couldn't come up with the perfect message or statement to make. And then, as I crouched in an overgrown hedge, I popped a few pills and the next thing I knew, the inspiration came to me. In bright red block letters, I sprayed "WHORE" across the side of the limo.

From there, I ran inside to a living nightmare. Wedded Bliss in Pepto Bismol pink. A hundred people, maybe two, with full wineglasses next to forgotten plates of half-eaten filet mignon. Exotic flower arrangements, even tropical fish swimming in fishbowls on tables as centerpieces. Lavish and gaudy. Everything I would expect from Jack and Jill. All bankrolled by me, of course.

I hid myself behind a coatrack, taking the whole thing in. There my dad and Jill were, swaying to "My Funny Valentine" smiling and nodding at the adoring crowd around them. It was just all so gross. Jill's tits falling out of a tight white cocktail dress so short that her blue garter was an accessory and Dad with his new hair plugs, pretending he was within a decade of Jill's twenty-four years. Fake. Like everything about him. His smile, his hair, his heart. Human garbage that hustled people for a living with his lemon cars and get-rich-quick schemes. He was a cheat and a pig that never gave a shit about my mom or my brother or me, unless he could get something out of it. Money or otherwise.

It was the "otherwise" that disgusted me the most. It was that moment, so revolted by his happiness, I realized how much I wanted to knock that happiness out of him like he'd done so many times to me.

Next to me was a table lined with presents. In a burst of fury, I rushed it and flipped it, sending boxes skidding across the dance floor. People stumbled, some fell, and I laughed at the sound of crushed glass as people trampled them. I then made a very nice imprint of my ass on the bottom tier of the cake, (Racer's suggestion) and told the guests they could all go fuck themselves, (my idea) before pulling the fire alarm and setting off the sprinklers. At some point, I might have mooned the videographer, too.

The scene in my head was almost amusing, but when I relayed the details to Tillie, they sounded less impressive. Okay, so I got Tillie's point. Crashing the wedding was a bad idea all around. He may be a d-bag, but so was I. And really in the end all it got me was a headline on the ESPN news crawl and a trip to this lovely place.

Tillie took a big gulp of lemon ice water. I felt bad I'd rambled on for so long. Even in the shade, she looked like she'd been smeared with butter. "So now what?" I asked. "When my dad visits, I have to beg for his forgiveness and tell him I'll mend my ways?"

"That's your decision. I'm not here to tell you that your dad is Mr. Wonderful. I have your family history here. I can see why you have problems with him."

"You do?"

"Sure. For one, you're aware of his infidelities to your mother. That's a violation of trust for your whole family. I know you have abandonment issues because he prioritizes his new family over you and your brother. I suspect you may have other beefs with him?"

She raised an eyebrow, and I caught her drift. I took a sip of my own ice water. "He's a horny drunk," I said. "But I'm faster and more coordinated, and my mom has just as mean of a right hook as I do."

Tilled just nodded. "But you do also understand that your relationship with your father directly affects your relationship with other men, so it's in your best interest to get your shit straight about that?"

"I guess."

"Which leads me back to Racer."

I groaned. "Look, Racer is a good guy. He may have a few problems, but he cares about me. Really."

I gazed at gray mountain peaks off in the distance over her shoulder. On-the-spot questions about Racer were the worst. When I first met him, I was still in school from time to time, and Dr. Pimco, the East Buffalo High psychologist, had me in his office for an hour one day, cross-examining me about "the nature of our relationship." I didn't offer much. I told him that I didn't ask him about his love life, so he shouldn't bother with mine.

But Tillie was different. She didn't judge. Okay, so she was a counselor with motives, but I liked the way she went about shrinking my messed-up head. A sudden breeze hit me in the face, and I took a deep breath. "He loves me," I said. "He's grumpy sometimes, but I like waking up and he's there, and I like cooking for him and hanging out with him."

"You enjoy his company."

"Beats being alone."

"Is that how you feel a lot of the time? Alone."

Again, I reached for my ponytail and gave a good tug. Most of the time, I did feel alone. At the pool, in an airport, at a restaurant or a press conference. There could be a million other people around, and I'd still feel like the solitary loser. It was like watching a movie or looking through a window at a reality I wasn't part of. It hadn't always been that way. I couldn't pinpoint exactly when it happened. It was sort of a slow drifting away rather than a clean jerk. "I guess I do get lonely sometimes," I conceded.

"And Racer fills that void?"

"Racer makes me feel good when I feel bad, and I'm not talking about the drugs or the sex. It's just him, and I feel like I owe him for that."

"Do you trust him?"

Tillie looked at me through her think glasses, her bottom lip caught between her teeth. She had something to tell me. Something big. Dear God, please don't tell me Chip and Dale were expecting a chipmunk sibling.

"Why?"

She reached down into her bag and pulled out a stack of papers. They looked legal with small dark font and red tags sticking to the sides. "I'm sorry to have to tell you this, Natalie. Racer's been arrested."

"Shit." I sighed. "They caught him with oxy again, huh?"

"No, not oxy."

"What then, coke?" I shook my head. "He's totally looking at jail time now."

"He's definitely looking at jail time," Tillie said with an anger in her voice I hadn't heard before. She reached across the table with her chubby hand and placed it over mine. "I'm sorry, Sweetie. Racer was arrested for rape, and a slew of other counts."

"What?"

"He drugged young girls he met at area malls, took them to his trailer, and videotaped having sex with them. The press found out that you're one of the victims." She slid the papers in front of me. "You should read this because you might be asked to give a deposition."

February 19, Friday
Mood: Triggered

Dear Annie,

Okay, so maybe you had a point about Racer.

The past few days have been pretty crazy. First, Show and Tell, then a few hours after that I get nailed with papers from the Buffalo police department. Racer's been arrested for doing all things perverted. They confiscated a bunch of videos. Guess who's a movie star?

You already knew all this, didn't you? Damn Channel Seven Eye-Witness News!

Anyway, I don't know if I can wrap my head around

this. I mean, I realize I was totally out of it, so it wasn't my fault that he took advantage of me, but it was my fault for putting myself in the position in the first place. How angry should I be? Is there a right proportion? And what about blame? Am I like 100% responsible or is it more of a fifty-fifty thing?

Tillie says he's pleaded "no contest" to the tapes in exchange for a plea deal. Once everything is processed (whatever the hell that means,) the tapes will be destroyed. Thank God, because the last thing I need is to have myself naked spread eagle on YouTube.

My parents are probably freaking out. Although not for normal parent reasons. Like Mom's probably trying to channel her inner Kris Kardashian to figure out a good PR spin to profit from it, and Dad probably has his financial advisor on high alert in case she doesn't succeed. I guess I'll just embrace the isolation rule. My parents and the vultures of the world can feast on the rotting carcass that was my career. I'll be in here, watching bad TV with Cass and eating apples with Onion Boy.

Today in my In-House Mail, I did get a message from Mitch. You remember him, right? Anyway, he must have heard about what happened (gossip flies fast around here) and felt bad about it. Here's what it said:

Natalie,

I heard about the Racer thing, and I'm really sorry. The last person you probably want to talk to right now is a guy, but I thought I would give it a shot anyway.

When I was a Level Two, my counselor gave me this little poem. Actually, it's a prayer, but I don't think you have to be religious to get something out of it.

Today I will be strong. I will not let someone else's short comings be an excuse for me to fall apart. I have strength within me if I use it. I cannot control anyone else's behavior but my own. If I am sincere in my path for personal growth, I will understand that the relationship I need to work out first is the relationship with myself. Lord, give me strength.

We're all behind you Natalie,

Mitch

Now, I am not sure if Mitch was put up to sending it, maybe by someone like Tillie or if he did it on his own, but either way, it was nice. And really, other than myself, I don't hate anyone right now, not even Racer. Maybe in a way, it's good I don't remember the whole thing. In fact, one of the nurses said that to me today. But really, I wish I did. Is that sick? I want the ability to go back and imagine telling him no.

If I hadn't been so whacked-out on whatever Drug du Jour, I could have.

You know what I remembered today? The first time I took one of my mom's pills. In the grand scheme of things, it wasn't that long ago. One year, five months and eleven days exactly. I remember I came home late that night after skipping swim practice that day, and Mom leveled into me. For an hour she went on about how one skipped practice, or one less trip to the gym, could upset the delicate balance of my unprecedented career. About the level of commitment she needed to see from me, what Coach Simms expected from me, what the world demanded. I remember I just wanted to disappear.

That was the day you told me something was wrong with you.

I never told her about our secret lunch that day. It wasn't hers or anyone else's business. That was between us. Of course, inevitably word got out and just like the cancer itself, it spread to every curious ear worldwide. And it broke *my heart. Our whole lives we'd been through everything together. Braces, boyfriends, birthdays. You are my one steady constant. I could not fathom you not being in the swim lane next to me. I still can't, and I won't.*

After my mother slammed the bedroom door, I went to the bathroom to dry my tears and opened the medicine cabinet for cleanser to wash my face. There, next to the Band-Aids and dental floss was my mother's full bottle of Valium. I figured, what the hell?

Minutes later. I felt nothing. Like that horrible lunch hadn't even happened, and if it did, it certainly wasn't in this reality. It felt incredible, to chill out. To be able to forget all my problems and dull the razor-sharp edges that now cut so deep in my everyday life. So, I took more and more, and that lead to booze and dope and the fucked up game where I chased the high and ran away from everything else that was too heavy a burden to bear.

Now I'm realizing in this situation, and hell, maybe in others, I really just want to feel something again. Take shit full-on without a filter. I am realizing that living life on this conveyor belt of medium, where nothing makes me exceedingly happy and nothing totally bums me out, is just a waste of being human. Maybe being numb isn't better after all.

Oh my God, am I saying that I'm glad Racer raped me?

No, but they say everything happens for a reason. Maybe that applies even to this.

EIGHT

THE NEXT WEEK or so I spent a lot of time just existing. Of course, news spread about the Racer situation. (Thanks to one of the Bikinis who "accidentally" saw some paperwork at the front desk when the UPS guy delivered it). Everyone was super supportive. Even Missy adopted the "If You Can't Say Anything Nice..." rule because she hadn't said a word. Not just to me, but she'd cooled off on teasing Cassidy, too.

The good news, which let me say has been in limited supply lately, was that I hadn't shot myself in the head yet. I'd officially survived one month at The Dunes. Truthfully, life without cell phones and internet access actually made for a pretty peaceful existence. But sometimes, I just felt gross. Like my skin was dirty with grime that wouldn't rub off. I decided to do something about it.

The Dunes pool was hardly ever busy, which I could never understand because lately it'd been ridiculously hot. It was a really nice pool, too. Six lanes, fifty yards long with a diving well. Almost identical to the one I trained in at home. I walked by it all the time on the way to tutoring sessions but until today,

I lacked the guts and a person to drag with me. That morning I put on my red swimsuit and talked Tillie into coming along.

So there I was, balancing on the side of the pool, dragging my big toe across the blue water. The black lines at the bottom distorted from bold and straight to jagged zigzags. "You coming, Til?"

Tillie sat in a lounge chair with her hand shielding the sun and a towel draped across her large lap. It impressed the hell out of me that she agreed to put a suit on much less consider swimming in it. Hers was red, like ours, but the cut was different. More like a "mom" suit with a high neckline and low on the legs. I wondered if that was just because of her size or was meant to set the employees apart from the residents. Either way, I was psyched. I guess the "if you want me to improve myself, you should try to do the same," guilt trip/motivation did the trick.

"I feel ridiculous," she grumbled.

"Come on, you'll feel great once you get in the pool."

"Do I look like a swimmer to you?"

She pulled off her glasses and rubbed her eyes. I could tell getting her the last few feet between the chair and the pool would be the greatest challenge yet. "No, you don't," I conceded. "But I think a part of you wants to be. I see you eating all that low-fat yogurt and drinking Diet Coke. You wouldn't do that if you didn't want to lose at least a little weight."

She laughed. "Now who's the shrink around here?"

"Please come swim with me," I said with my hands folded in front of me 'in prayer.' "I'm a screwed-up kid and it would make me feel so much better if you, an adult, would take the time...."

"You are so full of crap sometimes, Nat." With a grunt, she heaved herself off the chair and the towel she held over her thighs fell away. That's when I saw them. The deep purple scars that ran in lines and disappeared under her bathing suit bottoms.

Quickly she lumbered across the deck and cannon-balled into the water. The spray hit me in the face, but I barely noticed.

"Happy now?" she asked when she resurfaced, and doggy paddled to the side.

"What happened?" I blurted.

"Huh?"

Really, I hadn't meant to say it out loud and as soon as I did, I felt bad. The thing was, I'd seen marks on girls like that before. Fellow swimmers with no way to hide them because swimsuits left little to the imagination.

I sat down on the pool edge, shielding from my eyes from the sun so I could look straight in hers. "You're a cutter?"

Tillie swam closer and lifted her thick arm to harness herself on the side. "It's that obvious, huh?"

"I'm sorry, it's none of my business. But..."

"It's okay," she replied like she knew this was coming. "I figured you would see them."

Our roles felt suddenly reversed. Me asking her to divulge her deep secrets, while I listened without judgment. I knew full well I was no therapist, and really, who was I to even expect a response? But I wanted to be her friend. I felt like she cared about me, and I wanted to show her I cared back.

"There were girls I knew who were cutters," I said. "It's hard to hide when you're a swimmer because you show so much skin."

"Would you believe me if I told you I used to be a model?" She slicked her hair back and gave me a pucker-lip pose. "Bikini even. You're looking at a two time runner up Ms. Cocoa Butter."

When she laughed, I thought it was safe to do the same. To

reconcile the Tillie in front of me as any centerfold I'd ever seen was hard, but I didn't want to say that.

Tillie pushed herself off the side and treaded water in front of me. I could tell she was getting her thoughts straight by the way she watched the water slip through her fingers as she stroked. "It's like any other story in Los Angeles, Nat. I came to the West Coast when I was nineteen because I wanted to be a model. I know it's hard to believe but I used to be a cute little blonde. Nice chest, tight ass. You know, all the model things. Anyway, I got an agent who told me I'd be more marketable if I had other talents. Acting, singing..."

"You can sing?" I asked?

"No!" She dunked herself under the water and slicked the hair from her face when she resurfaced. "That's the thing. I didn't have any talent except looking good and when you have that much pressure to do your job, it messes with your head."

"I can relate."

She smiled at me. "I know you can. So, I had to make sure I looked extra good to compensate for the talent I lacked. But unlike you, I'm not an athletic person. I love to eat though, so I put on weight. Pretty soon my agent told me I was too fat to book, so I started taking diet pills. When those didn't work, I did cocaine. That held off my appetite okay but burned a hole in my nose. Along the way, I kind of dealt with the stress of it all by cutting. Somehow, feeling physical pain helped me deal with emotional pain."

"How did you end up working here?"

She paused a moment, wiping the water from her upper lip. "A close girlfriend of mine, a fellow model I'd met when I first came out here, died of a drug overdose. I realized I would end up the same way if I didn't make some changes. So I went to rehab, then to college. Became a counselor and wound up here. The end."

I nodded, watching my legs make circles in the water. "Ever still do it? I mean, cut?"

She shook her head. "No, but I do think about it. I mean, I see the scars everyday. I know how bad they look, but believe me, they looked worse years ago."

"And it's not like they're where everyone can see them," I offered. "You can hide them."

She shrugged. "Even if I couldn't hide them, at this point it really doesn't bother me. We all have scars, Nat, but they fade. You have yours, but they'll heal, too."

"Do you miss the model life in LA?"

"If I were still in LA, how would I have met you?" She smiled and teased me with a splash. "You happy now?"

"Thrilled." The breeze kicked up, wrinkling the surface, and I could smell the chlorine wafting around me. A weird sort of energy zinged through my body like it used to right before a race. Like all my senses were heightened. The sun was warmer, and my limbs were stronger and nimbler than a few seconds earlier. How fucking great was it to be talked "with" and not "at?" Like I was a person who could *contribute.* I swung my arms to stretch them out before taking a breath and diving in.

The water skimmed over my skin and silence swelled in my ears. When I broke the surface, I propelled my arms in quick smooth strokes just like I used to, like my body had a memory of its own. A few laps turned into a few more, and by the time I stopped at the opposite wall, I'd swam a half mile. Thirty-five laps. Not a world-record pace, but smooth. Funny what clear lungs can do.

"Wow, that was a show," Tillie said when she swam up beside me on the wall. "In the time it took you to do that, I only swam four lengths."

She panted slightly like she always did, but somehow her

smile seemed wider. Maybe I had a small part in making it that way. "Four is better than nothing, right?"

"Yeah, and I like this better than a treadmill."

"See. Exercise can be fun."

"Not bad." Tillie tipped over on her back and floated facing the sun. "Don't let me interrupt you. You keep swimming, and I'll just hang out."

For an hour I did a series of sequences, every stroke, even butterfly which I hate. For a cool down, I floated on my back like Tillie and stared up at the blue sky. It was the first time in a while I was enjoying myself. Truly on the plus-side of just existing.

"Hey, Natalie, we ran late. I have to change and get back up to the office."

I swam over to the side where Tillie stood, her beach towel looking like a dish rag against her large self. "I have to go and get changed. Can I trust you to get yourself out of here and back up to the dorm on your own?"

I was flattered that she even asked. "Sure. And hey, Tillie?"

She turned, squeezing the water from her hair.

"Thanks for talking to me. And I'm sorry about your friend."

She moved to block the sun from my eyes and stood above me. "And I'm very sorry about your friend, Natalie."

It was the first time since I'd been at the Dunes I didn't mind someone else bringing up Annie. It felt sincere. Like we now shared a secret or had made a pact. One I was totally committed to. After a last cool down lap, I headed over to the hot tub for a few minutes to relax my muscles. It was at the far end of the pool, out of the way and sort of hidden by a semi-circle of small trees and shrubs. It was cool to be by myself. The hum of a lawnmower filled my ears and the scent of rose bushes tickled my nose. It was peaceful. Something I hadn't experienced in a long while.

I didn't actually see Clint walk through the gate, but his trademark Johnny Cash CD blaring from his old-school portable player was a tip-off. When I peeked over the hedge, his golf cart was parked next to the shed, and he was clanking around the pump room humming off tune to "I Walk the Line."

After a few minutes he appeared rubbing his half-exposed belly like his lunch had been a doozy. He emptied the poolside filters, hosed down the deck and refilled the chlorine tank. After putting all his tools back in the cart, he got in and turned up his music.

When I figured he was gone, I settled back into the tub but before I could close my eyes, I heard the gate reopen. Clint stood there a moment with his hands in his pockets then headed to the First Aid box on the shed wall. He jammed whatever it was in his pocket into the box.

If the guy hadn't been so bad at being discreet, I probably wouldn't have thought twice about it. I also would have been more surprised when Missy arrived ten minutes later and retrieved whatever it was that he'd left.

———

"Did you guys read the letter from Fiona?" Staci asked over our mac and cheese dinner in the commissary. "It's hanging up at the nurse's station. It sounds like she'd doing really well."

I scooped a forkful into my mouth and passed the salt shaker to Ari beside me. She emptied half the contents of the damn thing on her food while the rest of us pretended we weren't disgusted. This was a normal thing for Ari. Whatever weird concoction of drugs she had taken on the outside had ruined her taste buds, so she salted *everything*. Seriously. The other day she even put some on her watermelon. She said she'd lost about twenty pounds since she'd been at the Dunes because eating tasteless food was no fun. Maybe that was Tillie's problem. Food just tasted too good.

"What did the letter say?" Ari asked, her arm still shaking wildly. "Is she at home with her parents?"

"I think she's living with her boyfriend in Birmingham," Staci replied. "She's hoping to hear about a new job this week."

"That's great," Tia said. "I was hoping shit would work out for her."

"I think she might relapse."

Everyone looked at Ari, who licked the cheese from her fingers.

"That's not a very nice thing to say," Cassidy said.

"What?" Ari asked. It's not like I'm trying to hate on Fiona or anything. I'm just saying. I spent a lot of time with her in tutoring, and we hung out a lot. I'm telling you, she may seem under control here, but on the outside. Whole new game."

Staci poured herself some milk from the pitcher on our table. "I don't know about that, she said. "Her parents will probably keep a close eye on her. I met them when they visited. They seemed nice enough."

Ari shrugged. "I hope you're right, but I say if she's back with her old boyfriend, she's in trouble."

The five of us looked at each other. Maybe it was the months' worth of Dunes head straightening, but I felt like Ari might have a point. I remembered the conversation I had with Fiona when we went to the gym together the day before she left. All that stuff about star-crossed love and her misunderstood boyfriend. If it sounded off, it sounded downright fucked up now. But what the hell did we know? If Tillie, Blaine, and the rest of the staff thought she was ready for the outside, how could she not be?

"Fiona will be fine," Cassidy finally blurted. "That's it. I don't want to listen to this anymore." She pointed her remote at us, pushed "mute" and picked up a piece of garlic bread.

"All Ari is saying is that in here, none of us can score anything anyway, so it's easy to stay clean." Staci waved her fork in the air for emphasis. "On the outside, different story."

"Speaking of scoring," I said. "Has anybody ever tried to from the inside?"

Four sets of eyes swung in my direction. Those in mid-bite had stopped chewing and the others dropped their forks to their plate. "Are you crazy?" Staci whispered. "Say that a little louder, and we're all in trouble."

"I'm not saying that I want to," I assured her. "I'm just wondering if it was possible." I watched Missy and the Bikinis across the room at their own table. I wasn't positive the little bag I saw Clint stash in the First Aid box was dope, but really, what else could it possibly be? "What do you guys know about Clint?"

Staci swallowed a gulp of milk. "You mean the maintenance guy? He seems nice enough. Friendly but not in a creepy way."

"You might have an issue with older men," Ari teased me. "But I support your revenge against Racer."

Everyone laughed. Recently, the girls had tried to make me feel better about the whole Racer thing by finding the humor in it. A little sick, but well-intentioned and I went along with it despite the fact it still hurt a lot. "No really," I said. "What do we know about that guy?"

"I don't think he's bad," Tia said. "When Fiona left and we changed rooms around, he helped move my desk. He talked a lot. Asked me about my family, my hobbies. Said he just liked to get to know the residents in case they needed help."

"That's nice. Seems harmless," Staci said.

"Yeah." Tia brushed her long dark braid over her shoulder and bit her lip like she was choosing words carefully. "But sometimes I wonder if he's too harmless. Like he's being extra nice because he's got something going on."

"Like what?" I asked.

She shook her head. "I can't explain it. Like a dude with an agenda."

I hadn't said a word about the day in the supply closet or what I saw at the pool. Not that I was specifically hiding it, I just didn't know what it meant or if it mattered. It also occurred to me that if Clint was a shady guy, if too many people were on to him, he could straighten up before he was called out. I'd just let the subject drop and took a last bite of my mac and cheese.

"Are we allowed to write to Fiona?" Cassidy asked after unmuting us with her remote. "I'm only a Two, but don't higher Levels get mail privileges?"

"Ari, Tia and I are Fours and we don't," Staci said. "Maybe when one of us hits Five, we could send her a card or something."

Ari laughed and rolled her eyes. "You're kidding, right?"

"No, why?" Staci asked

Ari tossed her napkin to her plate. "Let me ask you all a question. Do you think prisoners who are sprung from prison go back to see their old cell mate on visiting day? Fiona doesn't want to hear from us. She's got to move on if she's gonna stay clean."

"Well, she wrote to us first," Cassidy said.

"Take it from a girl who has been around. This isn't a magic land where people come here and leave and life is all good. Some come back three, four, ten times before they get their shit straight. You want what's best for her? Cut her lose. Otherwise, she's gonna slip up."

Ari scooped up her plates and dropped them off at the kitchen window. The rest of us followed. Suddenly, we'd lost our appetites.

NINE

I SAT OUT ON A WHITE DUNES' beach towel on the lawn and tried hard to stay focused on the Robert E Lee chapter of my American Pageant textbook. No dice. The sun was too hot, the weed whacker too loud, and my mind was too busy to concentrate. Lately, I was always *deep in thought*. Everything was a question or something to be explored. Staci even asked me a few days ago if I knew if, "What if" was my new favorite way to start a sentence. I hadn't noticed, but now that it was brought to my attention, I added it to my mental list of things to mull over.

Word around the place was that I would soon be a Level Three. Tillie hinted about it, and a few of the girls said they had a feeling. I had to admit I was better physically, but mentally still shaky. It was like my life was this huge tornado and now that the storm had passed, I had to pick up the mess. I didn't know where to begin.

I closed my text book and laid back with my arms behind my head. For February, the sun was amazingly hot. In the past, I hated the heat but since I'd been here, I noticed that it didn't bother me as much anymore. It could be that's what this whole experience was about. Doing new things. Search and discover. Tillie told me once that Level Two was like coming to terms with sitting ass first in a mud puddle. You have to get over the fact that you're there in the first place, before you can stand back up, clean yourself off and move on.

"Hey, Natalie, long time no see."

When I opened my eyes, a tall figure in a white tee and jeans stood over me. His head blocked out the yellow sun. I brought my hand to my forehead and squinted. "Mitch?"

"Sorry, were you napping or something?"

I hadn't talked to Mitch since the day he dropped me off here, but I had seen him milling around and on random days, he sat in on group. Mitch had a mysterious way of lurking. In a good way, in his unassuming t-shirt and jeans and a half smile at the ready. The letter he sent me when the Racer thing happened was probably one of the nicest things anyone had ever done for me.

"Hey, hi," I stammered as I sat up. "No, I was studying actually. I have a tutoring session with Staci Blinkin in a little while."

Getting ready to graduate, huh?"

"I'm not sure why. It's not like I'll be going to college in the fall."

He lifted his sunglasses to his shaggy blond head and shoved his hands into his pockets. "You gotta think positive, Nat. Who knows what could happen between now and then?"

"I suppose."

This was weird. A normal conversation with a guy. Dr. Blaine would be impressed.

"So, I thought I saw you in the pool the other day. Even more impressive to see you in action in person rather than on TV."

"You swim?" I asked.

No, more like wade. I'm a beach man myself. Looks like you'd still be pretty competitive, that is, if you wanted to be."

He looked at me like he expected a response. I was caught off guard. Did I even have an opinion on the subject? And even if I did, why would he want to hear it in the first place? "Um, I guess I should go find Staci and see what's holding her up," I said, getting up from the grass.

He gave a quick scan of the courtyard. "I hope I'm not the one that's keeping her away."

"Why, because of the love poetry thing?"

"I get the sense she's still a little embarrassed by it. She shouldn't be. I was flattered."

"That's nice of you to say." This was okay. Conversating. Comfortable, in a way I wasn't used to with a boy. Excuse me, a *man*. "By the way, I got your note about that whole Racer thing," I managed. "That was very cool of you. Really."

"Just offering my support. That's what this place is about, right?"

"Yeah, but you didn't have to. And you went out of your way to do it. That means a lot."

He shrugged. "I just wanted you to know you had a friend. Even if you hate guys right now, which you have every right to. I hope you don't hold that against me."

"I don't hate you. I'm still slightly annoyed with you for dragging me out here."

"Hopefully you'll get over it." He laughed and man, did I like the sound. Deep and easy.

"Listen, Nat, when you make Level Three, you're given a day pass out. I know you probably don't have any family or friends out here, so if you'd like to get a cup of coffee or something..."

"I'm in. Sounds good."

I wasn't sure what I liked more, the news that a day pass

might be in my future or that this guy wanted to hang out with me. Although if he was asking me out, I wanted to tell him that after Racer, I was swearing off older guys. Really any guys, and as an employee of The Dunes, even if he was attracted to me, wasn't that against the rules to have a romantic relationship with one of the residents?

"Great," he said. "I'll tell Tillie. When I accompany the Out-of-Towners on day passes, she likes to know ahead of time so it fits my schedule."

Of course, he was offering his babysitting services, not a date. Healthy people had healthy boundaries. I pulled a handful of grass and let it blow off in the breeze while mentally kicking myself in the head. "Sounds good," I said.

"So, I guess I'll see you soon. And tell Staci I said 'Hi.'"

"I'm right here," she yelled as she jogged up to us. She stopped with one hand on her knee and the other in the air, like she planned on saying something really important as soon as she caught her breath.

"You okay?" Mitch asked. "You look like you're gonna pass out."

She offered Mitch a little wave but kept her eyes to the ground. I was pretty sure this was their first interaction since the poetry drama. I wondered if her red face was exhaustion or embarrassment.

"They're here, Nat." she panted.

"Who's here?"

"My parents. Tillie just told me. They want to see me." She dropped her butt to the grass and covered her face with her hands. "Ugh, this is so the last thing I wanted to do today."

"Wait a minute. You didn't know they were coming?" I asked.

"They don't tell you," Mitch said. "They think your reaction is more genuine if you don't know about it."

"God, I was in boarding school for six years, and they never came once," Staci whined. "Why would they bother now?"

In the two months I'd been at the Dunes, I'd come to know most of my fellow residents' back stories. Staci's was one of the most interesting, and one I could relate to the most. She was the daughter of Miles Blinkin, the very popular and very conservative Massachusetts senator who was a big deal in The War on Drugs. Staci went to northeastern boarding schools since she was eight and started using marijuana when she was twelve. By seventeen she was a full-blown heroin addict living on the streets in Boston. When the press got hold of her story, they plastered her family's picture on every news magazine in the country. There was lot of pressure for her to get well. And she damn well felt it.

"There must be a lull between State dinners and PR events," Staci grumbled. "I bet they'll try to pull me out of here."

"You don't want to go?"

Mitch and Staci looked at each other before she glared at me. "Natalie, at some point in here, you're going to realize that this is an opportunity not a punishment. People care here. The counselors, the teachers, they actually give a shit about us. They listen. Do you know how long and how hard I tried to get my parents to give a shit? Babies on my father's campaign trail get more hugs and kisses from that man than I have. I'd be better off if my parents stayed away, at least until I'm ready to leave here."

Pissing her off was not my intention, but I was pretty sure her anger had little to do with me anyway. Mitch just stood there a moment before bringing his sunglasses back over his eyes. "How about I walk you in there," he offered. "Safety in numbers."

She pulled herself up from the grass and brushed herself off. "You don't have to..."

"Hey, um...what happens at these parents visits anyway?" I asked.

Staci sighed. "It's like this controlled thing, almost identical to your intervention. They sit around and tell you why you suck, and you agree with them now. Kind of a 'face the music' type thing. You get one hour, and then the counselors sort of judge you on how you handle it and evaluate it when they consider you for Level Five."

"Am I allowed to go with you?"

She looked at me like I'd offered her a kidney. "Oh my God, are you serious?"

"Yeah, we're supposed to support each other, right?"

We both looked at Mitch for the green light.

"She's got a point," he agreed. "I'd take her up on it, Stac."

Staci was not emotional. I mean, she smiled and laughed at things, but an extra funny joke or something would have to inspire it. I'd never seen her cry, though, until at that moment when she brushed a tear from her cheek. "Okay then, let's go. The Senator hates to be kept waiting."

"You call you own father 'Senator?'"

"When I was a baby, he was a circuit judge. Try learning to say 'Your Honor' instead of Daddy."

———

Senator Blinkin was the tannest man I'd ever seen in my life. It was obviously fake and so orange that the hue reminded me of a traffic cone. He was also short, bald, stocky and not at all the definition of the word "distinguished." Mrs. Blinkin, however, was the complete opposite. The woman was a statuesque redhead with the identical facial features as her daughter, and I could tell by the slightly unnatural slant of her blue eyes, that she paid good money to maintain them.

There were eight of us in the conference room. Staci and her parents, Tillie, Dr. Blaine and a few of the nurses, who were all seated at a long table with Staci at the head. I fully expected to be dismissed by Tillie or Teeth, but instead, they welcomed me. Even pulling up a chair right next to Staci. It was odd. We had group therapy in this huge, windowed room every day with twice as many people, but today it felt claustrophobic. The sweat dampening Staci's forehead told me she felt the same way.

We were instructed not to talk until everyone was seated and Dr. Blaine explained the ground rules about speaking one at a time and not raising voices. He then read a report on Staci's progress that made her sound more like a lab rat than a human. When he was done, people stared at each other with goofy smiles. Staci just sat there with her arms folded on the table.

Senator Blinkin cleared his throat and ran his hands down the lapels of his suit. He looked every bit like a politician preparing for a speech rather than a concerned dad having a chat with his daughter. "So first, my wife and I want to thank this wonderful staff of people who it sounds like have taken very good care of our daughter these past few months. As we all know, drug addiction is a disease that as a community we have to treat." He fixed his gaze on Staci at our end of the table. "Anastasia, you look well."

"Thank you," she said with a formality in her voice I hadn't heard before. "I feel well. Everyone here has been extremely supportive, and I look forward to continuing my work here."

Looks were exchanged and bodies shifted like everyone else knew something Staci didn't. Staci didn't flinch. In fact, a corner of her mouth twitched like she was holding back a smile.

"Darling," her mother cooed. "We were talking to this wonderful staff, and we think that maybe you could continue your therapy in an out-patient fashion."

"And we informed them we don't offer that option here." Tillie folded her arms like she was readying for battle. I swear, in the few weeks she'd been swimming with me, there was a force in her voice nonexistent when I'd first met her. It was subtle and I couldn't describe it if I had to, but it made me feel good either way. "From where we see it, she's half way home," Tillie declared. "She still has a service project to finish, and school work to complete. She's also made some good friends."

Tillie smiled at me, and I took it as a cue to join in. "Staci is my peer tutor. She's a wiz at American History. I wouldn't have passed without her."

The Blinkins' wrinkled noses told me they cared very little about my academics or my impressions. As for Staci, I really wasn't sure she even heard me. She just sat there with her eyes narrowed and her back straight like someone had jammed a rod right up her.

"Well then, your progress should be rewarded," the Senator declared. "I think what we have planned for her is much more productive and inspiring than a service project." He looked back at Staci. "How would you like to join the campaign trail with your dad?"

Everyone seemed to hold their breath waiting for her answer. Like one would wait for a bomb to detonate. After a moment, a smile spread over Staci's face. "Really? I mean you never asked me to do that before. I'm flattered, really."

"Our PR people figured we could turn this into good press. I'm up for re-election in November and with you, we can milk that whole recovering addict angle. A little sympathy vote couldn't hurt."

"And I've already arranged my stylist to help with your appearance," her mother added. "We'll tone down the hair a little bit, get some sleeved shirts to cover up those hideous needle scars. You'd be perfect."

Staci looked down at herself. I figured she was studying her clothes, which even I would admit, the well-worn Dunes white shirt, khaki shorts uni, didn't scream Senator's daughter. She heaved a breath and again stared at her parents at the other end. "You know, isn't this supposed to be a visit so we can talk about our issues and move forward?"

"That's what we're doing, Sweetheart," the Senator said.

"No, you're talking about risking my life so you can use me to score some votes," she argued. "How sick is that?"

"Staci, don't raise your voice at the Senator," her mother scolded.

"Ask Dr. Blaine or Counselor Tillie. They'll tell you I'm not ready to leave."

"I'm your father, and it's really my decision."

"No, actually, it's mine, Staci corrected. "I'm eighteen and I can choose."

"Oh, really?" The Senator scoffed and leaned forward on the table. "And whose money do you plan on using to pay for it?"

Wow, this was a strange position. I never figured a kid would fight their parents to actually stay in rehab. If it were my parents offering me an out, I'd jump on it. What was Staci so afraid of?

"That's really all I am to you, isn't it?" Staci challenged. "Something you take care of. You put more money into your yacht in Kennebunkport than your own daughter!"

"Anastasia!"

"Mother, why did you have me? I don't even have any memories of you. I had nannies and nurses and people who shipped me back and forth to boarding school."

"Excuse me," her father snapped. "But who paid for all the orthodontics for that horse's mouth of yours, and the world class schools you attended? You've had everything handed to you. How could you embarrass us like this?"

"That's all I am to you? A prize pony you can show off to your stupid friends."

Sitting there was like being courtside at Wimbledon the way words were flying back and forth. Tillie and the rest of the staff were all poker faced, and I figured that was probably planned. They were here as observers, and maybe referees if it came down to punches being thrown. I wasn't positive that was out of the question. I could hear Staci tapping her foot under the table. A good indication her temper wasn't far from completely lost.

"My first day of kindergarten my Nanny put me on the bus," she said. "When I got sick, it was a private nurse who hugged me and gave me medicine. I'd call you both at work, and you'd say you were too busy to talk to me."

"I had an important job," the Senator said.

"An important job doesn't love you back!" Staci leaned across the table like she might pounce on her prey at the other end. Even me, her ally, was stunned shitless.

"You two are selfish, uncaring, cold people who worry about nothing except appearances and bank accounts, and how you can use people for their own benefit. And you think I want to help you promote that?"

She stood up and I swear to God, she looked seven feet tall. The way she lifted her chin and the wideness of her emerald eyes was like a woman on a mission. Not crazy or out of control, just steady. Sturdy. Like these people could hurl a million stones at her, and she would not go down.

Her chest heaved with a deep breath before turning to the staff beside her. "Dr. Blaine, Tillie, I know I don't have the medical coverage to pay for this right now, but if you give me a few days, I am sure I can work things out. I know there are government health agencies I can contact. And if all else fails,

I'm sure the advance from my tell-all book should more than cover my bill."

She smiled politely to her parents, which I likened to a spit-filled "fuck you," and strode toward the door. After a few moments, the embarrassed Blinkins started into it with Blaine and one of the administrators, while Tillie, the rest of the staff and I exited quietly. They headed back to their offices across the hall. Me? I wanted to go look for Staci.

Man, did I want to shake that girl's hand.

TEN

CASSIDY SAT down on the millimeter of available floor space between our beds and dug through the bottom drawer of the dresser. It was almost ten-thirty, a half hour before lights out, and an hour later than when I'd intended to go to bed. The past week or so, I'd gotten in the habit of swimming before breakfast, which got me up at about five-thirty. Usually, Cassidy was a good sport and went to bed early too, but recently she'd gotten the munchies late at night. Any other person would suspect the obvious, we were in rehab after all, but I knew the real reason for her hunger had nothing to do with anything she was smoking.

"You know, maybe you should stop having dinner with Kevin." I told her. "You don't eat anything, and you go to bed hungry."

"But I like to have salad for dinner and he's afraid of it."

"Well, tonight it was burgers. Those don't have onions."

"But people put onions on hamburgers." She unwrapped a petrified Tootsie Roll and shoved it in her mouth. "I just don't want him to be afraid of me."

"Okay, then why don't you eat with the rest of the girls. You can't just live on candy."

"Trista would do it for Ryan."

I smiled and sat down next to her on the floor. In the six weeks we'd been roommates, I was confident I knew just as much about The Bachelor as she did and had heard loads about the most famous Bachelor couple. Sometimes, when she would use the damn show to further a point, I could do the same now. Here was a good opportunity to put the tactic to use. "Trista may do things for Ryan, but Ryan wouldn't ask her to," I said.

"Maybe you're right." She sighed. "Tomorrow is tacos. Maybe if I just put tomatoes and cheese on it, I won't hurt his feelings."

"I think it's worth a try. But how about right now we go raid the kitchen. See if Chef Biff has any leftovers or anything." I jumped to my feet and dragged Cassidy with me out the door.

"You know I saw you talking to Mitch the other day on the lawn. Lots of girls did."

"So?" I asked.

"So, I think he likes you."

"He works here. He has to like everybody."

"But what if he likes you more?"

I rolled my eyes. This was exactly the conversation I'd been avoiding since the whole Racer thing happened, and so far, I'd done a pretty good job. But this was Cassidy. There wasn't a vindictive or hurtful bone in her body, and if she did have one, she certainly didn't know where to find it. "He's cute, Cass," I admitted. "But he works here, and he's older than us."

"I heard he was a college student when he came here, and now, he's two years clean. He's smart and religious. Goes to Catholic church every Sunday."

"Maybe that's where he plans on taking me when we head into Los Angeles. Church."

"Getting better is fun, isn't it? And on my day pass I want to go to the Museum of Film and Television. It's like my life's dream."

I bit back a laugh. She didn't even know the place existed until last week when she drove by it on her way to her new service project, cataloging film at the US Network. Now it was all she talked about. Being a Level Three (a week ago today, thanks much) I also had my own service project to start, but I'd been so busy discussing the wonderful world of stock footage with Cassidy, I barely had time to think about it.

We strolled down the hall past the closed resident doors. The place was quiet save for a few muffled conversations, and the rhythmic thuds of the industrial washing machine when we passed the laundry room. Once the sun went down, The Dunes was not that happening a place. Sometimes girls would do schoolwork or once in a while raid the kitchen. Chef Biff didn't mind, and the staff was always around. Some nights it was popcorn. Sometimes pizza with the works. It was worth the long walk from our wing to the other, and we had to go by front lobby reception to get there.

The night staff hung out in the offices behind the front desk and beyond was the kitchen and whole other wing where new patients detoxed. Next to that was the big intake room. When we did pass by at night there was usually plenty of staff activity. Laughing, reading, watching TV, but tonight the place was totally abandoned. The TV was on, as were the computer screens, so people couldn't have gone far...

"Where is everyone?" Cassidy asked, "And why is the wind blowing indoors?"

I peeked around the long lobby desk and realized the admittance door to the outside was open. Insects swarmed around the flood lights and the wind rustled the hedges beside the stoop. When I leaned closer, I could hear voices in the darkness. Loud urgent ones and I wondered if I should usher Cassidy out of there. "I think we have a new resident," I said.

We both jumped when we heard a scream, the high-pitched, horror movie kind that sounded like a tea kettle. People shouted and a car engine revved. Someone cursed, and I swore it was Mitch's voice.

"What's going on outside?" Ari came up behind us, wiping the sleep from her eyes and hugging herself against the cold. "I was coming to get hot chocolate and I heard people yelling. Is everything okay?"

Suddenly, Mitch burst through the door carrying a wailing blonde flurry of arms and legs. A herd of other personnel scrambled in behind him, yelling at each other, barking orders, panic paling their faces.

"Please, it hurts!" she screamed. "Stop it! Stop it, please!"

The girl tumbled to the floor in a heap, flipping around like a fish out of water.

She had matted blonde hair and her white t-shirt was stained red, with what I had no idea. The stench of vomit filled the air, and I noticed that Mitch and one of the nurses were covered in it. Normally the sight of puke would make me want to puke myself, but I was so freaked out by the scene that I forgot to be disgusted.

"Let go of me!" the girl screamed. "Please, you're hurting me!"

"Calm down," Mitch soothed. He was on his knees with a hand on each arm. "You're okay. The nurses will take care of you."

"Fuck You!"

Her fist landed square on Mitch's jaw. He flew back but didn't lose his grip. He mumbled something like "I'm sorry" and just like that he flipped the girl over, putting her face down and her hands behind her back. "You guys are in charge, but someone needs to get the on-call doctor," he instructed the nurse standing over him.

"He's already been called," she told him.

The girl kicked her feet and wiggled like a snake, a few times knocking Mitch off balance. Seconds later, a different nurse scurried out from the back room with the biggest needle I'd ever seen.

"Mitch, what the hell is going on!" I yelled.

The words came out in an accusation, and I hadn't meant for them to. Mitch looked up at the three of us, but his eyes narrowed at me. "Damn it, Natalie, get out of here!"

"What's wrong with her? Why is she like this?"

"It's withdrawal," Ari mumbled in my ear. "She's freaking out."

The girl was sobbing now. Writhing and moaning with her face beat red. If I wasn't standing right in front of her, I would have sworn she was being murdered. By the way her eyes kept rolling back in her head, I wasn't so sure that death wasn't eminent anyway.

"I need her to be still," the nurse yelled, scurrying around her to get a clear shot. "I can't give her the tranquilizer if she's moving."

"Jesus, what the hell is she on?" another staffer guy yelled. "It's like holding down a horse."

The girl heaved just as Mitch turned her on her side. White foaming vomit spilled from her mouth on to the floor.

"Oh, my God, is she rabid?" Cassidy asked, franticly pushing the "channel up" button on the remote.

Mitch looked up in our direction again. His expression changed from controlled panic to anger when his eyes fixed on mine. "Natalie, take your friends and get out of here!"

Ari and Cassidy scurried like ants, but my feet seemed nailed to the floor. I couldn't move, couldn't breathe. I felt like I was watching a car accident. The whole thing. The impact, the carnage. A girl in pain, screaming while a crowd of people held her down.

Somehow, the girl wiggled out from under Mitch and grabbed a vase from the nurse's desk. She slammed it against the counter, the shards flying across the tile floor. It was glass, not usually allowed in the place, and it wasn't until I saw her point a jagged piece at a nurse that I fully understood why.

I gasped when security guards burst into the room. The same big, burly guys who had hauled off my paparazzi intruder that day at OccuTher. They put her in a head lock and held her tight to the floor. The nurse finally managed the shot.

After a minute, the girl stilled into a fetal position. If I didn't know better, I would have thought it was a crime scene with the vomit and the smears of blood thanks to the bits of glass Mitch and the nurses were pulling from their hands. The girl just lay there now, completely out and limp. Her skin was shiny like it was coated with sweat, and I could see fresh red scabs on the insides of her arms. For the first time, I could see her face. Even with her eyes closed, I recognized her.

"Oh my God." I gasped. "Is that Fiona?"

One of the security men shoved me aside, and I just stood there frozen. The next thing I realized was Mitch's hand wrapped around my arm. Somehow, he'd already changed his shirt from the puke covered one to a Dunes standard issue tee they must have stashed in reception somewhere and walked me down the hall toward the resident rooms. "What are you doing up at admittance this late?"

"Cass and I were getting a snack."

"I'm sorry you had to see that."

"Same," I agreed. We went into the darkened day room and Mitch snapped on the lights.

He pulled out one of the table chairs and sat me down. I

noticed his hands were already bandaged, albeit haphazardly, when he rested them on the table. "I didn't know you knew Fiona," he said.

"She was released a week after I got here," I told him. "What happened?"

"Her parents called us and said she disappeared with her boyfriend here in Los Angeles. We tracked her down."

"Is she going to be okay?"

"Should be."

I regarded his bandaged hands and the now blooming black eye that swelled the right side of his face. "How about you? You okay?"

"Sure, of course," he assured me with the slightest crack in his voice. "Maybe in a way it's good when people like us see stuff like that. Keeps us on the right path."

A chill swept over me, so I wrapped my arms around myself. "Scary. I know you're used to this kind of stuff but you're a human. That has to be hard to deal with."

He opened his mouth twice before words emerged. He forced a smile, but I noticed he couldn't quite look at me. "Just go back to your dorm and get a good night's sleep, Nat. Fiona will be fine, and you'll feel better in the morning, too."

"So will you, "I assured him because it felt like a nice thing to say, not because I believed it.

Finally our eyes met, and it felt like a genuine connection. Not a romantic one or anything, but like we both just shared a moment requiring both our efforts to process. I'm usually not a mushy person, but I wouldn't have minded a hug. Or, given his sad clown mangled face, giving him one. But instead, we both let the moment pass. He patted my shoulder like a big brother would, stood and headed for the door.

"Make sure Cassidy is okay," he said over his shoulder. "I can have some snacks sent down to you both, too."

"It's okay, I'm pretty sure we've both lost our appetite."

"You know, if swimming doesn't work out, I think you have a future as a standup comic."

I didn't respond. It was impossible while swallowing back the tears.

———

March, 18 Friday
Mood: Just WTF

Dear Annie,

You won't believe the shit show I saw tonight. Remember Fiona? The girl who was totally put together when she left? Well, she came back tonight in a puddle of vomit. Total relapse. It scared the crap out of me.

How many chances do we get? Like how many times can we make the same mistakes before it's game over? I hate that I am asking you this because from where I'm sitting, it's like the universe stole all your chances. I'm bitter because a good person like you deserves every and all of them. But Fiona, she was given another chance, and never had any intention to take advantage of it. Sounds selfish, greedy, and weak to me.

All the things people thought of me before I came here.

Tonight was the first time I thought about wanting another chance. Like, not just at swimming or whatever, but at life in general. I also want to be a positive influence and not a negative one. Where people could learn from the things I've done right, not the things I've done wrong. I suppose my swimming was a positive influence on people before. The word inspiration was thrown around a few times in interviews, but I'm not sure if it meant much to me. What

I do know, though, is I want a chance to figure that all out. I don't think I could come up with such deep thought on my own until I saw what I did tonight. What I do know for certain, however, is you deserve every chance in the world to get better, and if I had extra chances, I would give every one of them to you. You wouldn't waste them either. You're good like that.

———

Fiona's return was the top story for a good couple of days. According to The Dunes grapevine, Fiona had knocked over a convenience store in San Diego, prostituted herself in West Hollywood and stolen a car in Beverly Hills. I didn't take it as gospel. I'd been a victim of The Dunes rumor mill, and I had no intention in helping its cause. So, by the time Fiona showed up to group, I decided I would keep my mouth shut unless I was directly addressed.

Fiona sat in the corner chair in her Newbie white jumpsuit, staring at the floor and looking nothing like the smiling blonde Southern Belle I remembered. Three days had passed since she'd arrived, and besides not being covered in vomit and blood, she didn't look much better. Pale. Thin. Maybe Ari wasn't bullshitting when she'd called Fiona a streetwalker after all.

Dr. Blaine blew in, and after a few minutes, "welcomed" Fiona back and spewed off a lecture about perseverance and a lame comparison between all of us and the Little Engine That Could. Sometimes I wondered if he just liked to hear himself talk because he rarely made sense. He just repeated in different words what someone else said to him.

Odd.

"Natalie, I heard you were in attendance when Fiona was

brought in. How did seeing her in that condition make you feel?"

The sound of my own name startled me. Pointed questions like these were ones I usually fielded in private therapy with Tillie, not in front of a crowd, especially around people like Missy who could use my answers against me God knew how. I straightened in my chair and cleared my throat. "It was definitely scary," I said. "She was screaming, swearing at the staff. She hit Mitch, and she tried to cut people with broken glass. I think one of the nurses had to get stitches."

"Wow, taking it out on Mitch. That's some serious shit you were on," Missy said with a tease in her voice. "And I thought you were strictly a Jack Daniels girl."

The Bikinis giggled and I sat there silently. A month ago, I would have jumped up and cold-cocked Missy, but I'd learned something about getting by in this place. You had to treat it all like a chess match. A long, drawn-out game, that in the end if you make the right move, you win. In this case, letting Blaine step in was the best strategy.

"Natalie, tell us, what's your impression of Fiona's situation?" he asked.

A Situation? Was that an honest description of the horror scene the night before was? A situation? I was almost offended on Fiona's behalf. "The situation," I said, with finger quotes in the air. "Was the most disturbing thing I've ever seen."

"It was," Cassidy agreed, waving her remote in her hand. "I had to change the channel."

"And how did you feel about it?"

Dr Blaine's double talk annoyed the hell out of me. I glanced at Fiona, who still refused to look up. I leaned back in my chair and stared at the white marble floor. "It's scary to think that when you go back out there, you have to deal with the same shit as before. If you do it in the same way, you end up in a puddle of puke with six people holding you down to sedate you. How do I know that won't happen to me?"

The rest of the girls gawked at me, with the exception of Missy, who I was convinced possessed no human emotion. I got the sense they all felt the same way. Some nodded as I spoke, and a few Fives chimed in with agreement. "Fiona was so put together when she left," I added. "If she couldn't get her life together, what chance do any of us have?"

Suddenly something shifted inside of me. Like a light bulb snapped on over my dense head. Before the other night, I had never really acknowledged anything was wrong with me. At least not something I could control. I realized not only did I control my destiny, but I actually wanted to. Could I really be capable of making better decisions? Of living a less screwed-up life?

"But maybe it doesn't have to be scary." I heard myself say. "Maybe seeing Fiona can motivate you instead."

"Interesting," Blaine said. "So, you're saying there might be positive things we can learn from Fiona's experience. Make us more aware of the possible dangers when we leave here and make us more vigilant in avoiding them."

Again, the circle hummed with mumbles. Like I was on to something.

"So, you're saying that as a community we need to pull together and acknowledge our sadness and our fear?" Blaine asked.

I nodded. "That's right. And deal with the problems so they don't get out of control."

"And what a wonderful lesson that will definitely translate on the outside." Blaine nodded at me. "Good work today, Natalie. Really."

Tillie offered me a quick "thumbs-up" and the rest of the staff exchanged looks. It had been a while since any grown up had been impressed by anything I had to say. It felt pretty good. I was actually congratulating myself on the way out of the room, until I passed Fiona still slumped in her chair.

"I'm sorry you're here," I said.

When the last of the residents filed out and it was just her and me, she looked up at me like she just realized I was there. "I'm sorry I freaked you out," she said. "I was pretty out of it. Wasn't aware I had an audience."

Her voice was deep and harsh, like the vocal version of sandpaper. It matched the haggardness of the rest of her. I hoped I didn't sound like I pitied her, but it was hard not to. "We hadn't intended to be one. But hey, it'll be old news tomorrow."

"Speaking of news, you were in the headlines when I was out. What that Racer guy did to you is a big deal. I'm sorry."

I shrugged. "Guess he's a real asshole after all."

"They all are, it seems. And I didn't know your teammate Annie Madsen has terminal cancer. No wonder you lost your shit."

The sound of Annie's name on a virtual stranger's lips seemed vulgar. Like she was violating a very specific boundary I had no intention of conceding. Annie was a very large part of my life that was off limits to everyone. This place could ring me out like a sponge of whatever else, but sharing anything about Annie was off limits.

Fiona meant well. She wasn't a predator with any kind of an agenda and didn't deserve my anger. So, I just kept my mouth shut and headed to the door for a graceful exit and let the subject drop. "You know, you helped me when I first got here," I said, with my hand on the doorknob. "If there's anything I can do."

"Believe me, you won't have to worry about it."

"But I'd like to..."

"Save your breath for someone worth your time, Natalie. I'm a lost cause." She stood and moved toward me at the door.

"But that's the way I felt when I first got here," I said. "I can totally relate."

Her blood-shot eyes narrowed. The warm, friendly Fiona had been replaced by this cold angry one, and it felt like I was talking to a person possessed. Then she slipped her hand over her stomach. "Things are different for me now, Nat. Or will be. My days here are numbered. Save your time and concern for someone else."

"Huh? Why would your days be numbered? Wait, are you..?"

"See you around, Natalie."

The door shut behind her and I just stood there trying to match the girl who just left to the happy hopeful one I'd met months ago. And what had she just told me? A baby? Was that real?

It's crazy when you're stone cold sober and you're convinced the last few minutes of your life was a hallucination.

———

March 27, Thursday
Mood: Defective

Dear Annie,

Okay you win. I am an addict. I do deserve to be here. But today I realized something.

I really want to get better.

The rest of the staff must have recognized my change of heart, too, because they just awarded me Level Four. Tillie told me this afternoon at our meeting, and it'll be announced tomorrow when everyone meets together.

Today's group session was crazy. I won't go into the particulars, but I totally realized all I'm missing out on by being here and how much better life would be if I just dealt with my shit. Which brings me to my other big news.

I selected my service project today. I am working at the oncology unit at the local hospital. The staff is not convinced it's the best idea, but I wore them down so they agreed to "see how it goes." After the past few days, I truly believe it's the perfect thing for me.

I just want to be the best friend I can to you, and even though you being sick scares the shit out of me, I have to face it head on. That's what strong people do, right? And I want to be strong.

ELEVEN

THE DESERT MEDICAL Center was about thirty miles from The Dunes on an equally ridiculously beautiful piece of land with green lawns, pretty flowers and a building that looked more like a spa than a hospital. Not a bad place to spend twelve hours a week for the next month of my life.

At least it didn't look that bad from the parking lot.

After an 8 a.m. ceremonial fitting of scrubs and a tour of the place, I met Ginny. Ginny was the head nurse coordinator, the cruise director, if you will, for my maiden voyage at "Desert M.C." She introduced me to the doctors, nurses, and the rest of the staff. I admit, when I insisted on being placed in an Oncology unit, I pictured I'd be working with old-people patients. Not that it would be "better."A person dying of cancer at any age is horrible, but at least with an older person, I could tell myself that they'd had a good long life despite ending the way it was.

Pediatric Oncology was on the top floor with glass ceilings and walls lined with kids' crayon and fingerprint creations. Ambiance aside, it smelled like a hospital. That raunchy mixture of cleaning products, stale cafeteria food and urine that after a while permeated your clothes and coated your skin. Not that I was a frequent hospital visitor, but when I broke my finger after jamming it into the pool wall, having it set at Buffalo Children's was not a top-ten experience of my life. But facing my fears was a key to recovery, and cancer was one of my biggest tormentors.

Ginny wasn't much older than me but acted like she was, using big words to describe simple things, and wearing her long blonde hair in a no-bullshit bun AquaNett-ed into place. All morning she brought me from room to room where red-eyed families greeted her like she was Mother Teresa, relaying stories about test results and prognoses. I sort of just hung beside her. Listening, but finding myself wanting to block the whole thing out.

The last room we visited was labeled "recovery," which I thought was blatant false advertising because no one in the place looked like they were on the upswing. It was dark with the shades drawn, and instead of TVs turned on the Disney Channel, the only thing audible was the whirl and buzz of various machines at work. Nurses in cartoon scrubs hung over beds with smiles that I couldn't come close to faking. A doctor in a white coat stood in a corner, flipping through yellow forms.

"I like your hair."

I turned toward the tiny whisper. One that sounded painful to make. A bald-headed girl, maybe eleven years old, stared at me from her pink-sheeted bed. Her thin lips looked cherry red against her pale skin.

"Um, are you talking to me?" I asked.

"I used to have blonde hair." She lifted her IV harnessed hand and pointed to her peach fuzzed head. "Mine was curly though. Not straight like yours."

Her wide eyes traveled over me, and I realized she expected a reply. First I had to process that my hair wasn't green or any other color of the rainbow like it had been before I'd ended up at The Dunes. I looked normal now. *Traditional.* How would a normal, traditional human answer this poor kid?

"My favorite book is *Oh, The Places You'll Go*," she told me. "I know its little kid-ish but it works for me.

"I'm a Dr. Suess fan myself."

"It's right behind you on the table next to the ice chips. You want to read it to me?"

I nodded and retrieved the book. It looked worn. The cover frayed, water rings revealing it had been used more than a few times as a coaster. I opened it to the This Book Belongs To page where it said in kid's handwriting, "Natalie."

"My name is Natalie, too," I said dumbly.

She smiled. "I don't like it. It sounds like an insect."

"I've heard that before."

"I wanted to change my name to Samantha or Tiffany, but my mom wouldn't let me."

"We always want what we haven't got, I guess."

The words hung there in front of us, and I was glad that she probably wasn't old enough to understand my stupidity. Here this poor girl was, lying here looking like a human pin cushion with tubes and wires spilling over her bed sides, and I'm waxing philosophical about hair and name preferences. What was I talking about? What was I doing here? This kid expected me to comfort her? I couldn't comfort myself.

"So you work here, or are they making you be here?"

I pulled up a chair and sat down. "What do you mean?"

"Like are you a nurse? Or are you like a prisoner doing community service?"

I smiled at this girl's brutal honesty and lack of filter. She was a chick I could hang with. "I guess I kinda work here. I chose to be here, though," I said. "No one forced me."

"Are you here to help kids or yourself?"

Was that a question or a challenge? She raised her hairless brow and held my gaze. I recrossed my legs and cleared my throat to buy time to find an answer.

"I guess both," I said.

I flipped the page and read the first words, but the tremble in my lower lip distorted them. I sounded small, and weak, and useless. Tears flooded my eyes and spilled down my cheeks. I couldn't take it. I just wanted to disappear.

The next thing I knew I was halfway down the hall, panting and sobbing like my lungs would burst from my chest. Behind me I could hear my name being called. I wasn't sure if it was at me, or the poor little girl I'd just left who was probably wondering why the hell the crazy nurse had stolen her book.

For an hour I wandered the halls like a zombie. Somehow, I ended up in the break room at lunchtime. Unlike the rest of the building, the place was modest with nothing more than two card tables, a snack machine, and a small TV that had the Weather Channel on mute. I was eating a stale jelly doughnut when Ginny sat down across from me with her blueberry muffin.

"Are you okay?" she asked, folding her napkin in her lap.

I nodded and flicked the powdered sugar from my fingers. "I'm okay. I'm sorry I ran out like that. It's just this is the first time I've been off The Dunes campus in three months. Sort of weird."

"I'm sure it is. And I suppose a children's cancer ward is probably a hard place to re-emerge into society."

"Hey, I asked for it. I thought being around it would help me."

"When you say 'it', do you mean the cancer ward or cancer itself?"

I sighed. I just met this woman a few hours ago, and it seemed warped to unload all my personal shit on her. But then again, it might be easier that way. Tell a stranger your problems then walk away. Sounded almost like a relief.

"My best friend, Annie. She's sick."

Ginny nodded. "I'm sorry. What kind?"

"What kind, what?"

"What kind of cancer?"

My appetite suddenly left me. I shoved the donut aside. "Leukemia," I mumbled. "And I don't know the prognosis or whatever. The Dunes prohibits contact with the outside until you hit Level Five, so it's not like I can call or anything." I eyed the landline phone on the counter beside us. "And even if I did have the opportunity to call, I'm not sure I'd want to."

"It's easier to just forget about it, huh?"

I shrugged. If she thought less of me, oh well. It wasn't like I'd made a stellar impression so far.

"You can't fault yourself for being a sensitive person. Seeing people suffer is hard, and everyone deals with things in different ways. Your defense mechanism is to shut down and avoid it. Drugs helped you do that. You are finding a new defense mechanism, a healthier way of dealing with things that scare you, other than self-medicating."

"I guess." The speech sounded rehearsed, but I realized that I heard her do this all morning. Calm freaked-out parents with fact rather than emotion. I liked her method. Dr. Blaine could learn a few things from her.

"See, that's why I really wanted to work here," I said. "I thought if I just threw myself into fiery hell, after a while I wouldn't mind being burned."

She smiled. "I understand what you are saying and I admire your candor, but what I have a problem with is you referring to the children's ward as 'hell'."

"I didn't mean it that way."

"In a way, you're right. For many of these kids, what they go through every day is hell, but that doesn't mean they can be guinea pigs for your own healing. I can't have you breaking down in front of a sick child and scaring them."

I leaned back in my chair and sighed. Ginny was right. I wanted to be placed in the cancer ward almost on a dare to myself. If I could hack it, that meant I was "better." I didn't think about the other people that I would be affecting.

Story of my life.

"I guess I need to get a new project lined up."

Ginny patted my hand. "Tell you what. I do think you would benefit from working in a hospital setting, and I might have the perfect solution. How would you feel about helping out in the ER?"

"The emergency room? What could I do? I'm not a nurse or anything."

"We always need extra hands. Answering phones, paperwork. Sometimes getting snacks for doctors. There're a ton of things you could do. Maybe in time, you could come back up to the cancer kids if you're up to it."

I hated to admit failure in the cancer ward, but I would be lying if I said I wasn't relieved. Not that blood and guts and other bodily fluids that were the norm in the ER was something to look forward to. It just seemed a less horrible a place to be. "Sounds good, Ginny. Thanks."

"No problem." She slid Oh the Places You Go across the table to me. "How about you return this to the library, and we'll call it a day."

I released a breath I'd probably been holding since the moment I stepped foot out of the van that brought me there that morning. Bringing the book back to Little Natalie was the right thing to do, but I just couldn't do it. I passed the recovery room three times but chickened out. The mental to do list in my brain was lengthy now, but this task was added to the top. Somehow, I would get this poor kid her book back.

———

When I got back to The Dunes, I went straight to my room. It was dinnertime and I knew the girls would want to hear about the big awesome first day of my service project. What a joke. I lay in a bed and closed my eyes, wondering if massively screwing up good intentions had become my life's theme.

It must have been past 11pm when my eyes reopened, because it was dark and Cassidy was in bed asleep. My stomach growled, reminding me of my missed dinner. Failure made me hungry, evidently, because I could have killed for a thick PB&J. So, I put on my slippers and sweatshirt and headed on down to the kitchen.

I'd never changed into my pajamas which I wondered if the staff would think was odd if they saw me. When I walked by the front desk, no one cared about my clothes, but they did make it clear that they supported eating my feelings and wished me well in my snack hunting endeavors. Sometimes it was nice when people knew your business around here after all.

The kitchen was split into two spaces. The big main prep area and a smaller side room we called "the pantry." After dinner, the big prep area was locked up, to keep us waywards from the knives and such, but the pantry was open all night. It had a big fridge and freezer with all sorts of snacks and drinks, and shelves jam packed with cereals, crackers, and cookies.

Twice when Ari and I were hungry late at night, we came down for Cheerios, but the pantry had no milk. We broke into the main kitchen to snag some with a secret stickpin hidden in the napkin holder. It had seemed harmless at the time, but a broken rule is a broken rule that came with consequences if you were caught. Tonight, though, I was willing to risk it, because the pantry was out of grape jelly and I really, really wanted some on my sandwich.

So I closed the pantry door facing the main desk, left the bread loaf and peanut butter jar on the counter and retrieved the stickpin from the napkin holder buried in the cabinet. Finally, I found myself with the pin poised at the lock, but when I turned the knob, it was already open.

When we broke in before, it was completely dark. We had to feel around for the nearest fridge and used the light inside of it to find the milk and navigate out. This time, though, there were lights at the far end of the kitchen. A truck was backed up to the open loading dock.

Some of the girls here kept track of routines like garbage or delivery night in case the information might be valuable. That seemed too much to care about. I now saw why in a situation like that stuff would have been helpful to know. I was just about to abort my mission when I heard a truck door slam and two male voices getting louder as they approached the loading dock. If I made a break for it, they would see or hear me. Instead, I ducked down behind a counter and listened for whoever was there to leave.

"It's been a good week," one man said, and I could hear things being dumped onto one of the kitchen prep tables. "A girl that left a few weeks ago came back dope sick out of her mind. Had four ounces on her."

"It's funny what they think they can sneak in." The other voice chuckled. "You're lucky you work here. Decent supply line."

The one voice was familiar. I mean, I'm sure I'd heard it before since he worked here, but it was hard to place. I tried to peek my head up so I could look over the counter to see.

"I tried this stuff right here," the man who worked here said. "Pure, not cut at all as far as I can tell."

"Nice, what about this?"

"Came from the same kid. I'm sure it's just as good."

I lifted my head high enough to be able to see them. There they stood in the halo of light at the table closest to the loading dock. The one man was clearly the truck driver in his grey uniform and cap. The other had his back to me. He wore a black sweatshirt and a baseball cap. He reached into his back jean pocket and pulled out a baggy. "Got a bunch of pills here, too. Like I said, it's been a good week."

The delivery guy took it and held it up in the light. "Looks decent."

"Have I ever been wrong?" the black sweatshirt guy joked.

The delivery man reached into his pocket and pulled out a thick wad of cash. He put it on the table and dumped everything next to it into a fast-food paper bag. "Same time next week?" he asked.

The men shook hands and walked out the loading dock. I was dying to see who the guy was who worked here, but I realized if I saw his face, chances were, he could see mine, too. So, I figured I'd just stay under my table until he closed the loading dock doors and left.

But when the truck pulled away, he came back toward the kitchen and when he stepped into the light, that's when I saw his face.

Clint.

How did I not see that coming?

I realized if he didn't leave through the dock, he'd have to walk right by me to go through the pantry. If I made a break for it, he'd see the light from the other side of the door when I opened it. I had no choice but to hide under the table and hope he was too preoccupied in counting his money to see me huddled in the dark clutching a jar of jelly.

When I heard him come closer, I sunk deeper into the shadows. I didn't see the large cookie sheet hanging off the prep table above me until it came tumbling down and landed at both our feet with a deafening crash.

"Natalie?"

When I dared open my eyes, Clint loomed over me with his phone flashlight shining on my face. I had to say, he looked about as freaked out as I felt. He bit his lip then laughed placing his hand over his chest. "Good Lord, you scared me," he said with a quiver in his voice. "This is the second time I've caught you sneaking around here. You looking for something in particular? Or you just like me?"

"I was just coming in here for something to eat," I stammered. I stood to my full height and followed his cue of lightening the mood. "The door was unlocked, and I really wanted jelly on my peanut butter sandwich."

"You know being in here is against the rules. Sets you back a few levels. Even get you thrown out."

His smile faded and I realized his tone was more threatening than relaying information. It wasn't lost on me that while I was in the wrong for breaking in there, I'd just witnessed him commit about ten felonies. Who had who by the balls?

"So, I guess I'll just make my sandwich in the pantry and head back to my room..." Clint jumped in my path just before I reached the door. I had the feeling confessing my kitchen break in would be much better than sticking around and listening to what Clint had to say, but he wasn't letting me by. Instead, he looked me up and down as he relocked the door. Then he leaned up against it with his tattooed arms folded against his chest.

"How long you been in here?"

"Long enough to get a jar of jelly."

His narrowed lips twisted in a crooked smile. "Hungry, huh? Tell me sweetheart, what you in the mood for?" When he touched my chin with the pads of his scaly fingers, I jerked my head away from him.

"Get your hands off me."

He chuckled. "Oh, suddenly you're a prude. You don't fool me. I read about all the dirty things you did with that guy back in Buffalo."

"So, what's the deal with the delivery guy?"

He shook his head. "You have no idea what you're talking about. You messed up kids get delusional all the time. If you were smart, you'd keep what you saw tonight to yourself."

I flipped the jar of jelly from one hand to other as if mulling his suggestion over. "And why would I do that?"

"Because you probably don't want Blaine, Fat Tillie, or the rest of the world to know you've been dealing confiscated drugs, which is a bigger news story than being a whore."

"What makes you think they'd believe you over me?"

He ran his finger over my cheek. "Because I'm not the one who broke into the kitchen. I'm also not the mental case who spread her legs for a fix before she got hauled away here. I'm the good guy."

I followed his gaze to a lone butcher knife left out on the prep table beside us. He picked it up, letting the light bounce off the stainless-steel blade as he turned it over in his hand. "You know, stuff happens here. Suicides, overdoses. Unfortunate things. I would think you've had your fair share of unfortunate things to deal with, haven't you?"

With his free hand, he grabbed my arm and met me nose-to-nose. His sour breath almost gagged me and I dropped the jar of jelly to the ground. "I'm the heartbeat of this place, Sweetheart. I keep it going. If I wanted to make it look like you were running a drug ring in here, I could, and if all else failed, I could make sure you never woke up the next day to say I was wrong. Are we clear?"

"Let go of me." I snagged my arm away from him.

"What? You playing hard to get now or something?" He laughed and picked the jelly jar up off the floor at our feet. "I like you, Natalie. You're different than the rest of the girls here. You mind your own business, I'll mind mine, and we'll both get by just fine. We clear?"

When he handed me the jelly, it was all I could do not to break the thing over his crew cut head. The competitor in me hated for him to have the upper hand, or the last word. I had no choice but to bide my time. In this event, he may have beat me in the prelims, but I would smoke him in the finals. "Yeah, we're clear."

I watched him disappear into the darkness in the direction of the loading dock. It took a few minutes for my pulse to slow and my legs to work again before I could head out through the pantry door. I returned the stickpin to its hiding place and replaced all the sandwich stuff and the jelly to the cabinets. I went back to my room. Somehow, I'd lost my appetite.

TWELVE

WHEN I DIDN'T MAKE it to breakfast the next morning, I wasn't sure if I was grateful my friends let me sleep or offended no one checked on me. Around eleven, I got sick of thinking about it and was considering writing a letter to Annie when Cassidy burst in.

"Oh my God, I'm so glad you're awake." She ran over and gave me a hug like it'd been years since she'd seen me rather than hours. "I missed you yesterday. I thought about you during General Hospital and almost cried. I'm so sorry about what happened. Are you okay?"

Last night's confrontation with Clint flashed behind my closed eyes. I kicked off my covers and brought my feet to the floor. "How the hell did you know about that?"

"Your service project?" She looked at me like I was the clueless one. "We heard how you freaked out and had to be brought back early. Staci said to let you sleep through dinner because an embarrassment like that might be exhausting."

She wasn't wrong. I was exhausted and confused and pissed. Really, I could not think of any redeeming moments from the day before. Not that I was excited to get a start on the next one.

"Did you hear about Fiona? I figured you hadn't."

Sometimes Cassidy's fast, nonsensical subject changes drove me insane, but this one was a welcomed distraction, and I'd gotten good at keeping up. I grabbed a hair tie from my bedside table and pulled my hair back in a messy bun. "What happened with Fiona now?"

"She escaped two nights ago, and no one has heard from her since." She reached under her bed and pulled out her TV Guide box. "You ready for our Bachelor marathon this afternoon? Everyone is meeting in the day room. You promised, remember?"

Despite my speechlessness, I had a million questions, but I realized it was too late to ask them. Cass sat there already engrossed in her TV Guide magazine. Once her channel changed, it was hard to get it back.

When we hit the day room, it was clear to me the news about Fiona's jail break had spread like a bad rash, because everyone had a version of the story. The most entertaining being the one where her boyfriend was hiding in the bushes with his motorcycle, and they rode off into the mountains to smoke peyote with an Indian man named Horse head. I wasn't sure how credible that was considering it came from Cassidy, and I swore I saw a TV movie last week with the same story line.

The most generic and plausible one was that Fiona hitch-hiked back to LA to be with her drug dealer boyfriend. No one mentioned her being pregnant, so I didn't bring it up. Maybe I had misunderstood her.

And I thought I had problems.

Right now, my greatest one was convincing Cassidy to watch something different than the Bachelor After Specials, where the final couples dramatically detail all the reasons why they inevitably broke up. I was confident if I had to watch another bleached blonde sob and wipe the sad clown mascara from under her eyes, I would pull my fingernails from their beds. No kidding.

"You want some popcorn, Natalie?"

Onion Boy sat between Cass and me on the puffy day room couch, holding the microwave bag of Orville Redenbacher in front of me. Popcorn was one of the "safe foods" Kevin consumed without anxiety. The other two were bologna and cheese, but without bread I figured the combination pointless. "I asked if you wanted popcorn," he said again. "There's sprinkle butter on it, too."

"No thanks," I replied. "I'm not hungry."

"I think she's just thinking about Fiona," Cass told him. "I don't get it. I didn't think you knew Fiona that well."

"I don't have to know her to feel bad about her," I argued. "And not just about Fiona. I feel shitty in general. Like, you try hard and you still make a mess of things. What's the point?"

Cassidy and Kevin shared a look. Like they were the level-headed ones trying to straighten out my head. "Well, she made her choices and you make yours," Cassidy insisted. "You have to keep moving forward if you want to get better."

I smiled. "You've been watching the Motivational Network again, haven't you?"

"This morning," Kevin said. "Some guy was telling a crowd about how each of us is walking down a path, and sometimes there are people on the side of the path who want to pull us into a ditch. If we encounter one of those people, we should just keep going. Don't let Fiona's mistake make you feel bad about yourself. Don't let Fiona pull you into the ditch."

"Thanks, I'll keep that in mind." On second thought, I jammed a handful of kernels in my mouth.

"You know, the advice totally helped me when I met the

people at my service project at the US Network," Cass said. "One of the girls who works there is a B-I-T-C-H. But I decided if she's mean to me, I'm just going to be mean right back and not let her use my remote." She waved the thing in front of us like it was a mighty sword. "She doesn't deserve the privilege!"

"And I've decided I'm only eating cheese from McDonalds as long as Burger King keeps serving onion rings." Kevin stuck his hand back in the popcorn bag. "Maybe you would feel better if you let the Fiona thing inspire you to make something better for yourself. Something that moves you in a positive direction."

I figured since my last twenty-four hours started off with offending a dying child and having my life threatened and ended with eating stale popcorn with a boy who considered himself edible and girl who was convinced she lived in a TV, there was nowhere else to go but a positive direction.

"Natalie, your dad is waiting to see you."

The voice came from out of the blue, delivering unbelievable information. I turned to see Staci hovering behind me with a guilty look on her face.

"What?" I asked, practically choking on a popcorn kernel lodged in my throat.

"Your dad and your stepmom," she said softly. "They're in the conference room. Tillie sent me to get you. I'm so sorry."

Kevin and Cassidy shared a look before she pressed "pause" on her remote and looked at me with panic. "Mommy New Boobs, too?" she asked. "And what about the chipmunks? Are they here, too?"

"I did see two little boys running around in the hall," Staci added.

"Oh, God." I leaned back on the couch and closed my eyes. Horrible news, yes, but maybe the timing wasn't that bad. I could test this new Looking-to-Improve-Myself attitude and Motivation Network Theory. But motivated or otherwise, I was definitely not excited. Shooting the breeze with Cassidy and Onion Boy seemed much more entertaining and productive.

"Come on, I'll walk you." Staci held out her hand. "You know, you came in with me to my visit, I don't mind returning the favor."

"That's okay," I said, dragging my feet through the day room door. "Might as well just get it over with."

"Just think how much better you'll feel. I felt great."

"Yeah, the blackmailing the Senator for medical insurance did go over well."

"I wasn't blackmailing, I was making my case. Standing up for myself and facing challenges without self-medicating. Either way, staying here was the best thing for me. My service project is going great, and once you move on from yesterday's thing at the cancer ward, yours will be fine, too."

I stopped and looked at her. "How the hell has everyone heard about that already?"

"It's just me. I heard Tillie on the phone with that Ginny woman," Staci replied. "I don't know the particulars but whatever happened, it will be okay."

The big dramatic scene with that little Natalie girl wasn't something I was proud of, and I planned on righting that wrong somehow before Missy and the Mean girls could make it headline news.

We stopped at the closed conference room door. The cheap perfume step mommy Jill always tried to pass off as Chanel somehow permeated from the other side. My hand wrapped around the knob. "How do I look?"

Staci looked surprised. "That matters?"

For whatever reason, I kind of teleported myself to that moment right before any public appearance where I would be judged. A press conference. News interview. A meeting with my coaches even. I looked down at myself at my Dunes uniform and figured I looked put together enough. Although anything would be an improvement than the human disaster they'd shipped off here months earlier.

"Good luck," Staci offered.

Sticking pins under my fingernails would be preferable than talking with these people, and I'm sure the look on my face conveyed that when I walked in. They didn't look too happy to be there, either. Dad stood in front of the huge picture window with his sunglasses still on. He wore designer jeans and a salmon button-down shirt sans the top two buttons. His sleeves were rolled up, and I was sure it was because I heard Jill tell him once that the look was "very rocker." I sighed. It was one thing to be so blatant about your mid-life crisis in your hometown, but it seemed worse to take it on the road.

Jill looked equally cheesy in her glittered red tank top pulled over her blubber tummy that muffin-topped over white shorts and her boobs that barely fit inside the fabric. She stood at the table with the chipmunks seated in front of her, each with a huge rainbow sucker that was half-smeared over their faces.

If they weren't hard to look at before....

I stood at the edge of the table and waited for someone to acknowledge my presence. Chip saw me first then smacked his brother with his goo-free hand. "Hey, look! She washed her hair! It's not green like a Martian anymore."

The two boys laughed, and Jill put a hand to her mouth to stop hers. The red glittered tips of her nails screamed "trailer park chic." Could it be possible the woman was even trashier than I remembered?

"Well, there you are," Dad said, lifting his shades to his head. "We've been waiting. The kids were getting restless."

"Sorry." I pulled out a chair and liked how it scarped against the floor. The boys held their sticky hands to their ears.

"The doctor and that fat nurse were just in here, and they

said they'd be right back." Dad nodded to the office door. "This is quite an outfit I'm springing for. It's nicer than our hotel in Cancun."

"Cabana, Pookie," Jill corrected. "We stayed in a cabana."

Jack and Jill made goo-goo eyes at each other, and I swallowed the vomit surging to my throat. It impressed me that I didn't lash out at the dig about my hair and more so at the "fat nurse" comment about Tillie. It also downright astounded me I didn't remind him it was actually my money that was bankrolling this journey. Three months ago, I would have unleashed an f- bomb or perhaps thrown something. But today I simply took a deep breath and kept the four-letter words to myself.

Dad pulled out his own chair at the other end of the table. He was obviously studying me, and I made a point to meet his gaze during the once over. As much as I dreaded this reunion, I now realized the build-up was worse than the actual event itself. Here I was, alive. Suffering, but marginally so, ready to take him and Jill head on. "Face the music" as Tillie called it.

"So, I'm sure they invited Mom," I said. "Is she coming?"

He folded his hands together on the table and shook his head. "Guess not, and I've given up trying to reason with her. She seems to think there is something of your career left to salvage. And between you being here and the legal situation with that pervert you were involved with, she's busy dealing with your 'professional reputation,'" he scoffed. "She left me to clean up this mess."

Blaine and Tillie came through the other door. It amazed me how their entrances were always incredibly timed. I never thought about the possibility that it could be a planned thing. Maybe the room was bugged or there were cameras mounted somewhere in one of the plants. If so, I appreciated their sneakiness.

The staff took their places at the long table. They had their handy dandy notebooks front and center, and a pen poised at the ready. Tillie spouted off a few pleasantries and a ten second recap on my three months there. She used words like "talented" and "thoughtful," "driven" and "sensitive." Adjectives I hadn't heard applied to me in a long time. I tried them on like new clothes, and I liked how they felt. I sat up straighter in my chair.

At the other end of the table, I could see my dad's forehead wrinkle. His fists clenched when Blaine declared me "receptive," outright laughed when he dropped "open-minded," and I think Dad was just as stunned as I was when Blaine put a positive spin on my cancer ward freak-out.

"Well, it certainly sounds like they're whipping you into shape," Dad said with a sarcasm in his voice I wondered if only I could hear. "You're a new woman."

"I feel good," I said. "I've been doing my school work. Even started swimming again."

"Swimming, huh? I guess hope springs eternal after all." He looked at Jill who giggled right along with him. "So, while you've been lounging around by the pool, have you been practicing your apology to Jill here for ruining her wedding? She's been waiting for three months."

"I assure you, Mr. Collins, that Natalie has had her plate full with other things," Blaine said. "She's done all that's been asked of her scholastically, has worked on relationships within the community, and next week she'll rejoin her service project at the hospital."

"Oh great, so she can graduate high school and get into what college? And, of course, you put her into a hospital so she can sneak into the pharmacy and score some pills."

"Mr. Collins, your daughter is a Level Three now, soon a Four," Tillie added. "She's earned the right to be trusted in a situation like this that is controlled."

"Trusted? Are we talking about the same girl?"

Sigh. It had been a long time since I'd dealt with my father sober. When I was stoned, his verbal target practice didn't seem to hurt as much. But here, I was vulnerable and the darts were beginning to fly. Funny, but I just didn't feel like ducking. It seemed strangely empowering to take it head on.

He bit his lip and closed his eyes. This was what I called his, "I've-Been-Wronged-Lecture-Face." A blow hard speech was eminent, and I felt sorry for Tillie and Blaine who were sitting so close to the hot air. "Do you know how much trouble this girl has caused me?" he declared. "I am an upstanding citizen in Buffalo. A businessman. She has ruined my reputation and has jeopardized my family's livelihood."

"We had to wait to put in the new pool and tennis courts at home," Jill said. "How do I explain to my boys that they can't take tennis lessons because Natalie's in the looney bin?"

"Daddy says you be a waste of space," Dale chirped, waving his lollypop. It fell and wedged itself between Jill's cleavage.

"A waste of space," Tillie repeated with disgust on her face. "Quite a strange way to refer to your own daughter."

"What else would you call her?" Dad stood up and stuffed his hands in his pockets. He began pacing the length of the table, like some lawyer on a legal drama about to make his case. "This girl was a world champion swimmer. Olympic star. American sweetheart. She had product endorsements, appearance requests, even movie offers."

"That sounds exhausting," Tillie said.

"It sounds like a selfish girl who only thought of herself when she decided to go AWOL and ruin all the lives of the people who supported her. She quit when it got too tough. Her mother refuses to take care of her, and now I'm shelling out money to send her to drug rehab, never mind the legal fees in dealing with the lawsuit."

"Lawsuit?" I asked. "You mean with Racer?"

He cleared his throat. "Jill and I decided to file a civil suit. With all the embarrassment it's caused us, we thought we were entitled to some compensation."

Even Tillie and Blaine couldn't keep poker faced for that revelation. I saw their wide eyes as they both scribbled something in their notebook. I couldn't help laugh, because I felt the lunacy was more hilarious than anything else. "Wait a minute, how is it that I get raped and you get money for it? What are you, a pimp?"

"Watch you fresh mouth!" He leveled a pointed finger at me.

"I'd like to respond to some of your comments," I countered. "One, it's my money that's paying for my stay here. And since we are all being honest, I bankrolled your wedding, trip to Cabo and those fake tits Jill hauls around."

"I thought you said she was making progress here," Dad snapped at Tillie and Blaine. "She just talked back to me. Didn't you hear her? She's disrespecting me!"

"Oh, believe me they hear everything," I said with a steel in my voice even I was impressed with. "They hear shit that isn't even said. Truths."

"What are you high right now?"

"Coach Simms can go to hell," I told him. "He's an abusive heartless asshole who should be banned from the sport. If and when I swim again, he's history. Mark my words."

"Do you hear how disrespectful she is?" he yelled at Tillie and Blaine. "Inexcusable!"

"I didn't think she was disrespecting you, Mr. Collins," Blaine insisted. "I think she was making a point."

"Daddy says you're a slut," Dale blurted. "Stupid little slutty slut." The chipmunks erupted in a sugar overload, chasing each other around the table.

"Perhaps if we remove your wife and kids, we can better focus on you and your daughter's issues," Dr. Blaine yelled over the kids. "This is really an issue between the two of you anyway."

"No, this is between all of us. She owes my wife an apology."

"Maybe you owe your daughter one, Mr. Collins."

Tillie could have slapped him in the face, and I think the reaction would have been the same. He opened and closed his mouth three times before he replied with a voice about two octaves higher than his norm. "Owe her? I don't owe her a damn thing. I've already given her too much, and clearly she thinks she's entitled."

"Entitled?" Blaine asked.

"She should count her blessings!" He looked back at me with a sneer. "How about Annie, that sick friend of yours. She's a breath away from the big sleep, and you're here throwing away your charmed life. Selfish."

Annie's name on his lips was like a kick in the head. I took a deep breath, folded my hands on the table, and leveled the sincerest look in his eye I could muster.

"Look, I shouldn't have trashed your wedding. I am very sorry for that. I'm also sorry for any pain I caused you, but I'm not sorry for being here. At least not anymore. And if being here means I can turn myself around, I'm actually grateful, and it will be the best money I've ever spent."

Yes, the last comment was a dig, but the rest was the best I could do. Lashing out further wouldn't have helped my cause and sitting there quietly just wasn't in my nature. An apology for wrecking his wedding I could handle, the comment about Annie I would let pass, but I damn sure wasn't willing to concede I was a human failure because he said so. Maybe it was the competitor in me. In any case, with a clear mind and wide eyes, I realized there was more to me than he knew. To not cut myself a break would sell myself short. Selling myself short was what got me here in the first place.

Again, the chair scraped against the marble when I stood up. I cleared my throat and squinted at the yellow sun spilling through the surrounding windows. "I'm not sure exactly what you want out of me, Dad, but I'm pretty positive I can't give it to you anyway. When I leave here, I don't know what kind of career I'll have left, or what will happen with the Racer thing. All I do know is I want to surround myself with people who appreciate me rather than people who try to put me down." I turned to Tillie. "I'd like to be dismissed."

Tillie and Blaine just blinked at me, and it felt like the Olympic press conference the instant after I hit a British reporter in the head with a water bottle. Like I had thrown a verbal grenade in the room, and everyone was frozen waiting for it to explode. This time, though, I was pretty damn proud of myself.

"You mean that's it?" Dad yelled. He ran his hands through his balding dark hair that Jill insisted he gel. "The four of us changed our flights from Mexico for this, and you decide you don't want to talk anymore?"

"I think that's an excellent plan." Dr. Blaine closed his folder. "I think today was a good jumping off point for us dealing with familial issues. The staff will be delighted to show you out, and of course, we'll be in touch."

Tillie came to my end of the table and led me to the door. When we were safely on the other side, she brought me in for a big bear hug, the full body kind. "Okay, so maybe you had a point about them."

"Who, my parents?"

"Her boobs. They're bigger than her head." She winked,

then headed back down the nurse's office hall. "Go for a swim or something. We'll chat later about all this. Good job, by the way."

My body shook, and my palms were wet so I wiped them on my shirt. The whole thing happened so fast I'd barely had time to think while I was in the room. Now, of course, I came up with a bunch of things I could have said. Tell them off. Set them straight. I was half temped to run back in and do so, when someone tapped me on my shoulder.

"So how did it go in there?"

The deep baritone voice startled me. "Mitch," I said with a hand over my heart. "Hi."

"Wow, you look like you've been crying. You okay?"

I ran a finger under my eyes to catch any tears that escaped. "Yeah, I'm fine. It's just dealing with my dad is exhausting. And maddening and frustrating..."

"Parent Visit Day, huh?" He slid his hands into his jean pockets. "I remember him from your intervention back in Buffalo. He doesn't strike me as a very understanding guy, unlike others you know."

His dimples deepened when he smiled, I couldn't help but smile myself. "Yeah, you're probably one of the few decent men left on the planet."

"So, you're totally over me dragging you here, huh?"

I studied him as I considered the question. I mean, I legit looked him over. I hadn't realized until that instant, but he was the only guy I'd ever felt comfortable meeting his gaze. Even Racer, I spoke to his chin and I told myself that was because his lower lip piercing was so distracting. But I realized now, it was about confidence. "Yeah, I'm glad you dragged me here," I said.

"Hey, I'm free next Saturday, and you have your day pass still waiting to be used. How would you like to head into Los Angeles for the day? Clear your head a little. Take a break from this place?"

I waited for sirens to wail or the sky to fall, but nothing happened. Was this me having a healthy interaction with a male? Was this me relating?

Was this me being normal?

"Sounds good," I said.

"Great, so next Saturday 10 a.m. I have to confirm it with Tillie, but it shouldn't be a problem."

This was the part where any normal girl my age would say something cool like, "I'll have to check my calendar," but mine was painfully wide open and he knew it, so what was the point in bullshitting. And as it turned out, he wouldn't have heard me anyway.

He was already halfway down the hall.

THIRTEEN

AFTER THE FREAK show family reunion a few days before, I was super motivated to break the apparent genetic chain of douchebaggery. So, I convinced both Blaine and Nurse Ginny to let me go back to the cancer ward to set things right with Little Natalie. It was clear to me now that the common ingredient on my vast buffet of issues was that I did not handle emotionally complicated, pressure-packed situations well. Or in layman's terms, I was a *wimp,* or what Coach Simms would say, *pussy.* Now was the time to change things up.

At 11 a.m., with my belly full of nurses' lounge donut holes and weak coffee, I headed on down to Little Natalie's room. Ginny told me she was out of recovery from whatever procedure she just had and back in her private room. That pleased me for two reasons. One, she was in recovery and two, a private room spared me from begging for her forgiveness in front of a crowd. Although, if I had to, it wouldn't be the first time.

Little Natalie's door was at the end of the hall where the long term residents stayed. Walking by, I noticed some of the doors had fancy signs with pictures or art, personal touches that made it more kidlike than the other wings. Little Natalie's door was decorated with multicolor cut out flowers spelling her name. The door was open a crack so I knocked and peeked in.

The room looked like a glitter bomb had exploded at a flower stand. There Natalie sat in her bed, surrounded by fluffy pink and purple pillows and covered with a matching faux fur comforter. Today there were far less machines and wires, but the air still sported that hospital smell of antiseptic and old soup. She had street clothes on, rather than a gown. A purple track suit with a matching scarf tied like a do rag over her bald head.

"Hey," she said, pulling the ear buds from her ears. "Sorry, I didn't hear you. I was watching Top Chef on my IPad."

"Top Chef is cool," I said, coming closer. "My friend, Cassidy watches that show."

A nurse appeared from a closet behind her bed, carrying a bag of dirty linens. She smiled at me and then rested a hand on Little Natalie's shoulder. "Hey you, naptime in twenty minutes."

"One more episode?" she asked, and it amused the hell out of me at how she used a sweet little voice that was almost a full octave higher than what she had just used with me. "Please?"

The nurse rolled her eyes and laughed. "Fine, I can't say no to you."

Little Natalie flashed a toothy grin before the nurse walked out to the hall. When she was out of earshot, Little Natalie chuckled and pointed to her do rag covered head. "Cute kid with brain cancer gets the sympathy every time."

This kid was impressive. Cute, resourceful and a penchant for rebellion. I took another step closer, feeling more at ease.

"I think I like the food shows because I couldn't eat like a human for so long. Food tubes suck, by the way." She set the Ipad aside and smiled up at me. "You look familiar. Are you the new social worker?"

The other day I had on scrubs, but today I had on my Dunes

white shirt and khaki shorts uniform. It made me feel slightly better when she didn't recognize me. Maybe I didn't scar her fragile psyche as much as I'd thought I did. "No, we actually met the other day. I came in here and I took your Cat and the Hat book."

"Oh yeah, the girl who freaked out." She laughed, like the memory amused the hell out of her. "Thanks for returning my book. The library lady brought it down."

"I meant to bring it back myself."

"It's fine. It took the scenic route but the destination was the same." She picked up the same copy of Oh the Places You'll Go from a stack of books on the shelf above her and waved it in the air. "Safe and sound."

"Well, at least that's something."

Hey, you want some fruit? I don't have much of an appetite back yet."

She pointed beside her to the bedside table littered with nail polish and jewelry beads. In the middle of it all was a barely touched edible fruit arrangement. A big cardboard poster stuck out of the middle of it said, "You're Awesome, Natalie!"

"That's okay." I shrugged. "Maybe your family will eat it."

"I could use a break from them." She pulled out a stick of melon and handed it to me. "Here, humor me and have some."

I hated melon, but I took it anyway. It seemed like small penance for my behavior the other day.

"So why'd you freak out?"

I tried to swallow my big bite. "What?"

"The other day, you ran out of the recovery room like you were on fire. Why?"

It looked as though this would be a lengthy conversation. At least one that went beyond, "Sorry I'm a loser for bailing on you the other day. Peace out." So, I grabbed a chair and pulled up next to her bed. "I have a friend," I explained. "She has cancer."

"Is she dying?"

I sat down to get my thoughts straight. "No, at least I hope not."

"We're all dying, Nat. Some say we start dying the moment we're born. We're all on borrowed time." She picked up a Hi-C juice box from her stash of goodies behind the fruit tower and gave it a deadly stab of the straw. "I read that somewhere."

"Wow," I said. "I don't think Dr. Suess ever said anything like that."

"So why aren't you with her?"

"What do you mean?"

She took a sip of her drink and thoughtfully leaned back against a purple glittered pillow. "What I mean is, if your best friend in the whole world is dying of cancer, why aren't you sitting next to her talking about stupid stuff instead of sitting next to me talking about stupid stuff?"

If felt like her words were like tiny jabs I had to duck and weave to keep from landing. She just sat there with blue eyes wide, clearly expecting a response with substance. All I could manage was a goofy half-smile.

"Well?"

I blinked. "Well what?"

"Why did you bail on her?"

"I didn't bail on her." I took a breath and squared my shoulders. It was hard to believe she was just a kid because I felt like I was chatting it up with Cassidy or Staci. Someone *on my level*. I had to remember to deliver a short, PG rated explanation rather than the sordid full truth. "So I'm not there because she lives in Buffalo, which is like a million miles from here. I can't be in Buffalo because I made some bad decisions, and I got sent out here to this place called The Dunes to learn to make good ones."

"Drug rehab, huh?" She laughed. "That's rough. You better now?"

I considered what would qualify as 'better.' "I'm working on it, I guess."

"That's good to hear. If you don't mind me saying so, it looked like you really lost it at the Olympics. Flipping that table at that press conference was great TV but bad PR I'm sure."

The nurse lingering by the laundry cart giggled, so clearly my cover was blown. I guess it was something I needed to get used to when I hit the outside.

"So this best friend with cancer in Buffalo? She got a name?"

It suddenly struck me that in the whole time I'd been out in California, with all the people who'd poked and prodded my fragile psyche, not one human soul had asked me that question. Hell, I wasn't certain I'd be willing to share it anyway but Little Natalie seemed like a good first set of ears. "It's Annie," I told her, like I was out of practice saying it. "Annie Madsen. She's awesome. You'd really like her. She has long brown hair and green eyes. And she's funny. Tells a joke like a stand-up comic. She's such a diva, too. Gets her nails done twice a month in these really pretty glitter colors. Sometimes she drags me with her. There's no point because I bite mine, and believe it or not, long nails make you slower when you swim. And she's good at everything. Like she can sing, and I can't carry a tune. She can draw and paint and even tap dance. We both took dance classes when we were little kids, but she was actually good at it. I know I was the better swimmer, well I'm a better distance swimmer, but she's the better..." I stared at the ceiling searching for the word, but I realized I'd already gone over my quota.

"Well?" Little Natalie prompted. "You're the better swimmer but she's the better..."

"Person." I heard myself say it like I meant to all the long. "Annie is a better person. If the roles were reversed, she would have made all the right decisions and been next to my bedside."

This girl maybe only eleven or twelve, but any idiot could see that I was now just having a conversation with myself. To Little Natalie's credit, she seemed to dig it. Her thin red lips twisted in a half smile as she folded the edge of the bedsheet over and over in her hand.

"Sometimes I wonder if she's mad I'm not there with her," I said.

"What makes you think that?"

"Just a hunch. I mean, I might be mad if my best friend wasn't there for me, and I was feeling bad."

Little Natalie crossed her skinny arms against herself. I could tell she was considering her words by the way she studied a long, clear tube that discreetly snaked across her lap. "Let me level with you, Nat. As a person who can relate to Annie, I don't really care about being mad at someone over stupid stuff."

"I've been told that."

"What about swimming? You miss it?"

No one had asked me that either. At least point blank, like she did. I mulled it over for a second and went with my gut reaction. "Yeah, I do, I guess. Maybe a lot."

She pursed her lips and nodded, like she was impressed as hell at my answer. "So, if I were you, I would think about how you could make your time away from Annie worthwhile. Cuz right now, what I'm thinking is how lucky people are they get to live, not how unlucky I am I might die. Catch my drift?"

I wasn't sure if I did, but I didn't want to admit it. "Sure."

"What I mean is, get your head straight. If you want to swim, swim. If you don't, don't. But believe me, Annie wants you to live your life. She wishes she could live hers. Life can suck and be hard and unfair, but you got one, so that's something."

The wisdom bestowed in the last few minutes was probably more valuable than any I'd stumbled upon the last three months. The nurse also seemed pretty captivated by the conversation given the way she hovered and folded the same sheet like three times. Who could blame her? Little Natalie made sense.

"Nap time, Nat," The nurse said, giving me a look I took as the visit was over. It was funny, when I figured I would be hellbent on getting out of there ASAP, but I found myself sad to leave. Like we could have shot the shit all day, eating gross fruit. I stood and headed for the door. "How about I stop by again next week when I'm here?"

"You know where to find me," Little Nat said, arranging the pillows behind her head. "Thanks for bringing my book back."

"No problem," I replied, halfway out the door.

"Oh, and send good vibes to Annie. Everyone could use some good vibes, don't ya think?

I looked back at her and smiled. "For sure, but make sure you keep some for yourself."

"Noted," she said, and I closed her door behind me.

———

The past week or two I'd gotten in the habit of bringing other people with me on my morning swim. Most of the time it was Cassidy, who liked to do handstands in the shallow end, but this morning she was having breakfast with Onion Boy, so Staci offered to keep me company in her place.

We strolled across the lawn down to the pool gate, Staci slathering on sunscreen as she went. "You know, it's too bad Fiona isn't still here. She probably would have liked swimming with you."

"I thought about that," I said. "But she didn't look like she was in that great of shape anyway."

"Withdrawal takes a lot out of you. You may not have had it that bad, but with heroin..." She made a face. "Man, just the fear of going through withdrawal again is enough to scare me straight."

"Heroin wasn't my drug of choice."

"Lucky you, because it's horrible. Lance told me when he was withdrawing from it, he ripped half of his hair right off his scalp."

Staci had been working at Lance Bates's studio for over a month now, and it was all she ever talked about. Before, I didn't even know what "pop art" was, but now I could spew off major artists, their influences, and a general idea of what part of the country they were from. I was sort of developing a second-hand interest myself. "You know, you spend so much time on your service project that I barely see you anymore."

"You'll be in the same boat next week, once you do yours more regular. You'll be so busy improving yourself, you won't even have time for me to bore you with Lance Bates stories anymore."

"I just want to do a good job. I feel like there's extra pressure because I screwed up the first time."

"You'll survive. You lived through the visits with your dad and Cruella. Once you face this, you'll be fine. Just think about next weekend. You have your day pass with Mitch, right?

"Yeah..."

"Well then from where I'm standing, life looks pretty good for you right now."

We headed through the gate and set our towels and clothes down on one of the starting blocks. After a count to "three," we jumped in the water together.

"Shit," Staci said when she surfaced. "I forgot about my contact lenses."

"There're goggles in the pump room. I can get some for you." I swam over to the side of the pool and hoisted myself to the deck. Even with wet feet, the concrete was hot, so I jogged over to the shed.

The door was ajar. Not that I was looking, but I didn't notice it being that way when we came in. Clint's cart wasn't near the gate, but that didn't mean much. Since the night in the kitchen, I'd noticed he'd been kind of watching me from a distance. Not stalking per say, but definitely clocking me. He'd pass by when I was studying on the lawn or drive his cart past when I was in the pool. Like a reminder to keep my mouth shut. I had, and now, since no one else knew about it and time had passed, I could almost mindfuck myself into pretending it didn't happen at all. Like it was some sort of delusion or bad dream I had the night after a really bad day. Maybe I just felt guilty that I hadn't spoken up about it.

But now as I stood there with my hand on the pool shed doorknob, for whatever reason, I was acutely reminded that it happened. It wasn't like I possessed a sixth sense or anything, but I had a really creeped out feeling there was something on the other side of the door I should prepare myself for.

"What's wrong?" Staci called, resting her arms on the side of the pool.

I brought my finger to my lips in the "shhh" sign and wondered why I felt it necessary to do so. She must have, too, because she hopped out of the pool, grabbed a towel, and hurried over behind me.

When I opened the door, I wasn't exactly prepared for what I saw, but I can't say I was surprised either. Clint stood in the middle of the shed with his bare ass facing me, giving it hard to a girl bent over an old wooden worktable. I couldn't see her face, but the faded full sleeve rose tattoo on her left arm clinging to the table edge gave her away.

"You can't come inside me, you perv," Missy gasped. "That wasn't the deal."

"The deal was I get what I want, and you get what you want." He yanked her by her long black ponytail and shoved her nose square into a freezer baggie of white powder beside her head. "See that, Whore? You want it? Pay for it."

He slammed himself in her, like an exclamation mark at the end of his sentence. I covered my mouth with my hand to both keep from screaming and from vomiting at my feet.

"Oh my God," Staci gasped in my ear. "What do we do?"

I gulped. Even Missy didn't deserve this, and in a strange way, I could relate. Even if I couldn't remember Racer doing what he did to me, I certainly didn't like it. And maybe even if Missy was a willing participant in this, it had obviously gone too far now. "Go get help," I whispered to Staci. "If we catch them ourselves, Missy will deny it, and who knows what Clint will do. Hurry."

Staci sprinted across the lawn. I waited behind the chlorine barrels, trying to block out the rhythmic pounding, trying to figure how the hell Missy had ended up like this. How any of us did? What was it about getting stoned that made us want to suffer for it? Wasn't feeling shitty about life why we got stoned in the first place? Was getting high really a cure? It definitely didn't sound like a cure, her begging him to hurry up, and him slamming into her like he was nailing her against a wall.

I covered my ears and closed my eyes, but I could still feel the vibration in my chest. It was like it was happening to me, when I was as helpless and she was. When I hated myself. When I thought my life was so worthless, it didn't matter if I gave it away.

Suddenly the air rushed around me, and the sunlight spilled in through the door. The same burly guards I saw that night with Fiona barreled inside, knocking over stacks of kickboards and swim buoys. One of them grabbed Clint by his collar and tossed him against the wall.

I'm not sure of the rest. A lot of yelling and screaming. Cussing and crying. Tillie somehow showed up and sat next to me with our feet in the pool. Neither of us said much. Probably because we both were dumfounded by Missy's defense of Clint to The Dune administrators who had shown up like a SWAT team. We waited thirty, maybe forty minutes, before I was asked to give a statement. Clint was taken away in handcuffs by some police officers I didn't remember arriving.

When the rest of the shitshow dispersed, Tillie and I remained. We sat in the lounge chairs watching sunshine fade to twilight. "I have a confession to make," I said.

"She took a long gulp of her bottled water and looked at me with a wrinkled brow. "Oh yeah, what's that?"

"A few weeks ago, I broke into the kitchen late at night to make a snack. I saw Clint in there. He was dealing drugs confiscated from new patients. He sold them to the food delivery guy. I probably should have told someone, but I chickened out. I'm sorry."

I figured there would be consequences. I mean, I did break a rule after all, but maybe they'd be lenient and not kick me out. Although, had I spoken up, Missy wouldn't have been spread eagle over a rotted table in a pool shed.

"I'm happy you finally spoke up."

I shrugged. "It's about time I did. Don't ya think?"

Tillie and I were leaving the pool when Missy skulked by us with security guards on either arm. She looked tense and wide-eyed. like an animal fighting captivity. When her gaze met mine, she snarled and loud enough for Tillie to hear what she said to me, "Payback's a bitch, Nat. I'd remember that if I were you!"

I had to agree.

Really, nothing about the last hour of my life would be easy to forget.

FOURTEEN

March 31, Thursday
Mood: Almost April Fooled

Dear Annie,

It's amazing how clearly I see things now through sober eyes. I'm not sure that's always a good thing. All I know is that after the Olympics, I self-medicated a lot because I liked being on auto pilot. I feel like in this place, they are easing me into having the controls back on the duct-taped Lear jet that is my life. Lucky me! I'm finding decision making is a skill I haven't used in a while. People have been deciding everything for me. What to eat, what to wear. What to say even. In real life, I have to have an opinion on those things. Like, do I like almond milk? The other day at break-fast I thought about that for at least a few minutes.

It felt pretty good.

So much has happened since the last time I wrote. The abridged version is this guy who worked here was doing some bad shit, and I made the decision to call him out on it when I had to. I mean, I didn't handle it perfectly. But I handled it sober and with reasoning behind it. I had a thought process. Haven't had one of those in a long time.

In any event, I'm getting better, I think. I also told Tillie to send my mother a message to fire Coach Simms. Tillie told me I could just contact him directly because it would be me making the decision, so I did. I fired him and it felt good! Me! No longer would I have to listen to his name calling and toxic lectures. Let him get into a pool and circle swim for hours on end. I'd help him into cement shoes...

Sorry. That was anger driven.

So anyway, I'm my own girl now, making my own decisions, or at least independent girl in training. I was thinking when I get back and you're better, we could maybe get a house together and be roommates. Like we used to talk about. Be independent!

Okay, back to work.

———

THIS WAS the first time ever I sat in morning group, actually looking forward to it. Between Fiona's arrival and jail break, and Missy's horror scene in the pool shed, the rumor mill was working overtime and everyone had been far too pleased to pump me for information. Being an eye-witness for most of it made me the Go-To-Gal for the juiciest gossip. So far, I had gotten by with "I didn't see much," and Cassidy urging others to change the channel.

Missy sat in her usual spot across from me, shooting daggers at me with her eyes. The news about her and Clint was that the sex was consensual and they were in love, but pretty much everyone knew it was Missy who was in love with his dope. Clint was arrested, and thanks to an anonymous tip about his dealings with the food delivery guy, it looked like federal drug charges would stick and he'd be in prison soon enough.

The residents might have seen sick entertainment value in the whole thing, but the staff was super shaken up over it. For a good week everyone from the cleaning crew to the tech support people had to go through emergency seminars about appropriate conduct with the residents. Now they all sported heinous Halloween orange shirts with "Staff" plastered across the chest.

Classy.

If the in-house news wasn't enough, I was also stressing about my service project that started back up Monday morning, and next Saturday's Los Angeles day with Mitch. An extra thing to look forward to on my day pass was street clothes! I got to wear what I wanted on my day pass. I wish I remembered what I'd packed in my duffle bag when I came here.

Blaine walked into group sporting his Let's-Have-a-Meaningful-Conversation face and took a seat with his clipboard. Tillie and the two other counselors filed in behind. Instead of the orange shirts, they sported orange tags. Good thing, because poor Tillie would've looked like a big old pumpkin in one of those tops. Even though she'd dropped some noticeable poundage since I'd first dragged her to the pool, she still got teased from time to time. No need to add salt to the wound.

"So, we've had a few shakeups in the community recently, huh?" Blaine said like addressing toddlers at preschool. "This is a trying time, isn't it?"

We all gave an obligatory nod except for Missy, who just stared at the floor.

"On the outside, we all self-medicated when situations got uncomfortable, scary, sad. Tell me, how is everyone dealing with it now?"

"Please," Missy mumbled, spitting a fingernail from her mouth. "How is it anyone else's business?"

"You made it community business when you were discovered by the residents, and you made it the staff's by participating in self-destructive activities in the first place."

"Self-destructive." She laughed. "How is a good fuck self-destructive? I thought this place was about learning to get pleasure in ways other than drugs. Sex is pleasure." She leveled her gaze at me. "I was just working the program until she showed up."

There was no doubt in my mind that had we been anywhere else, she would have come at me fists, feet and all. Thankfully, all the fire power she had right now was her mouth. "You're no better than me, Natalie," she said. "You think I'm a whore? Well, so are you. At least I stay awake for it."

The jab grazed me, but I didn't flinch. Neither did the rest of the room except for Staci who sat up in her seat. "Missy, why are you blaming her for your shitty decisions?" Staci asked.

"How are your actions Natalie's fault?"

"Fuck you. None of you know jack about me or what I do."

"What you *did* is prostitute yourself for drugs on The Dunes property, putting yourself and the rest of the community at risk," Blaine declared. "We as a staff have offered our apologies and made steps to rectify the situation. Now it's your turn to take care of business at your end."

"I ain't apologizing to anyone who deserves what they get."

"Missy," Blaine said as he recrossed his legs. "You seem to have a problem with anger toward people. Do you want everyone to hate you? Look down on you? Pity you? Because if so, you're succeeding."

Heads whipped around the room like they were on swivels. Blaine was never that blunt, and his even keel voice always made us wonder if he took the chill pills he preached against. But today his face was red, and he looked at Missy with a wrinkle in his forehead. She'd pissed off Teeth. A milestone for sure.

"You, my dear, take delight in hurting others," Blaine told her. "Because you don't like yourself. You think you are worthless and insignificant and want others to feel the same way. How do you feel now that I've said that?"

Tillie and the two other counselors shifted in the seats. This was definitely not a group therapy session I was used to. Usually, it was hand holding and sweet talk and obviously ineffective as far as Missy was concerned, because she had been stranded in Level Three purgatory as long as I'd been here. Right now, she was pale-faced and sunk down in her seat like someone had sucked the air out of her usual puffed-up self.

She pulled at the cuticles of her fingers and sighed. "It's bullshit," she mumbled. "Fucking bullshit."

"What's bullshit?" Dr. Blaine asked.

"People like Fiona and Staci. Posers." She looked across to me. "Especially you, Nat. I could tell the minute I saw you in the day room that you were bullshit. Even before I knew you were some swim star. You're just a goody goody that got caught smoking Daddy's cigarettes and got sent to her room 'for her own good.'"

I scanned the room. It was good to see everyone else looked as confused as I was. My dad's cigarettes? And what did that have to do with Fiona or Staci?

"You're here for your own good too, Missy," Blaine said. "All of you are."

"We're not the same!" She stood up with her hands on her hips, again leveling her gaze at me. "People like me and Ari and Tia, we're the real addicts. Heroin. Meth. We're street kids. Throwaways. My grandma was a crack whore, my mom was a crack whore, and now I'm one. You guys have no clue what that's like. I was born in a fucking flop house. We slept on sidewalks, sold ourselves to anyone who'd pay, fought rats for food in dumpsters because we had to. We came from nothing, and we still have nothing."

She took a step toward me and stared harder. Her brown eyes were black, and she tapped her foot like she might lash out with it and kick me. "You got everything. A nice house, a good school, food to eat. You're a fucking celebrity. Okay, so your mom is crazy and your dad is a bastard. So what? Your best friend is dying from some disease, and you're sitting here whining about being misunderstood? Fuck you!"

When the tears began to fall, I swore the whole room held back a gasp. The ice girl was having a meltdown in front of our eyes. Even Blaine was mesmerized. Missy stood in the middle of the room with fisted hands, shaking her head like she was fighting something inside it. We all waited, curious, at the edge of our seats. The tea kettle was ready to boil.

"I do what I have to do to look out for me," she yelled. "I like to use because being high is better than feeling like shit. You know how I got in here? My parole officer, who also deals dope by the way, is paying for my stay here. You want to know why? Because he used to be a John of mine and gets off on being a sugar daddy. He thinks in here, I'm not fucking anybody else. He thinks he controls me, but you know what? I control me. I do what I want when I want to. So, I like being high? So, what?"

She took a breath and I held mine, and I assumed the rest of us did, too. The hairs stood on the back of my neck, and I realized I didn't know where to look. At Missy or the floor. So, I opted for closing my eyes and letting the words find their own way to my ears.

"So, fuck Fiona and Staci and to all you people who were given everything and fucked it up. Because you're nothing but stupid and selfish and that's why I hate your asses."

The slam of the door echoed in my chest. No one, not even

the Bikinis, moved to follow. Maybe they realized they should be offended, because as I now knew, they were the twin daughters of a kagillionaire movie producer in Malibu. Staci stared at the ceiling, and I could see her throat bob when she swallowed. "Selfish" was a word I heard her parents hurl at her. She was probably sick of hearing it, and out of Missy's mouth, it was probably worse.

And then there was me. I felt naked. Like someone had ripped my clothes right off of me. Tillie told me once that my using drugs was my attempt to hide myself. If that was so, I was painfully exposed right now.

"Well, I guess we've chatted enough this morning," Blaine finally said, pulling his folder closed. "Let's have a good day, a restful weekend, and start fresh Monday."

———

March 2, Friday
Mood: Sorry

Dear Annie,

I think I owe you an apology.

I've been thinking about my intervention. (Yes, I can say the word now) Many of you told me I was selfish. It made me angry then, but now I see you (and they) might have had a point.

I have never considered myself as fortunate, but I am beginning to think that just like luck, it's relative. I know my house may not be a mansion on the rich side of town, but at least it's not a refrigerator box homeless people sleep in. My parents might be crazy, but they don't beat me or rape me. And maybe I'm not the prettiest or the smartest or the best swimmer, but bottom line, I'm alive. I

*have a future and opportunities and things to look
forward to.*

*No offense, but there are some people like you who can't
say that.*

*I get that there are people who have more opportunities
than others. What I have to do is stop blaming others for not
giving them to me. If opportunities are something I have to
work for, that's not a bad thing. What's bad is wallowing in
self-defeat instead of taking a chance .*

*Today I told Tillie what I just told you, and I swear I
saw her eyes tear up. That's when she revealed that she and
the rest of the staff awarded me Level Five status. It will be
official next week sometime. I'm excited and proud of
myself, but also, I'm freaked out because now I have a lot to
live up to. The good news is that I can continue my service
project, and next Saturday I get a day pass to spend the day
in Los Angeles. It's progress. Slow but steady.*

*I miss you and love you. And again, I hope you can find
it in your heart to forgive me. You're the least selfish person
and most unlucky person I know. And I mean that as a
compliment.*

———

Friday nights usually weren't prime time for scheduling one-on-
one meetings, or any other kind of meeting for that matter,
which was why I was shocked when Tillie informed me midway
through The Bachelor Season Four finale that someone was
waiting to see me.

It was still daylight outside but felt much later, the remnants
of this week's happenings still hanging around in my mind. I
totally was not in the mood to go another round with Dad, and I
considered telling Tillie so, but when I looked through the

window on the conference room door, it wasn't my father on the other side.

I never realized before how much Annie looked like her mom. Mrs. Madsen was short, and as far back as I could remember, sort of chubby, but in her tan shorts and pale pink golf shirt she looked like she'd lost some weight in the months since I'd seen her. Her shoulder-length frizzy brown hair hung in her face, and her eyes looked tired. Her Western New York skin was pale, almost as ghostly as her daughter's the last time I saw her.

The knob slipped in my sweaty palm when I opened the door. I felt my legs go weak. Somehow, though, I managed to bridge the distance between her and me. No words, just motion. I couldn't think of anything to say.

"Your hair is blonde again," she said as a greeting, in a faraway voice that sounded more like a child's. "You always had such beautiful blonde hair."

She ran her hand through the strands, and I found I sort of liked it. It was nice not to bother with pleasantries and exchanges about the weather. Just straight to the heart. "That's the first thing they did when I got here. Wash the dye out."

"This is quite a facility. Your staff showed me around. It's beautiful out here." She wandered over to the windows. "Not a bad place to be, is it?"

"No. No, it's not."

I stood behind her, appreciating the view of the sun setting over the mountains. We were silent for a few moments, and it was nice I didn't feel obligated to fill the space. Obviously, Annie wasn't here, but she might as well have been considering her existence in the room was bigger than either one of us standing there. "Annie misses you a lot," she told me. "She wanted to write and call, but it wasn't allowed."

"I know. That's okay. I'm glad she didn't waste her time."

Mrs. Madsen turned toward me and wiped a tear from her

cheek. "You, my darling, aren't a waste of anything. Can you please just come here and give your second mother a hug."

I let her arms fold around me. She smelled like Annie. That fruity scent of strawberry shampoo and Ivory detergent that always seemed to stick to me after leaving their house. I took a deep breath and let it settle within me.

"I heard your dad came out here a few weeks ago. He said you still have a lot of work to do. I thought I would come and see for myself."

"It's a long way to come," I stammered.

"But it's worth the trip."

My legs felt weak, so I pulled out a chair and folded my hands in my lap. "Um, I've finished my school stuff. I do volunteer work at the local hospital. I've even started to swim again."

"You know, you don't have to," she said. "I know you've had so much pressure. From the press and everything. And I never liked that Coach Simms you had. Annie said he was pushy."

"She wasn't wrong," I told her. "If I come back, he won't be involved, believe me. I'll find a new coach. I already fired him."

"You and Annie are such talented athletes. I'm happy you're picking it back up." She smiled. The way I wished my own mother would. Prideful. Sincere. The kind of smile that made you feel ten feet tall.

"I've made a lot of changes. Positive things. I'm trying to make my life better."

"That's wonderful. I was hoping that maybe a change of scenery would do you some good."

"How is she, Mrs. Madsen?"

The question seemed to knock her off balance, because she pulled out the chair next to me and sat down. "Annie is home. Scrapbooking, isn't that sweet? Of the whole family, her friends, swimming. We've all been so worried about you, so I thought I would come out and see for myself how you were doing. I don't think she'd be strong enough to make the trip anyway."

I felt knot in my stomach. "She's getting worse, isn't she?"

"The doctors say the end of the summer."

There was no need for elaboration. The tears rolling down her cheeks said it all. I pulled a tissue from the box perpetually on the table and handed it to her. "I just wanted to make sure you knew. I didn't want the last contact you had with her to be a message that...she'd passed."

I gulped. "I don't want Annie to see me like this. I want to show her I can get well."

"Annie wants you to get better, and honey, that's the best thing you can do for her. Not throw your life away."

"Thank you for saying that but..."

"There's another thing. The Tillie woman I spoke to said you should be done with the program in a month or so. If it's at all possible, I want you to come home and stay with us. I made an arrangement with the administration here so they contact us not your parents when you're released. You're not a child and you have control of your own affairs no matter what your father tells you."

"Mrs. Madsen, I really don't feel comfortable putting you out like that. And you damn sure don't need an ex-drug addict hanging around."

"Oh, please." She batted her hand and sniffled. "You're like a daughter to me. We want you to be there. And of course, after...you're more than welcome to stay."

I felt my body seize, like someone injected ice water in my veins. "Me...why? Why would you want me under your roof? Your family is already going through so much. I'd be an embarrassing burden."

"You are not an embarrassment or a burden. You're wonderful. Smart and kind. Special. Just like Annie."

If she intended the comparison between Annie and myself to flatter, I took it more as an insult on her daughter's part. What exactly had I done that was so smart? Wreck my life? Alienate my family? Spend the last months of my best friend's life keeping touch through one-way letters? Why would Mrs. Madsen want anything to do with me?

I closed my eyes until I felt her hand slip through my hair. "Sweetheart, I know it hasn't been easy on you, and I hate to see you punish yourself for things that aren't your fault."

"Some of it is," I whispered. "Most of it."

"Being vulnerable is nothing you should feel guilty about. You're a world class athlete put under world class pressure."

"I didn't handle it very well," I said.

"And we all should have done more to get you away from that Racer guy."

"It wasn't your place, Mrs. Madsen."

"Well, I want you to know that Mr. Madsen's legal practice has taken it upon themselves to make sure that man won't see the light of day. We can do that much for you."

I suddenly realized how good a job I'd done at compartmentalizing my life. Organizing things into little boxes. Natalie the friend, the student, the swimmer. East coast and west coast, stoned and sober. A presence in multiple worlds. Ignoring the Racer thing was easy because I was thousands of miles away from it all. But now that Mrs. Madsen was here, someone who really knew, all of a sudden it infected me, consumed me like a virus. *Something to address.* I took a deep breath and stared at my folded hands.

"Mrs. Madsen, I put myself in the position of letting Racer do what he did to me. I know it's not my fault. It's his, and I need to accept what has happened, take something positive away from what I went through and move on."

When my own words hit my ears, I didn't recognize the

voice they were spoken with. It was clear and strong. Like there was resolve behind it.

"You've come a long way, Natalie. I'm proud of you."

We sat there silent for a minute before she got up and went to the door. "Take care of yourself, Natalie." I didn't see her leave, but I heard her footsteps recede while my face was buried in my hands.

Tillie came and got me and walked me back to my room. I'm not sure I said a word. I just remember climbing into bed and pulling the covers over me, letting my tears lull me to sleep.

FIFTEEN

MY SERVICE PROJECT reboot started Monday morning, which was great because I was ready for a distraction. The Emergency Room blood and guts atmosphere was not my idea of a pick-me-up, but anything was better than blowing my nose and staring at the ceiling while Cassidy tried to get me to watch the God Network and actively search for Jesus. I could say, however, that Jesus definitely was not in any of the bed pans I'd emptied thus far that morning.

Not that I looked that hard.

Last week in the interest of preparing myself, I sat down and watched a few old Grey's Anatomy episodes. They were pretty good and if all the doctors were as cute as Patrick Dempsey, maybe it wouldn't be so bad. So far, my favorite part was answering phones. No latex gloves required, and it didn't smell that bad at the front desk.

Ginny had been my constant companion all day. I think more for her security than mine. If she was fearing another meltdown, it wasn't necessary. Contrary to what you see on TV, I realized the ER was not such a dramatic place, in rural California anyway. A few Mexican children with ear infections. A migrant farm worker with an infected hand and an old man who had forgotten to take his heart meds on the golf course. Nothing I couldn't handle. So at 8 pm, I sat at the desk playing solitaire with a half a deck of cards and nibbled on the chocolate cookies that always seemed to be stashed at the nurse's station. Ginny seemed pleased, and even said I could pay Little Natalie a bedtime visit if it stayed slow. She headed to the break room for the first time all day.

Suddenly the door burst open. Two shirtless guys in torn jeans and dirty faces held an unconscious girl by her arms. Her muddied blonde hair fell over her face and her mouth hung open like a silent scream. One of the guys screamed for help before scurrying out the door, leaving the poor girl in a heap on the linoleum.

"You guys we got an OD!" someone yelled behind me. "Bring a gurney STAT!"

All at once, people converged. A few nurses, doctors. I was pushed to the side. A bed with wheels was snapped into place and just like that, the girl was whisked away.

"Where did she come from?" one orderly asked another.

"Didn't see."

"Two guys dropped her off and bolted out of here," I informed them. "Maybe we should go try to find them and ask what happened." I took a few strides to exit but stopped when I realized they weren't following me. "Well, we should get them, right?"

"Why bother," a nurse said. "They probably don't know any more than we do. And if they do, they wouldn't be honest about it."

"But maybe if they told us who she was and what happened..."

They turned back toward the nurse's lounge, but I stood there with my foot still in the door. Two things struck me. One, was I supposed to blame this girl for her own sickness? Okay, so maybe she was a drug addict. Did she choose to be? Did the farm worker earlier choose to expose his open wound to dirt, and the old man choose to play golf without heart medication? The doctors were more than happy to treat them.

Two, was I a hypocrite? Four months and four levels ago, I was a drug addict myself. It could have been me being dragged into the ER and people blowing me off. When exactly did I switch sides? And who said there were sides in the first place?

So, I ran out of the ER entrance. A couple taxis lined the curb, and a police car idled next to a parked ambulance. Other than a few nurses chatting by the bus stop, and a security man standing guard by the door, there wasn't a soul in sight. Not a sound except for the hum of the huge industrial air conditioner behind me.

I trudged back through the door and took a breath, pretending it was the sour stench of hospital that was making my eyes water. A few nurses I'd seen attending the OD girl were behind the desk with their foreheads pushed together in private conversation. I wasn't looking to interrupt. I just returned to my perch and my riveting, yet nonsensical solitaire game.

"That must be a wake-up call for you," one nurse said to me after the other disappeared. "Drug addicts and OD's."

"I guess so. It makes you think about stuff."

"I just don't get why people would want to make themselves sick. I see sick people every day who are willing the sell their soul to get better, and then there are girls like that one. Healthy as a horse. Pregnant even." She picked up a cookie and took a bite. "Ends her life and a helpless baby's life, too. Why? What for?"

I blinked when the words registered. "Excuse me, ends?"

The attending doctor flanked by two nurses emerged from

the far curtain and made their way down the hall. They were frowning and dragging their feet, but I also sensed an odd sort of anger radiating from under their scrubs. "We need to get an ID for this girl," the doctor said. "Tell Ginny to get on the phone. And, Natalie, can you clean everything up in there. Somebody from the morgue will be here in a minute to claim her."

I nodded dumbly and squeezed around the crowd. It didn't bother me that I was going to share the space with a dead person. It was more important to me why she died and what for. When I pushed the curtain aside, somehow, I felt the same anger I sensed in the rest of them. Maybe I was a little peeved myself.

I wasn't cold, but for some reason goose pimples raised on my skin. For a few minutes I went about my business, sweeping, wiping down, marking out my check list for clearing the room. The bed was pushed up against the wall. Under the pale blue sheet, I could see the human silhouette and the small bump of a pregnant woman. I just stood there while all sorts of monologues ran through my head. I wanted to tell this girl I understood where she had come from. How I could relate to the loneliness that led her to self-medicate in the first place. How I was pissed at the doctors and nurses for blowing her off and sympathized with feeling like no one cared.

When I was done with my tasks, I snapped off my gloves and took one last glimpse of the body on the bed. One foot was sticking out from under the sheet where the blank toe tag was attached. It seemed cruel she was nameless. Like her existence on the planet was erased. Could it be that this corpse never made a single impression on anyone in her whole life so that she would die anonymously and disposed of like trash?

That was when I spied the tattoo "Julian" written in delicate calligraphy on the top of her exposed foot.

I don't remember walking over to the bed or lifting the sheet, but I can totally recall the sinking feeling in my stomach when I saw her. The paleness of her skin, how her hair stuck to her lips. Her eyes were closed, but I didn't have to see them to imagine the brilliant blue.

"Hey, Nat," Ginny called from the door. "Are you okay in there?"

I swallowed the lump in my throat and wrapped my trembling fingers around her lifeless ones. "Fiona Tannenbaum," I mumbled to Ginny when she came up beside me. "Tell the doctor she's not a Jane Doe. She's Fiona Tannenbaum. My friend."

———

March 15, Monday
Mood: Wrecked

Dear Annie,

I had a hellacious day at work. It involved a drug OD, and I'm not going to depress you with the particulars, but I really need to vent. Spoiler Alert: Excessive nonsensical whining ahead.

So, this girl Fiona. So nice, had everything. Good parents, good home. Pretty, smart. Why would a person who had everything choose to block it all out with drugs and booze? At first, I was so sad for her. People referring to her as a "victim" lamenting how her "disease" finally got the best of her. Boo-hoo.

Is it bad that I'm mad as hell at her?

*Somebody used the phrase today "better living through chemistry." I guess it means some people use drugs and alcohol to enhance a life that is already pretty good. I think those are the same people who use drugs "recreationally"

*like going to an amusement park and riding a rollercoaster.
But at what point is the roller coaster ride not fun anymore?
When you throw off your safety bar, jump from the cart, and
puke in the trash can? It seems like that's what happened to
Fiona. She never got her head out of the trash can. I know
the analogy is ridiculous, but if you get what I'm saying,
then my point is made.*

*So, I guess there are different ways addicts become
addicts. I don't know if the difference is a big deal, but to me
it seems like it should be. I liked to be high so I didn't have
to think. About school, or my parents' divorce, or my over-
achieving brother, or my swimming career. I was medicat-
ing. Like, if I had bronchitis and the doctor gave me
antibiotics.*

But it wasn't curing me.

*I'm so confused about the whole damn thing. Sorry to
bug you with this, and maybe by the time I do get to send
mail to you, I'll omit this letter all together. Just needed to
knock things around my head.*

———

It might have been just me, but it seemed people treated Fiona's
death more like an inconvenience than a tragedy. It was the first
thing addressed in group the next day, and Tillie and I talked
about it that afternoon. People hugged a lot. I even saw a few
tears, but mostly it was business as usual. School, work and rehabilitation.

Not much else.

Not that I'm the sentimental kind, but I felt I needed more.
Something meaningful. Life confirming. So, I went down to the
pool to swim a few laps. Fast and tiring ones. All butterfly. Once
my lungs sufficiently ached and my eyes stung from the chlo-

rine, I decided I was angry. A few more lengths, I settled on who I was mad at.

The world.

Fuck it. I hopped out and called it a day.

It was on my way back for dinner when I saw a familiar face in one of those God-awful orange staff shirts. Mitch stood next to a pile of dirt, maneuvering a new rose bush into the ground. "Hey, Natalie," he greeted me, wiping the blond hair and sweat from his tanned forehead. "How was your swim?"

He barely looked at me, instead enthralled with his handy work at the base of the trunk. Man, he looked good in jeans, and the orange t-shirt didn't look half as hideous as it should have. "So, are you a landscaper now?" I asked.

"Not quite. The staff got this bush this morning in Fiona's memory. I wanted to get it in the ground before it dried out."

"That's nice."

"I thought so, too." He stuck the shovel in the pile of dirt and leaned on the end of the handle. "I heard you were there when she came into the hospital."

"I was the one who told the doctors who she was."

"That must have been hard."

In twenty fours, I'd heard a million people utter that same phrase. Usually followed by "I feel so bad for you" to which I would think, who cares about how I feel? I'm not the one on ice in the morgue with a name tag hanging from my big toe. "I'm all right."

"Have a seat and keep me company. If I have someone to talk to, maybe this will go faster."

I doubted it, but I plunked myself down. "Haven't seen you around lately," I said for lack of anything else. "Have you been busy?"

"Depends on the day. How about you? You think the new service project will work out?"

"We'll see." I pulled out a handful of grass from the lawn beside me and let the blades float away in the breeze. "I don't know how cut out I am for sick and dying people, I've decided."

"The ER isn't a better fit than the cancer ward, huh?"

"Not when you have to identify a dead friend of yours. No."

"That's rough," he agreed. "But it seems to me in situations like that, you start to count your blessings. Better to be the one standing than the stiff one on your back."

"Gee, don't be cold or anything."

He stopped mid-shovel, balancing a mound of dirt. "I'm sorry, Nat. I didn't mean it that way."

Usually, I wasn't one to take offense easily, but this whole Fiona thing had really messed with my head. Relatively speaking, there was a lot for me to feel good about. My pending Level Five status was a huge win. I'd completed my school requirements, and I already told Teeth I was determined to see my service project through. We were scheduled to have a memorial service in the chapel on Sunday, and a bunch of us sent cards to Fiona's parents, but beyond that everyone around here was pretty much chill. "Mitch, can I ask you something?"

"Sure."

"Do you think people care more than they say they do, or less?"

Mitch brushed the dirt from his gloves. "You mean generally speaking, or about Fiona?"

"I don't know. In general, I guess."

He sat down on the edge of the garden and took a gulp from the water bottle beside him. "I think some people can detach themselves from stuff better than others. Like, some nurses can handle working with real sick kids in the cancer ward. Some can't. It doesn't make you a bad person, just different is all."

"It's just that people knew Fiona here, and now it's like she never existed."

"You're sensitive. A lot of addicts are. We feel things deeper than most and sometimes it gets so bad, we just want to block it out all-together."

"Which is why we become addicts in the first place."

"That's right. You can't worry about what other people do. Human nature is to just move on for sanity's sake. They have to."

"Desensitize," I mumbled. "It's just so weird. Like even with the whole Racer thing...." I bit my lip. I never talked about the "Racer Thing." In fact, I'd never called it anything out loud before. To Mitch's credit, he didn't react. He just looked at me and waited for me to finish my sentence. "....with the Racer thing I wasn't really aware. This is just so...in my face."

I was babbling. Babies and morons babbled. I cursed under my breath and pulled my knees to my chest.

Mitch took another drink of water and replaced the cap. "Maybe you'll feel better Saturday when you get a break from this place. I got big plans for your day pass."

"Oh yeah, like what?"

"Not telling. It's a surprise. All I can say is that you'll have a good time." Mitch stood, pushed a hand through his dirty blond hair before glancing at his watch. "Maybe you should head back for dinner. The staff already has problems. I don't want to be blamed for you being late."

"Good point." I stood up and brushed the grass from my towel. "Good luck with the bush. It looks great, by the way."

With a wink, he jumped back into the garden. I watched him jam the shovel in the dirt a few times just for entertainment's sake and then headed back inside.

SIXTEEN

March 10, Saturday
Mood: Fashionably challenged

Dear Annie,

Who the hell packed my duffle bag?

Either Johnny Cash raided my closet or I had really awful taste in clothing when I was stoned, but everything I own is black. Shirts, sweatshirts, shorts, jeans. Who in this century wears black jeans?

I'm sorry you were ever seen with me. How embarrassing for you.

Today I have a day pass. Mitch is taking me to Los Angeles, and it's the first time I've had access to the street clothes I packed. The only thing with any color is my favorite Janis Joplin t-shirt. Remember the purple tie dye-ish one? I think it looks suitably retro-rock star in case we make it to the Strip (how's that for So Cal lingo?) It's also the only shirt that doesn't smell like you could roll it and smoke it.

Funny thing...now that I'm sober, I feel naked without makeup. When I quit swimming and jumped into my

*downward spiral, I got away from the whole makeup thing.
I probably could have used it, according to my mother who
never missed an opportunity to tell me how crappy I looked.
Is it weird that I am into my looks again? Okay, I was
before, but in a different way. Like the green hair and black
lipstick made everyone look at me, but no one saw me. They
only saw the hair and the lips and the rest of me could just
disappear. It was like walking around invisible.*

Do you get where I'm coming from?

*I'm also super nervous about being recognized. I was
spared all the bad press when I came here, but I haven't
spent much time thinking about dealing with the media
now. When I had my Olympic meltdown, people were
straight up pissed. I didn't do my job. I was un-American. A
national embarrassment. I wondered if people would ever
show some sympathy. It's like the rest of the world doesn't
understand us athletes aren't machines. We're humans with
vulnerabilities and breakable hearts. Some of us are more
fragile than others and I'm still handicapping where I might
land on that spectrum. I'll get a preview on my Saturday
day pass, I'm sure.*

*Okay, so I guess I'll go with the Janis shirt and jean
cutoffs. I'll tell you how it goes.*

Maybe I can at least score some Chapstick from Tillie.
Love,
Natalie

———

SO HERE I was riding shot gun in The Dunes van (patients
always sat in the back. I was a big girl now!) with no makeup
and my head full of split ends pulled back in a rubber band I
found next to Tillie's copy machine.

Cute, if I do say so myself.

It was warm and sunny and totally beautiful. A typical Southern California morning in the desert. I sat there with my nose practically pressed against the glass. Damn, it felt good to be out. "So where are you taking me?" I asked, feeling like a third grader on a field trip. "Everyone talks about all the cool stuff to see in Los Angeles."

"I told you it was a surprise." Mitch sat beside me with his shades over his eyes, looking amazing in khakis and a white collared shirt that showed off his tan really nicely. He may be a babysitter, but he was definitely a good-looking one. "Sit back and enjoy the ride. Morning in the desert is beautiful, isn't it?"

"The view is incredible." I squinted at the yellow orb of the sun, even brighter against the sand's reflection. The mountains surrounding us reminded me of the old west. I liked cowboys. The ones on my mom's old romance novels with five o'clock shadows and easy smiles.

I wondered if Mitch had a Stetson hat.

The narrow dirt roads turned to divided highways, and soon we hit West Hollywood traffic. It was thick and slow. The kind of gridlock that would turn Racer into a road-rage poster boy. Sports cars mingled with Pimp My Ride SUVs, and I could feel the base from their stereos in my chest. Colorful billboards hung over us, and beautiful people walked by us on the sidewalk. Most were blond, fit and very tan with dark sunglasses. Maybe that was all LA was. A city full of clones from the mother planet, Surfer.

Mitch slumped in his seat with one hand on the wheel and the other resting on his lap. His head moved slightly to the classic rock barely audible on the van stereo. I smiled as I sucked in a good hit of car exhaust. "So, this surprise of yours," I said. "Do I at least get a hint?"

"Well, we could do the usual Los Angeles things like watch

Kardashians go shopping or stuff ourselves with In-N-Out Burgers. Of course, they're always the tar pits or the studios tours, but I had a better idea."

"Oh yeah, like what?"

"Lance Bates, the guy whose gallery Staci works at, has a big show about once a year. It's today, and I thought we could check it out."

"Oh yeah, Staci may have mentioned it."

"His stuff is pretty popular. I just thought you could do the tourist things anytime, but this was sort of a one-time-only kind of thing."

We slowed down near a white stucco building with a windowed ceiling and fountains near the entrance. Land Rovers and BMWs jammed the parking lot, and it took forever to find a space to park the van. I didn't mind. I'd never seen a tiled parking lot before.

On the outside, the building was cool, but indoors, the joint was spectacular. Marble floors with high walls and ceilings. Funky fountains and odd chairs and benches I wasn't sure were meant for sitting on. In front of us there was a huge flight of stairs, and I could see people milling around at the top. Mitch nodded in that direction, and I followed. "Lance is a really good guy. I think you'll have fun."

"You know him personally?" I asked.

"We were at The Dunes together. I'm actually not an art person, but I love music. I am a big fan of some of the album art he does."

"Album art?"

"Art that goes along with the album for press release or whatnot. Vintage vynals have it right on the cover. He's designed stuff for Maroon 5, Billie Eilish, Taylor Swift."

"That's definitely a variety."

"I know, he's that good. Not bad for a heroin addict who five years ago lived in a sewer."

The top floor was just as incredible as the lobby, with equally beautiful people milling around. If I weren't so excited to be wearing *any* street clothes, I probably would have felt underdressed. Some of the woman looked like they just stepped out of Vogue magazine with rhinestone sunglasses and purses I was sure cost more than the van that brought me there.

"Are you coming?" Mitch was a few paces ahead of me, standing in front of a colorful likeness of Bono under a psychedelic fruit tree.

"Um, yeah," I stammered. "I've just never been to an art show before."

"Well, that's what rehabilitation is about, right? Exploring yourself. Testing waters. Getting to a better place of understanding."

We sidestepped a few mingling people, and a waitress or two serving fancy finger foods. People oooed and aahhed over champagne glasses and cheese puffs about structure and texture and angle and interpretation. Art lingo. I tried to eavesdrop to see if I could follow, but I needed more than Staci's tutorials to understand even half of their conversations. That's when I first noticed it. The heads on a swivel and the gazes that fixed on me and did a once-over. I was dying to know what they whispered to each other. Although maybe I was being hypersensitive, Maybe it was me that was imagining the attention.

That was, until Mitch slid up next to me and said in my ear, "Maybe when we leave you should wear sunglasses and a hat. More incognito."

"How would I have those things at the ready?"

"I stashed some in the glove compartment in the van." When I smiled at him, he shrugged. "I came prepared."

After the initial entrance, the vibe chilled and I found

myself actually relaxing. Straight, and the pride I felt in that made me enjoy myself more. Mitch stopped in front of a beautiful floor-to-ceiling canvas. He slipped his hands in his pockets and tipped his head to look up. "Hey, Natalie, this is one of my favorites. I think you might like it, too."

I stood next to him and lifted my eyes. It was an oil painting (I think) of a mythical looking male angel with purple wings surfacing in water. An ocean, I guess. The water behind the angel was dark and murky, painted with dark and bold strokes, but in front of the angel the water was bluer and brighter until it almost sparkled when it reached a stark horizon. In his hand was a wand made from stars and streaks of gold speckled above it in the dark sky. The details were endless. Moody shadows but also vibrant colors. It looked magical and mystical and more complex than any music art I'd ever seen. "What is it?" I asked, wanting to reach out to touch it. "It looks like something religious."

"I guess it could be," he replied. "This is the first oil painting Lance ever did. At The Dunes, actually."

"Wow, was there some sort of inspiration or whatever?"

"The way he explained it to me is that everybody has a point in their life, a defining moment, that's sort of like standing on a cliff before jumping off of it. Making the right decision means the difference between drowning in the darkness or making your way out toward the brightness at the horizon. He pointed to the bottom of the cliff. "See, the dark water is despair. Addiction. The clear blue water signifies the good place. The right choice. Prosperity."

"I get it." I took a step closer. I'd never taken an art class in my life, I never even liked to color when I was a kid, but somehow, I felt connected to this painting. Like someone had trusted me with a deep dark secret. "What's the thing in the water and why does it have wings?"

"The creature in the water is you, or me, or anyone. The

wings represent the power within us all to rise above our fears and doubts to excel. The wand of stars in his hand represents the opportunities we make for ourselves."

"Jesus, Mitch, you know my work better than I do." A tattoo covered man in a stylishly torn tank top, camo pants and combat boots extended his black nail-polished hand to Mitch. "Hey, bud. Glad you could make it."

"Lance, great to see you. I brought a friend, too." Mitch nodded in my direction. "This is Natalie."

"Hey, you're a Dunes' kid, too, huh? Staci's friend, right?" His pink shaggy hair skimmed his shoulders as he pumped my hand. "Great, I love to meet people from my alma mater. Staci is around here somewhere."

"That's okay." I held up my hand. "You guys look really busy."

"This is a gathering of friends," Lance said. "No work required."

"I was telling her how you painted this when you were a resident." Mitch winked at me. "She was totally impressed."

"Yeah, it's my first and favorite. That's why I hang it right up in front where I can see it. It reminds me to keep myself straight."

"Does it have a name?" I asked.

"Yeah, I call it, Treading Water."

For whatever reason, I laughed. "Wow, that's so funny cuz I'm a swimmer, and I tread water all the time."

It suddenly occurred to me how stupid I must have sounded. Art people had more sophisticated minds that wouldn't take things so literally. To Lance's credit though he didn't call me out. Instead, he kindly validated my infantile interpretation with a wide warm smile and patted me on the shoulder. "So I heard Mitch explain the painting to you, but the basic meaning behind it is how humans feel things deeply and that's a good thing. What's bad is if you get caught up in the stupid stuff. Focus on the light side, where the water is clear and blue. The muddy water on the dark side doesn't nurture anything. We addicts constantly find ourselves negotiating between the two places."

"The dark muddy water is like 'drag,' then." When I saw the blank-faced stares, from Mitch and Lance, I realized I needed to explain myself. "In competitive swimming, sometimes we train with weights or things to make us slower in water. Drag. The dark muddy water is drag."

Lance nodded his head like I'd just deciphered some earth-shattering mystery. "Yes!" He exclaimed with a clap of his hands! "You get it!"

Staci bounded up behind me, looking as equally punked-out as Lance in her black leather skirt and white lace top. She offered an awkward wave before attacking me with a hug. "I'm so glad you're here, Nat! I was hoping you'd get to see the gallery."

"Yeah," I said. "Mitch was just showing me some stuff Lance did when he was a resident." I did a three sixty and glanced at the colorful walls. "Looks like there's a ton more to see."

"God, you don't know the half of it. Did Lance tell you about his new project?"

Lance smiled. "Staci, don't go bragging about stuff we don't know will pan out."

Staci leaned in with her forehead to mine. I think her inten-tion was to whisper, but she couldn't quite pull it off. "Trent Rezner, the lead singer of the Red Hot Chili Peppers, asked Lance personally to do his new album cover. He walked right into the gallery this morning and asked him."

Normally, I would have been more interested. Hell, I liked the Chili Peppers as much as anyone else, but I was so wrapped up in my personal revelation and the painting in front of me that I was too busy to gush about it. "Lance, Mitch said you painted this in residence. How long did it take?"

"About three months. I did other stuff in between, but I made sure I worked on this a little each day. It's weird, but when I look at it, I can see my progress." He came up beside me and leveled a black-painted finger at the swirls of color. "The short brush stokes here look jumpy and non-committal. An infant Level Two. Up here, the strokes are longer, confident. Level Five. The work isn't just what you see, but the journey that got it on the canvas."

"It's wonderful," I stammered. "Really, I'm kind of speechless. I'd love to see the rest of your work, Lance."

"Cool." He stepped back and waved his arm. "Please, make yourself at home."

Staci took me by the hand and led me back through the crowd. I was met with a few more stares, weird looks and whispers, but this time I didn't care as much. I was a girl who felt things deeply and that was okay. I was a lucky one, and today I wanted to embrace it.

———

"So, I'm not that bad a host after all, huh? I told you Lance was talented."

Mitch leaned back, allowing the waitress to slide his plate in front of him. He insisted we have lunch at the Sunset Diner. It was rumored their burgers were the best in Los Angeles, so here we were sitting face-to-face in our booth, watching the midday rush move around us.

The unwanted stares and people whispering had bothered me more than I thought, so I took Mitch up on his offer for the baseball cap and dark sunglasses. The celebrity uniform for going incognito. To be clear, I didn't consider myself a celebrity. I just didn't want to be seen. And I wanted to enjoy the huge slab of cow covered in ketchup sitting in front of me. Greasy meals were a fave of mine when I was stoned. It looked pretty good sober now, too.

"Dig in," he urged. "The Dunes food is good, but this is incredible."

I scooped up my bacon cheddar burger and let the blood drip to the plate. It tasted better than it smelled. "Two for two," I said through a mouthful. "You were right about the gallery and the food."

"I'm happy you had fun."

"Lance seems like a cool guy," I said, dragging a napkin over my lips. "It's interesting that you two are friends. Other than The Dunes, I can't see that you have that much in common."

"Oh, you mean my preppy clothes and his leather and piercings."

"I guess. I just think it's pretty nice of you to bother with residents at The Dunes. I thought once people got better, they'd want to run in the other direction."

He mixed a spoonful of sugar in his iced tea. "That probably is a good idea for some people. Make a clean break. I can't speak for Lance, but I sort of feel like since people helped me with my problems, I feel duty bound to return the favor. I'm studying to be a crisis counselor. I get my Masters next spring."

"Wow," I said, doing math in my head. "So that makes you... twenty-four?"

"Twenty-three. I doubled up my classes for two years to get my undergrad on time and Masters ahead of schedule."

I took a healthy bite of my burger and washed it down with my soda. It was weird how put together Mitch was. Two years ago, he was like me, now he was a master's student who knew exactly what he wanted to do with his life. "Can I ask you a question?"

"Sure."

"How did you end up at The Dunes?"

I caught him mid-bite. He dropped his burger to his plate and wiped his hands. "I used to play football at Pepperdine," he said.

"Pepperdine University?"

"Yeah, here in Southern California. You heard of it?"

"The swim coach there recruited me. Wow, you must be pretty good. I thought football players were bigger than you?"

He chuckled. "Yeah, don't remind me. That's pretty much what landed me at The Dunes in the first place." He lifted his iced tea to his lips and held it there longer than needed for a sip. "Steroids," he said simply, like the one word told the whole story.

I noticed his grip tighten around his glass as he lowered it back to the table. His brown eyes clouded and his easy smile now looked more like he was forcing it. "I'm from a small town in Idaho. Not exactly a hotbed for football. Anyway, I came out here on scholarship. It's Division One, so there's lots of pressure."

"So, you tried steroids."

"When the kicker can bench press more than you, you get desperate."

"Then what happened?"

"I had a heart attack."

I must have made a face because he laughed and patted my hand. "It's okay. I lived," he joked. "But I woke up to an intervention in the hospital with tubes in my nose. I was released a week later and escorted to The Dunes."

"And now you're clean."

"And retired from football." His gaze wandered to a group

of loud college kids leaving and piling into a pickup outside the door. "Retired from a lot of things. I may have missed out on a college career, but at least I have a future. The Dunes pays pretty well, and it helps me to stay close to the program. I live near campus, made some good friends. I hang out with Lance and some other people still around that I knew from The Dunes. We kind of support each other."

"You're good at that, offering support."

"Fortunately, the staff at The Dunes think so, too. That's why they hired me. Their theory is that some of the tougher teen cases respond better to someone my age than an older white coat doctor."

"Yeah, someone like me."

Our eyes locked. The red in his cheeks told me he'd embarrassed himself, maybe forgotten who he was talking to. "I'm sorry, Nat. I didn't mean it like that."

"No, that's okay. I deserve it. I was a tough case, and I'm glad you were there." The words rolled off my tongue so easily. They were the ones honest words I had spoken that didn't have strained thought behind them. "I like spending time with you. The gallery was a lot of fun. I've never been to a gallery before."

"Really? I would think a public figure like yourself would be invited to stuff like that all the time. Maybe on your travels through Europe."

It had been a long time since I'd fielded questions like this. It felt like I was remembering a past life, or even speaking for a person I barely knew anymore. I stirred my straw in my Dr. Pepper, listening to the ice cubes clink against the glass. "When you're training and competing, it's not like you're out seeing the world. It's hotel, pool, gym, meals in between. That's really it."

"Sounds exhausting. Was it worth it?"

That was a question I tried very hard NOT to ask myself over the years, because yes or no meant different consequences.

"I'm not sure," I settled on. "I mean, there are things I miss and things I don't."

Two Beverly Hills looking girls with armfuls of shopping bags came in the door and paused when they saw me. They whispered and giggled before taking a table on the other side of the diner.

"Is that the stuff you don't miss?"

"It's not even when people recognize me," I said. "It's what they're recognizing me for. I'm a human, you know? If I have a bad day or I'm in a bad mood or nervous or worn out, it's talked about on ESPN. I didn't set out to be the Poster Girl of Nervous Breakdowns. Sometimes private things should be private."

"Like Annie?" Our eyes met, and we stared at each other a moment before he held his hand up like he meant no overstep. "I saw that press conference at last summer's Olympics," he explained. "That had to be a hard way to find out your best friend's cancer was terminal. I would have hit that reporter in the head, too."

I leaned back in my seat and thought a second about the scene many considered the beginning of the end. "It just all happened so fast. Annie got sick right before the Olympic trials last spring and couldn't compete. No one knew what it was, exhaustion, anemia whatever, but she was in the hospital for tests for a few weeks and I was off to Europe for the games."

"You had no idea, huh?"

"My coach did but he kept it from me." I laughed at the unbelievable memory. "He actually blocked Annie's number from my cell phone so she couldn't contact me. Anyway, I swam my prelims, made the finals and everything was going fine. It felt strange not having her with me, but I figured no news was good news."

"Until the press conference," Mitch said.

Again, I picked up my soda. I noticed I drank it like I would a cocktail, waiting for it to burn my throat, warm my stomach and eventually dull the edges of the sharp images running around my head. That press conference. I remembered the guy, the smug asshole standing in the back of the crowded room, yelling over the shutter clicks of cameras. He was tall, slim, wore a blue baseball cap, and sported a five o'clock shadow that attempted to hide what I could only describe as a shit eating smirk. He cleared his throat and folded his arms against himself before asking point blank. *So Natalie, how do you feel competing now that your teammate and friend, Annie Madsen, is dying of terminal cancer?*

When my gaze again met Mitch's, I realized I'd zoned out. Not in a stoned sense obviously, but in a way I could easily snap out of. A refreshing change. "Sorry, can we change the subject. I haven't thought about it in a while."

"Probably not sober either." Mitch's brown eyes twinkled, and he shifted in his seat. "I'm just glad you don't hate me. You were pretty pissed at the intervention and on the plane ride out here."

"I'm over it. It wasn't you I hated; it was the circumstance. Turns out it was probably good my leaving town after all."

"You mean the whole legal thing with that guy back in Buffalo?"

I tossed my napkin to my empty plate and wondered what capacity he was asking me the question. As a guinea pig for a social work project, curious Dunes staff member or concerned friend? I didn't know how to answer. "I guess it's a big deal. But I don't remember it happening, and I'm not sure if I should feel guilty or grateful about that."

"I suppose you could just suspend your judgment. Or try to take some positive away from it. You can't let other people's short comings ruin your life."

"That's what your note said."

Outside the window, a sports car with the stereo blaring slid up to the curb. A fresh batch of kids in UCLA regalia piled out of it like it was a clown car at the circus. They burst through the door and made a bee line for the counter. "Have you thought about after?" he asked, watching the kids settle in for lunch.

"After what?"

"After here. You know, when you leave The Dunes?"

The look on my face must have been a doozy, because he looked like I shot his dog. "I'm sorry," he said. "Sore subject."

"No, it's not that. I'm excited to get on with my life and all...."

"But...."

"Mrs. Madsen, Annie's mom, offered for me to come live with her. I didn't say yes, and I didn't say no, either."

Mitch waited while the waitress cleared our plates. When she left, he rested his hands where his plate had been. "What do you want to do?"

"I don't know. It's just everything else is starting to fall into place. I'm done with my school work, I've dealt with my father, I'm working past the Racer thing, but...."

"There's Annie," he supplied.

"I just feel like life is giving me a second chance, and I don't want to fuck it up. I just want to set everything right."

After a few more minutes of chit chat, Mitch grabbed the check. I thanked him and finished my soda while the brunette silicon-enhanced waitress flirted to bolster her tip. "We should head back," Mitch said, grabbing his wallet from his pocket. "Late on a day pass pisses off the staff."

I watched him pitch a few dollar bills on the table. "I'm ready," I replied feeling odd using those words and led the way to the door.

SEVENTEEN

March 25, Saturday
Mood: Whatever

Dear Annie,

Three weeks have passed since my day pass with Mitch, and I haven't written. Bad Natalie! Time is flying here. So much to tell!

First of all, I am now a Level Five. Thirty days and counting, and I will be a free woman. A new woman, too. This incarnation of myself is much happier. Confident. A well-conditioned swimmer who shaved .3 seconds off her 100m backstroke (thanks very much), who now applies mascara daily and can quote every word ever uttered on seasons 1-7 of the Bachelor. I've cut onions completely out of my diet and now am an amateur weight loss consultant to Tillie, who has dropped four dress sizes and picked up a mean breaststroke. I also have developed weird interests. I now enjoy art and filling out college applications. I use phrases like, "thems the breaks" and "life goes on" and believe in positive thinking.

I also smile. Sometimes, I show teeth.

My attitude isn't the only major change. On a sad note, moving day for Cassidy, Kevin, and Staci have all been scheduled for tomorrow. THE SAME DAY! Was that necessary? But I guess if they all leave at once, it will be like ripping a Bandaid off of a wound. Quick. Relatively painless.

See, that's me "looking on the bright side."

Anyway, Cass and Kev both have jobs now, too. Cass's service project at the US Network has turned into a full-time thing, and Kevin's fear of onions evidently did not interfere with him operating the Cinnabon oven (while supervised) at the local mall. And get this, they're living in the same group home. How cute.

Cassidy always loved happy endings.

Staci's life is also on the upswing. Her parents' guilt has manifested in a purchase of a Malibu beachside bungalow, which is why we now refer to her as Malibu Staci, a Simpson's reference that Cassidy came up with in one of her moments of relative clarity. The Blinkins even offered to pay all the expenses. Staci could afford it herself with her job at Lance's gallery, but barely, so she reluctantly let her parents help. Not that she will admit it, but her relationship with her parents has actually improved. Word around The Dunes is they are visiting her next month when she is showing her own stuff next to Lances at the gallery. I'm really proud of her.

As for me, as soon as I'm released, I'm heading back to see you. Annie, you've been the one who has kept me motivated through all this. I can't tell you how good it felt to put my charm bracelet back on. It really was like you were there. By my side.

My BFF.

I can't wait to see you. Maybe we could head to the pool. Swim a lap or two, hell maybe just float. I have so many plans for us. I want to make a list.

1)

"NATALIE?"

I nearly fell off my bed when I heard his voice. Deep and out of nowhere. I sat up with my hand to my chest and waited for Mitch to come all the way in the room. But he stayed frozen where he was, his hand on the knob, his usual smile blatantly absent. "Hey, you got a minute?"

"Sure," I said.

His presence in the female dorm alone was enough to give me an ooky feeling. The sick pain in your stomach you get when you know bad news is coming. Normally, he made a point of looking into my eyes when he spoke. Not so, today.

"What's wrong, Mitch?" I croaked.

"Tillie sent me to get you. Mrs. Madsen called."

I gulped. "What did she say?"

"I'm sorry, Nat. But I think it's time for you to go home."

———

I'm not sure how I actually ended up on the plane. Mitch took care of the arrangements and since I was still a resident at The Dunes, it was strongly suggested that I have an escort. Lucky for me Mitch was free, and he was willing, so he came along.

Existing on a plane usually tweaked me out. When I used to travel the world for meets I silently suffered from panic, but now for some reason, I didn't have it in me to be afraid anymore. Maybe my mind was too busy with other shit. Like pretending that I was really pissed about missing my good friends' moving day instead of fearing my best friend's death. Anger, fear, it was all the same. It was like I had been picking at the same scab for months, letting it bleed and then re-heal. The thing was just scar tissue now. Just numb.

Everybody was pretty vague about Mrs. Madsen's phone call. All I knew was Annie had been taken to the hospice unit at the hospital, and when we landed, a rental car would be waiting to take us there. Thank God for Mitch. My hands were shaking already. Who knew what kind of condition I'd be in to drive.

"What happens in a hospice unit?" I asked, the puffy clouds floating outside my window.

"It's where they make sick people comfortable," Mitch said softly.

"You mean, die peacefully, don't you?"

I took his silence as a yes.

Did people really ever die peacefully? It's not like anyone has come back afterwards to reveal their experience. It could be just like falling asleep. I shook my head and cursed the thought of Staci, Kev and Cass at that moment having a grease fest at the Sunset Diner. "What am I going to say to her?" I asked myself but said out loud.

"Whatever is in your heart," Mitch answered. "I know that sounds like a line from one of Cassidy's TV shows, but really, it's the truth."

I turned from the window and looked in Mitch's dark eyes. "I don't know what's in my heart."

"Well, you love her, right? Start with that." His confidence was something I really liked about him. Something he had in premium when I had barely any. I wished I could borrow some, and I think that was what he sensed when he took my hand in his.

"I did all this for her," I whispered. "I mean, coming out to California. Going to The Dunes."

"Natalie, she may have motivated you to work the program,

but it was all you who got on the plane, stuck out detox and worked your way up five levels to get where you are now."

"And where am I now? An ex-drug addict on a plane, going to see her dying friend. How is that any better?"

"You're not the dying friend," he said it in a blurt. Like a slap in the face or a dousing of cold water. He gave my hand a squeeze before releasing it. "I'm sorry, I didn't mean that the way it sounded."

"I know how you meant it." I leaned my head back in my seat and closed my eyes. "It's just I was so angry when Fiona died. I don't want to feel that way about Annie."

"You won't. And don't feel like you're alone in this. I'm here if you need me."

There was that confidence again. That weird warmth to his voice that calmed me. I opened one eye a slit and smiled. "Mitch, why have you been so nice to me?"

"I'm a nice guy."

"No, I mean you just seem different with me than with the other residents."

He sort of flinched. Like the question knocked him off balance. It seemed strange. A vulnerability.

Like Superman to kryptonite

He angled his body to face me. His mouth opened twice before words actually came out. "Look Natalie, I know you're younger than me, and I don't want you to think I'm being inappropriate, but when I first met you, I felt like I could relate to you. With your swimming and my football. When I heard about that Racer thing back in Buffalo, I felt terrible. I guess I just wanted to make sure you knew not all guys were assholes."

"So, you're telling me you're friends with me out of pity?"

"What I am saying is that we are eighteen and twenty-three-year-old works in progress. Life is a journey, ya know? And it helps to have someone you care about with you on the trip."

Man, those eyes. I could get lost there. I weaved my fingers in between his like I'd seen couples do at the mall and held it on my knee. It felt good. Right. No other guy ever held my hand either, my father included. Maybe that was why the action felt so intimate. "As long as I get to see her and talk with her, I'll be okay," I said, turning back to the window. "I just want her to know that I turned my life around. After that we can hop a flight back to LA. The quicker I can get back to the program and make my release date, the better."

"Are you sure?" he asked. "Maybe we should stay a few days."

"What for?"

"I don't know. I just don't want you to regret anything."

The sun was drifting below the clouds, and I squinted against the orange haze. It was beautiful. Peaceful. Like the whole world had just fallen asleep.

We landed four hours later.

Three hours too late.

———

Blaine liked to use the analogy that a person in recovery often takes three steps forward then two steps back. Today I felt like my legs had been hacked off by a jig saw.

No one actually told me Annie died. When Mitch and I stepped off the elevator at the hospital, I saw a crowd of people at the end of the hall. All red faced and slumped with eyes to the floor and hands in pockets. It didn't occur to me it was on Annie's account until I saw Mrs. Madsen pick her head up off her husband's shoulder.`

Beyond the crowd there was an open door. The yellow hue of the light bounced off the white sheet. Resting on the side of the mattress was a bony hand. A thin purple bracelet that matched mine hung from her wrist.

Anger, fear, pain, swirled around me like a violent storm. A knife in the heart would have felt better. My chest hurt and my vision narrowed. I felt sick. I wanted to disappear.

So I did exactly what I did the day I met my namesake in the cancer ward back in California. I ran. Far and fast. Nowhere in particular. Stairways and back halls. The more lost the better. Eventually, I ended up in some side parking lot. Buffalo in winter. Wet, cold, dark. A fat man in a bulky Bills parka and a Marlboro in his mouth balanced himself on a snowbank and heaved garbage into a gigantic dumpster. It smelled like piss and vomit. I breathed in deep.

Somehow, God knows how long later, I ended up back in the parking garage sitting on the hood of our rented Corolla. My jeans were soaked to my ass and my sneakers were covered in muddy slush, but I didn't mind. In fact, it felt good to suffer.

Maybe if I was lucky, I'd get frostbite.

I stared out at the city beyond. White lights in darkness, cold and oblivious through the cloud of my breath. I wasn't crying. Somehow the sadness wouldn't register in my brain. This was the most horrible thing that could ever happen, and I couldn't shed a damn tear? Maybe that's what the drugs had done to me. Made me a heartless zombie.

"Natalie!"

Mitch jogged down the parking structure ramp and stopped in front of me. For a second he just stood there, his hands on his hips, panting softly. His forehead wrinkled in either concern or bother. I just sat there enjoying the sound of my teeth chattering in my ears.

"Now what am I supposed to do?" I snapped. "She's gone. Now what? What happens?"

"You grieve."

"What the fuck does that mean?" I slid off the hood and kicked a chunk of ice that wedged under my shoe. "Annie was it, Mitch. She was the only one I had! Don't you get it? Everyone else has shit on me or given up on me, but she never did! She loved me for me! Tell me, who else in my whole life can I say that about?"

My own voice sounded unfamiliar to me. Shaky, higher, with an echo that wasn't necessarily the garage acoustics. I wanted to be angry. Pissed. *Put out.* But I couldn't do it. I just could not pull it off.

My eyes locked on to his. He came toward me with his hands outstretched and I braced myself for the contact. And just like that, my head was against his heart and I held him like a last breath.

And then the tears began to fall.

Horns honked, and car tires whined as traffic maneuvered around us. I realized we were in the middle of the lane, but Mitch didn't seem to mind the headlights moving around us. He felt hard and warm. Something I wanted to cling to. It was like I was falling, reeling, into some black abyss where I'd be swallowed whole. Maybe if I hid right there and held on tight, the horrible despair would give up on me and just leave me alone. "I can't think about it," I blubbered. "It's just too much."

"You have to, Nat." His hand traveled over my head and down my back. "You'll be okay, I'm right here."

"Bullshit!" I screamed and shoved him away from me. "You're here because you're fucking being paid to be!"

"Natalie..."

"I don't believe you, Mitch! *Nobody* is a sure thing."

If I couldn't cry before, I couldn't stop now. My body shook and my legs tingled like they'd give way. When I breathed, the sounds that came from my mouth didn't sound close to human. I picked up an ice chunk and hurled it across the parking lot. "That's it, let's get the hell out of here," I said.

"Where are we going?"

"Back to Los Angeles."

"Why?"

"Because there's nothing left for me here!" I seemed to be drawing a crowd now. A security guard peeked at me from his perch next to the lot attendant's little house. An old man with a shopping cart wheeled his way up the ramp. I cursed and grabbed the keys from Mitch's denim jacket pocket. "Let's get the hell out of here."

"You shouldn't drive," he said.

"You shouldn't stop me."

Mitch took a long blink, and I could tell it was an effort to keep his own shit together. "What about the funeral?" he asked softly.

"Are you fucking crazy? And turn it into a public spectacle?" I opened the car door and slipped inside.

"But it's a funeral."

"Exactly, and I love her too much to ruin it for her."

Mitch ran at me and grabbed the door before I could close it. He kneeled down to my level and lifted my chin so I'd look at him. "Well, it seems to me that you have a choice to make. You can handle crisis like you always have. Avoid it, buy drugs like you used to, or you could truly honor your best friend and show her that you are a better person than the girl I left with three months ago."

His chocolate eyes stilled me. "How am I supposed to do that?"

"Right all the wrongs. Not just with Annie but with your family. I know in your mind you've made peace with your dad, but being a 'Level Five' is laying the groundwork for the rest of your life."

"So you think I should treat this as some sort of test?"

"It is a test, Natalie." He didn't wait for me to reply. He just took the keys and directed me over to the passenger seat. "So you gonna give me directions, or do I have to find the way on my own."

"Where are we going?" I asked, climbing over the gearshift.

"Home, Natalie. You're going home."

EIGHTEEN

AFTER WE LEFT THE HOSPITAL, we drove by my house three times, but I couldn't force myself out of the car. It was after midnight anyway, and I was cold and tired. Mitch suggested sleep might make my mind clearer, so I agreed to a motor lodge by the airport.

I don't actually think I slept. Mostly, I watched the Weather Channel and wondered what Mitch thought of me on the other side of the thin wall. I thought about Cass and Kevin and Staci living under roofs other than The Dune's. All the things that were going to change.

The next day I just existed. Ate fast food and watched TV in between. I wondered if Annie's family tried to get in touch with me and then wondered why they would bother. My own family probably hadn't. I wasn't sure if they even knew where I was. Mitch didn't offer much information, and maybe that was on purpose. That afternoon he dragged me out of the room for a drive, just to make way for housekeeping. Really, I think it was just a series of right hand turns to pass time. Strange, because I was sure time was standing still.

The second morning, Mitch knocked on my door with my

complimentary Buffalo Times and announced that the funeral was at two p.m. We had tickets for the evening flight back to Los Angeles. Depending on my plans, we could take it or re-book.

The problem was I had no plans. Mitch made them for me, which was how I found myself sitting in the passenger side of our rental car outside my mother's house a little before noon.

"Do you want me to wait in the car?" Mitch asked.

For the second time, I reached for the door handle, and again I bailed on the effort. We'd been sitting there with the engine running for ten minutes at least, watching neighbors snow blow driveways and walk their dogs. A few kids in Sabers jerseys played hockey in the street. Typical late winter activities for suburban Buffalo. Also typical, my house was the only one still with a foot of snow in the driveway.

"Mom won't even cave for a plow man," I told him. "She insists my dad should be the one to pay for it, and she's not one that takes 'no' for an answer."

"Sounds ruthless. I suppose that's a decent quality for a business manager."

"Not so much for a mother, though." I reached for the door handle again, and this time, I actually got out. My sneakers sunk into the snow, and I made a mental note to add boots to my list of things to grab. I already told Mitch I wanted to pack up some of my summer clothes and personal things to send back to The Dunes. I didn't picture myself coming back to Buffalo right away after my release. Not that I had a clear vision of what I'd do in California either. It just seemed to make sense, and Mitch didn't tell me not to.

"You know, I don't mind coming in," Mitch said. "I can help you pack some of your stuff."

"That's okay. You've been so nice to me, making you hang out with my mom seems cruel." It was the obligatory thing to say. The truth was that walking in there and seeing my mom was something I had to do on my own. Mitch knew it, and so did I.

Annie was dead. What was left to fear?

I looked over at him in his khakis, white long-sleeved button down and denim jacket. Perfectly preppy, but drafty for Buffalo this time of year. "I'm sure my dad still has some clothes here. I'll make sure to grab you a sweater and a jacket."

I shut the door behind me, scaled the gigantic snowdrift courtesy of the snow plow and trudged toward the front door. I hated winter. The cold, the way the snow would turn dirty after a few days, and the darkness that always came about four o'clock in the afternoon. Depressing. Funny how the season can affect your mood. Like the north wind blew the "hopeful" right out of you.

It also amazed me how everything looked the same. I know I'd only been away for three or so months, but somehow it felt more like years. The same white house with a matching picket fence that sometimes made me laugh because of the American Dream implication. A pink flowered wreath a neighbor brought over last summer still hung on the door, and I wondered if my mother'd had any visitors since. Sad. It wasn't just the winter, either. Even in the spring, with the garden full of tulips and green grass, there was nothing happy about this place. It was all very impersonal. Like a hotel where strangers came and went. Nothing that screamed a family lived here. Hell, not even a whisper.

I flipped up the "Happy New Year" welcome mat I got her a decade ago and picked up the key from underneath. Unfortunately, it worked. The door creaked open.

The smell hit me first. Lemon pledge mixed with my mother's real Chanel perfume. Normally, she wasn't a perfume wearer, but she claimed it counteracted the "airport odor." When I was younger, I knew a business trip was planned when

I woke up to the smell. In a way, I actually looked forward to it. It meant I didn't have to make my bed for a few days, and I could eat in the living room in front of the TV. Not a frozen dinner, carefully consumed over my placemat at the kitchen table. Now she traveled on my business and always sounded just as put out.

The place was immaculate like always. Freshly mopped tile floors and recently shampooed oriental rugs. It reminded me of a museum. Mom's beautiful things on display. Art, silver, dolls from the orient. Mementos from all the places she'd been. The only things she didn't display were photographs. Not one hung anywhere in the house. I'm not sure we ever owned a camera. That always bugged me. For as many press photos I'd posed for over the years not a one was ever framed. I couldn't begin to fathom why.

"Mother?" I called but got no answer, and I would have looked upstairs, but the fresh vacuum trails on the carpet warned me not to. I kicked off my shoes and headed on into the kitchen.

"Mom?"

She was sitting at the table in a black power suit with her luggage beside her and her cell phone balanced on her shoulder. I knew she heard me because she held up her hand. Her international signal of 'don't bug me, Mommy's working.' In front of her was a flight itinerary, and obviously incorrect, considering how she was reaming out the unfortunate soul on the other end of the call.

"Listen, I don't care who you have to bump off that flight. I have to get to Denver tonight. I have clients to see in the morning." She sighed and grabbed the pill bottle beside her. She dumped a couple into her palm, and she tossed them down her throat. "Great, good. I'll be at the airport ASAP."

She dropped her phone to the table and swung around in

her seat. She gave me a tight-lipped smile, the kind I'd seen her use with clients or business contacts on my behalf. After a moment, she stood and extended her perfectly French-manicured hand. "Natalie, darling. You're here. I wasn't expecting you."

I took her hand and shook it stiffly. Hugs and kisses were usually reserved for greater accomplishments like securing an energy drink endorsement or scoring a Time magazine cover. Me showing up after almost four months in drug rehab was not an occasion worthy enough for her to show affection. I was shocked I got the handshake. "I know this was unannounced," I said. "But I made plans at the last minute. Annie's funeral."

"Oh, yeah, I know I'm so sorry." She rubbed my shoulder and brushed a strand of her corporate blonde bob behind her ear. "I wish I could make it myself, but I sent them a card. They should get it this week."

"A card?"

"I didn't have time to call for flowers."

This was a classic Mom conversation. If crisis didn't happen when it was convenient, she just wouldn't deal with it. "You didn't have time to come see me in California, either."

She walked around the kitchen island to the sink and pulled a crystal glass from the cabinet. She checked it for watermarks before filling it under the tap. "Your father went. I figured if one of us visited, that would be okay."

"But weren't you at least curious about how I was? Weren't you even worried about me?"

"Of course, I was worried. Worried about your reputation now that the world thinks you're a drugged-out porn star." She nodded to a stack of files on top of the new stainless-steel refrigerator. "The legal end of that whole thing has been taking all my free time. But I must say I think I've handled the damage control pretty well. I've even been asked to consult others on media spin. Not bad for a former traveling cosmetics rep."

She gulped down her water then wiped the lipstick spear from the glass. Like that required more consideration than me standing in front of her. "I'm sorry," I said, not exactly sure why but because it felt like it was what was appropriate. "I just thought maybe you'd be concerned enough to come see me. That's all."

She laughed and shook her head. "Don't think just because you've screwed up your own life, everyone else has to screw up theirs to rush to your side. Especially when it involves cleaning up your mess..."

"I resent the way you've ignored me my whole life, and I feel like you're exploited me and my swim career."

There. It was out there.

It was not an accusation, but rather a declaration of statement. According to Tillie there was a difference. But by the look on my mom's face, she didn't seem to share the sentiment.

I watched her throat gulp down the last of her water before she placed the glass gently into the sink. "So that's what they're teaching you out there, blaming others for your failures? I knew sending you there was ridiculous, but your father insisted that this place was new age."

"If you thought it was ridiculous, why did you let me go?"

"It got you out of the way of that pervert you were sleeping with."

"I think it was more getting me out of YOUR way."

"You little selfish bitch." She walked around the island and stood in front of me, her steel grey eyes glaring at me with an anger I'd never seen before. "Your life is the mess it is because of you. You. You had a nervous breakdown. You are a world-wide disgrace. You said 'yes' when someone offered you a joint and you put yourself in the situation to be taken advantage of. Don't expect just because your life has gone to hell, you can take others down with you. And you damn well don't need to aggravate Annie and her family any more than you already have. It was good that you were gone."

I heard the front door close and footsteps pad through the foyer. When I turned, Mitch was standing in the doorway. I cringed when I saw his shoes were still on, making puddles with snow stuck to his Nike Airs. "Hey, excuse me for barging in, but there's a taxi waiting outside. Was I interrupting something?"

"It's okay," I said quickly. "Mitch, this is my mother, Nancy Collins."

"I know," he said, offering his hand. "From the intervention."

She eyed Mitch and folded her arms in front of her. "You go everywhere with her?"

"No, I'm just here for support. As a friend."

The corner of her mouth turned up, in what I could only describe as a sneer. "Right, a friend. I'm sure that's all it is."

Mitch looked at me, and I stared at the floor. Mom feared public embarrassment, but somehow, she was never opposed to making a scene herself. I could tell by the way she tapped her foot that a big one was painfully eminent.

"So where are you two staying? In a hotel together?"

"Are you kidding?" I stammered. "You think I'm sleeping with him? Mom, he works for The Dunes. He's doing me a favor by being with me."

"Yeah, just like Racer did you a favor." She grabbed her coat from the chair and pulled it on. "I have to get to the airport, and don't suppose that just because I'm gone, you can shack up here." She snagged the key from my hand and grabbed her luggage from the floor before heading toward the foyer.

I watched her maneuver outside with her bags, and I realized that was how I remembered my mother, even as a small child. Her back to me, always with one foot out the door. So many times I'd have things to say or questions to ask, that she'd never have time for, or I could never get out fast enough to interest her. In almost nineteen years, that never changed. I would be stupid to think I could change it now.

But at least now I had the balls to try.

"Mom, wait."

The screen door hit her in the back, and she lifted her eyes to mine. I gulped. I didn't think she'd actually stop.

"Look, I'm not proud of the things I've done, and I realize that I'm an adult now. I may have gone down the wrong road, and I take the blame for that. But as my mother, you could have tried to keep me from going down that road it in the first place."

The words spewed from my mouth so easily, it was almost like I'd rehearsed them. Even my voice was stronger than usual. I realized I liked it. *Assertive.* Calling it how I saw it. A trait of my mother's that suddenly I realized I didn't mind having. And just like that, I wasn't angry at her anymore. "Go catch your plane," I said. "I'm just going to grab my stuff and be on my way."

When the door closed behind her, I just stood there waiting for something to happen. Like in a movie when the music came up or some stupid montage of scenes of my childhood conveying one act ending and another ready to begin. When I heaved a deep breath, I felt a hand slip over my shoulder. "You okay?" Mitch asked.

"Yeah," I said with confidence. "I feel pretty good."

"I know it's hard to face your demons like that. If it's any consolation, I think you did a great job."

I went to the window and watched her pull away. The taxi lumbered down the slushy road, disappearing around the corner in a cloud of exhaust. "It's like Tillie says, you can't change people, but you can change how you react to people. It makes sense."

"You want me to help you pack?"

I let the curtain fall back and turned around to face him. "We can do that later. I want to make one more stop before the funeral."

He smiled down at me. "Okay, where?"

I slipped the keys from his hand and held open the door. "How about you let me drive. See if I have it in me."

It impressed me he didn't tell me no. I wasn't even sure I was trustworthy yet behind the wheel.

———

A journey to hit the fastest burger drive-thru ended up being a half-assed tour of the Greater Buffalo Area. The Bills Stadium, Lake Erie. I even drove him by my old high school and the YMCA where Annie and I swam most nights. Mitch told me it was all very "full circle." To come back home with a clear head, make peace with my past. Honestly, I wasn't much interested in any kind of future at the moment that didn't involve Annie. Yet for some reason, I found myself with a death grip around the steering wheel, waiting to make a left hand turn into the hellscape that was Happy Acres Mobile Home Park.

I kept the car in the middle of the road avoiding the potholes, the knocked over garbage cans and the random skinny dogs milling about them looking for a meal. Driveways looked like junkyard lots with scrap metal piles and rusty old cars. Some were jacked up with no tires and piles of trash bags stacked in between them. The mounds of dirty snow didn't help the whole scene much. It looked like an abandoned slum after an apocalypse.

"Is this place somewhere we should be?" Mitch asked.

I wasn't sure if he meant if I intended to drive us here or if it was safe that we were. "Don't worry." I assured him. "We won't be here long."

We pulled up to a driveway of a multi-colored trailer with rotted front steps and a front door that hung off one hinge. The window immediately to the right of it was boarded up, the same way it was since someone put a hammer through it when the Sabers lost in triple overtime.

"Natalie, who lives here?" Mitch asked.

"Hard to say," I said, honestly. "Depends on the day, I guess."

I suddenly realized what this might have looked like to him. Me falling back into my old ways. Coming to the shit part of town to score some dope. "Mitch, I just gotta talk to someone."

"Listen, Natalie..."

"That's all it is. I promise." When he looked at me with those wide brown eyes, all I knew was how important it was that he absolutely believed what I'd just said. That I wasn't trying to deceive or manipulate. I threw the car in park and killed the engine.

"Natalie, I get what you're after here, but I'm telling you now this isn't the best idea. I'm not even sure you're allowed in there. Tillie told me he's on house arrest and there's a restraining order."

"I'll be fine."

"Maybe later. In a few months okay, but right now, you don't know what you're walking into."

"Oh, I know exactly what I'm walking into. It's just a matter of me handling it right." In all honesty, I was surprised I even got this far. In my head this was more of a drive-by, hurl-a-good "fuck   you"-out-the-window-before-turning-back-onto-the-highway type situation. But somehow, I had the guts to pull into this place. And here I was ready for confrontation. It's what Doctor Teeth back at The Dunes would call "closure."

I wanted to close my fist and pummel Racer's face.

Mitch just sat there clean shaven and still tanned from the perpetual California sun. He looked so out of place. A good guy who now scanned the street like a neighborhood watch. "You know I'm not supposed to let you go in there by yourself, right? I'm your escort for a reason."

I could tell as he looked me over he was deciding if he could trust me. I couldn't blame him. It's not like I had a great track record. "Then come in with me but I am telling you now, I'm going in there. It's something I just have to do."

"You know you're not gonna get the answers that you want, right?"

I shrugged. "That might be true, but that doesn't mean I don't deserve to ask the questions."

"Fair enough. I just don't want you to be disappointed."

"I'd be disappointed if I didn't do this." I opened the car door. Mitch just sat there, I guess waiting for me to change my mind. "I don't have anything to hide," I assured him. "If you want to follow me..."

"I'll hang back for now," he said. "But know I'm right here."

I looked out the windshield at the snow-covered driveway. Not really a driveway, just an area where previous cars had packed down the snow. Of course, nobody around here would bother to shovel, so the only path to the door was made the same way as the driveway, the traffic of Racer's visitors. I heaved a breath to rally myself and stepped out of the car.

Overflowing garbage bags lined the front stoop, reminding me that back in the day, the only person who ever bothered to take out the garbage was me. I shuddered to think what the inside looked like. I was reminded of the times we used the dirty cat box as an ashtray and when we stepped over the remnants of an overflowed toilet for a week.

"You get five minutes," Mitch called from behind me. When I turned, I saw him leaning against the car like a tough guy with his arms folded. "Five," he repeated. "That's all."

"Got it."

Carefully I scaled the crooked steps, half-expecting them to give out under my weight, but they held. I took it as a sign that the mission should not be aborted. I placed my hand over the knob and gave a good shove.

The smell hit me first. Like if I wasn't sure-footed, the sheer power of the stench would have knocked me to the floor. A mixture of sweat, rotting food and a forever backed up septic tank made worse by the fact the place was at least 80 degrees. Sure enough, to my left, propped up on the broken kitchen linoleum was the space heater cranked up to 'high.'

The rest of the place looked like it awaited an insurance claims adjuster. Garbage overflowing, old pizza and take out boxes lining the counters. I turned to the right where the living room was. Really just a long narrow space with stained carpeting, a table and a few chairs and old ripped bed sheets tacked over the windows. I took a few steps into the room and stopped when I'd reached my destination.

There he was, sprawled out on the sagging three-legged couch in a pair of ratty old boxers and his brown terrycloth robe hanging open. He was passed out, of course. Not like anyone would willingly fall asleep with a full box of Captain Crunch spilled all over him and an open jug of milk resting against his hip. Slowly I padded over, kind of wanting him to wake up but also hoping he didn't, so I could really look at him and in my mind have the conversation I knew I probably wouldn't have the guts or the chance to have if he was awake.

He looked the same for the most part. The same long, dark greasy hair that stuck to his equally greasy beard. The same pizza face complexion of a 15-year-old kid with acne, and not the forty-year-old man he was. His mouth hung open as he snored loudly, giving me a good glimpse of his piss yellow teeth.

So was this it? My big redeeming moment? I imagined a movie scene with background music and me in a spotlight, unleashing all the shit I'd rehearsed in my head the past few months since I'd found out all the ways he'd fucked me. Literally and figuratively. But now, with my clear head and my tired heart, all I thought to say was "I'm sorry."

So maybe this was a monologue, where the importance was only felt by me who would deliver it. I was sorry. Sorry, for the choices I'd made, the people I'd wronged, the ways I'd disrespected myself. Sorry I couldn't turn back time. Sorry about how I'd dealt with my parents, my coach and my swimming career. Sorry this guy got the best of me and Annie was not here to see me attempt to right my wrongs.

He groaned and shifted on the dirty cushions, and I felt my heart pound in my chest. I wondered what he would think when he opened his eyes and saw me standing there. Would he care? Hell, would he even recognize me? Back at the Dunes, I had speeches. Some mean, some angry. Some punctuated by my teen girl tears with the general theme of "how could you?"

For whatever reason, my parting shot was simply picking up the milk cap from the floor and screwing it back on the milk jug before putting it back into the refrigerator. I figured the good deed would really solidify me as the bigger person. But when I opened the refrigerator door, I didn't realize the bigger showdown was actually now right in front of me.

There behind the expired orange juice and the plastic container of green God-knows-what was a baggie of white-grey powder. It just sat there, secured tightly in a double knot. I took a long blink, licked my lips and felt my heart skip in my chest. I recognized this as my default reaction. Score! Not too long ago, I would have taken that bag and bolted out the door or just sat down on the dirty linoleum and cut a few lines. Hell, I could see a razor blade and a rolled-up dollar bill sitting conveniently next to me on the windowsill. It was so fucked up how a few seconds alone with that stuff could totally derail the last four months of my life. There it was. Self-destruction nestled in a two-ounce baggie.

But this was a new day! A whole new game! Exactly what this competitor trained for!

Maybe.

If I wanted to, I could feel so much better. But then, so much worse. I looked back over at Racer still snoring away. Would it be worth it? My sweaty hand detached itself from the refrigerator handle and wrapped itself around the bundle. It was lighter than I expected. I felt the grainy texture of it, pressed my fingers against the plastic. Imagined its bitter smell. I studied it. Considered it.

And then, like a switch that flipped in my brain, I stabbed my fingertip through the baggie and dropped it into the kitchen sink. There under the broken faucet I dumped out the powder, letting it spill over the stack of dirty silverware and cracked cereal bowls. It slipped through the tiny holes of the drain like sand through a sieve. Little by little. The clump became a trail became a spec and then, gone.

I felt my lips pull into a smile and a chill rolled down my back. I realized, this was the confrontation that mattered. This was exactly what I needed to say. To myself.

When I got back to the car, Mitch didn't ask questions and I didn't offer answers. It impressed me that he trusted me enough to sit in the car and wait. I also appreciated his smile though, and his observation when he put his seatbelt back on. "You look like you got somethings off your chest."

"Yeah, I did," I said, backing out and throwing the car in drive. "And I think I'm ready for a funeral."

NINETEEN

I'D NEVER BEEN to a funeral before, but even a newbie like myself would know that showing up late to one was the epitome of rudeness. When I was at my mom's, I stole a black dress and heels and got dressed in a Burger King bathroom down the road. It looked fine on the hanger, but in reality, it was tight and too short. Inappropriate and drafty. My hair remained in its uniform ponytail and makeup, I no longer owned, so there was no help there either. Also, I had no coat. Oh well. Hypothermia didn't sound so bad, relatively speaking.

I didn't come from a family who attended church much. We were more of the Easter/Christmas type Christians, and I use the vague description Christian, because I have no idea what kind. Mitch on the other hand was Catholic. Practicing and serious about it. He was also unhappy he wasn't wearing a suit. Personally, I thought he looked great in his jeans and my dad's navy sweater he threw on. I wondered if he was apologizing to Jesus when he dipped his finger into the Holy Water and made the sign of the cross on our way inside.

"What's that for?" I asked.

"Like a greeting," he whispered. "Think of it as taking your shoes off in God's house."

The place smelled like incense and flowers. The musty old church aroma that reminded you to be reverent. The priest stood on the altar steps in full regalia, droning on about God's Master Plan and the promise of Heaven. After he recited a poem, one of Annie's about rainbows and hope, he urged us all to pray. When he was done, Mitch took me by the arm. "Come on, Nat, we're late. Let's take a seat."

The door shut behind us with a thud. The priest stopped mid-sentence and every head swung around to my direction.

"Um, excuse me," I stammered. "I don't mean to interrupt. I just...."

Mrs. Madsen's head popped up in the front pew. It took a double take to realize it was her. The woman I saw only weeks ago barely resembled who I saw now. Her shoulders slumped, unfocused eyes, her face was drawn, and her hair was haphazardly pulled back in a lopsided barrette. "Natalie, oh my God, you're here!" she gasped.

She slipped past her husband and came down the aisle. When she barreled into me and held on tight, it felt nice. Sincere. I buried my face in her hair and closed my eyes, realizing like I had when she visited me in California the smell of her was both wonderful and heartbreaking. Totally Annie. I held her closer.

"Natalie is her best friend," she announced when she finally let go. "She flew in. All the way from California." She stared at me with red-veined eyes, her shaky hands cupping my cheeks. "Oh goodness, you're here. It's so wonderful that you're here."

Mr. Madsen rushed to his wife's side and gently rubbed her back. He was pale-faced and red-eyed himself. I didn't remember him being completely bald, but he was now. His blue veins bulged on his forehead. "Natalie, we were hoping you'd make it. You look great."

"Thanks," I said. "I'm glad I could make it. And this is Mitch. He escorted me..."

"I'm a friend." Mitch rested his hand on my shoulder and extended the other to Annie's dad. "I've heard so many wonderful things about you and your family. Natalie loves all of you very much."

The words sounded so sincere from his mouth. I wondered if I had said them myself, if the room would have laughed in my face.

Mrs. Madsen led me to the front of the church. The rest of the mourners just sat there and stared. I was flattered she'd want me to sit with her family, but instead of the pew, she led me up to the pulpit. "I want you to give the eulogy...I want you to tell everyone how much you loved her."

"Honey...." Mr. Madsen mumbled. "Maybe Natalie would just like to sit down.

"Annie loved Natalie. They've been best friends since pre-school. Best friends." It was like Mrs. Madsen was talking to everyone and no one at the same time. With an unfocused gaze, she turned toward the congregation. "Didn't Annie love Natalie, Frank?"

Mr. Madsen shook his head, like he was having a hard time following his wife's logic. "Yes, dear. Yes, she did."

"And we love you like a daughter, Natalie." She dragged a Kleenex under her red nose. "Please. Tell us."

Mr. Madsen stood beside his wife and gave a little nod. Maybe he was a little nervous about it. After all, the last time he saw me, I was standing next to a limousine stoned with a can of spray paint in my hand. But I could tell he wanted it for his wife. Normally, this woman was a rock. Irrationality and sadness were traits I attributed to my family. She stood there in her frumpy black dress, tendrils stuck to her tears, and I melted inside. I couldn't say no.

I wouldn't.

The priest stepped aside, and I climbed the steps to the pulpit. My heals echoed against the stone and my heart pounded in my chest. Someone cleared their throat and another sneezed. I took a long blink and gulped before I faced the crowd.

And suddenly there I was, standing above the sea of blank-faced, black-clothed people with a lump in my throat and a tremble I was sure Mitch could see from the back pew. All eyes fixed on me. People I had known my whole life. Our school principal, our bio teacher, our old swim coach, but also people from the swim community over the years. Coaches, fellow competitors. One girl, a freestyle sprinter like Annie, who I was pretty sure made the trip from Uzbekistan smiled up at me. Press people and officials. Maybe a hundred people. Or more. They all looked at me now, with that wrinkled forehead look of confusion.

Cringy

After four months of being away from these people, I could understand the reaction. Kind of like watching a freak show at a carnival. An oddity that amused you, but you felt sorry for at the same time.

"Um...that poem..." I adjusted the microphone when it shrieked over the speaker. "The priest was reading is one of Annie's," I told them. "She loved to write. Poetry, short stories, songs. Annie could do anything. I always envied that about her. I envied a lot of things about her. Her favorite phrase was lemons to lemonade. She always saw the bright side of stuff. Never gave up on anything, or anyone."

I was babbling. Like whatever came into my head just fell out of my mouth. No one reacted. Mitch just sat there but when our eyes met, he smiled. And somehow I knew what to say.

"So, there's this painting I saw recently at an art show," I heard myself say. "Of this mythical guy and he's swimming in an ocean. Behind him the water is dark and scary and in front of him it's clear and bright and it leads to this beautiful horizon. It means, that if we just stay looking to the bright clear water, we will eventually get where we need to go. The swim is easier for some than others. It's kind of magical and mystifying. Annie would have loved that because she loved that kind of stuff.

Where was I going with this? In my head and heart, I knew how huge this moment was but how do you say that? How do I tell these people in a very real way I owed my life to Annie's death?

The Madsens both looked up at me from the front pew, clutching each other with expressions somewhere between despair and oblivion. In front of them was a casket. Annie's casket. White and adorned with the biggest, most beautiful pink and purple roses I had ever seen. I didn't want to look at it, but at the same time I couldn't look away.

"Annie didn't ask to get sick. She was sort of shoved into the dark water, and if getting better meant a full sprint freestyle to the clear water at the horizon, she would have beat all of us there..."

I saw a few smiles and heard a chuckle or two. Maybe this was somehow coherent. I sniffled and shifted my weight in my mom's oversized heels then kept going. "I swam with Annie since the beginning and I know she's gone, but I can't, and I won't see this as the end. I know when I get back in the pool, she'll be with me. I'll get her to the horizon. I've always been the distance swimmer. She'll always be my anchor."

When I saw more smiles and even a few approving nods, I realized that maybe I didn't totally embarrass myself after all. The organ playing the opening chords to Amazing Grace told me I was done. An arm--I'm still not sure who it belonged to--led me back down to the front pew next to Annie's mother. I don't remember the rest of the service.

Afterwards, people assembled to the front pew and offered hugs and handshakes. I tried my best to stay out of the way. When the last of the guests filed out to the courtyard, Mrs. Madsen led me by the hand to the side chapel next to the altar. There under a weeping statue of the Virgin Mary we knelt in front of the coffin.

"Your mom sent a beautiful card," Mrs. Madsen beamed, and your father is on vacation with his family..."

"Key West, I think," I supplied. "And I'm sorry they couldn't be here. I'm sorry for a lot of things."

Mrs. Madsen smiled in a far-away way that reminded me of Cassidy. As if the action was totally detached from the moment. "Pictures," she finally mumbled, and then said again louder, before taking me by the hand and leading me up to the small table of photo albums. "Look, Sweetheart, Annie and I picked out some beautiful pictures. We were going to have an open casket, but her hair is gone."

"Yeah, Annie was pretty manic about her hair. Anybody's hair. She cried when I dyed mine green."

Mrs. Madsen laughed. "Annie was very sensitive about other people."

"I'm going to miss her so much, Mrs. Madsen. Really."

"Annie loved you like a sister, and you're like a daughter to me. Please, Honey, do what you have to so you can get your life back."

I looked up at the vivid stained glass, now just mangles of color through my eyes. I said something to the effect of "I will, I promise." Meaningful in my head, but I'm sure unintelligible through my sobs. My body shook and sweat clung to me. I felt like a snake shedding my skin, or like something foreign inside me was trying to make an escape. Any questions or fears or insecurities I'd ever had in my whole life seemed to converge at that very instant.

"I won't disappoint us," I said with a steel in my voice even I could hear. "I promise, Mrs. Madsen, I won't."

"Annie and I are proud of you."

When the priest came over to offer his condolences, I reached inside my dress pocket. I pulled out the folded letters I'd been saving and slipped them in her coffin. I knew it was pointless. Totally symbolic. But in a weird way, I felt like Annie would be mad if I didn't. I knew when I was writing them I couldn't send them, but I always knew I'd get them to her somehow.

The rest of the day was a blur for me. The people, the places, all sort of a fever dream. Funny, but grief itself seemed like a drug. I felt clumsy and uncoordinated. By the time I was back at the airport, I was too drained to be freaked out by the flight.

I was officially out of tears.

Mitch took care of checking our bags and everything else. We didn't talk much, which was fine because I had pretty much said it all at the funeral. He did however offer his hand during take-off, and this time I was compelled to take it.

"Mitch, do you know where the swim coach's office is at Pepperdine?"

"Sure. Right down the hall from the football offices. A real nice one. It looks out over the pool." He looked at me and smiled. "The pool is huge. Outdoors, Olympic size with three or four bulk heads. I can take you there when we get back if you like."

"That sounds nice." I shifted in my seat to face him. "Do you think you have to be a student to use the pool? I mean, what if I wanted to train in it or something?"

"I don't know. Maybe that's something you could ask the coach."

"Maybe." I fingered the purple charm that dangled from my right wrist. "There's so much I want to do. I just hope I have it in me."

He pulled out a pad of paper, identical to the one he gave me on our first flight from Buffalo together. "Maybe you'd like to write some of this stuff down. Make a list of things so you don't forget."

"That's a good idea." I took the pencil from his hand and held the tip to the page.

EPILOGUE

September 12, Friday?
Mood: Pumped!

Dear Annie,

So, I know it's been a while since I've written in our journal, but it's just because I've been busy "living my best life" as they say. So much to tell!

I got into Pepperdine! Believe it or not, my GPA and exceptionally high SATs scores (I'm a good test taker. Who knew?) got me in. I'm taking classes in social work. I kinda like what Tillie does, and it would be cool if I could work at The Dunes when I graduate. Look at me, planning my future! Anyway, I'm starting off with a few classes and will be fully matriculated in January. They're letting me train with the swim team, too. Of course, if you were here, you'd be the team star, but for me, it's just cool to participate.

Everyone else is good, too. I'm still living with Staci at her Malibu beach house. Staci's parents continue to be the picture of support since she threatened a tell-all book. And now that Staci has made a name for herself in the pop art world, they're almost sincere about it. They also told me I could stay here rent free which is great because the West Coast is expensive, and I am East Coast broke, at least until my attorneys I can wrestle control of my finances back from Mommy and Daddy.

Not only is Staci's place free, but it's also close to Cassidy and Kevin's group home. They're doing well, too. They come over for dinner once a week or so and order pizza. Still no onions allowed in the house. Ari and Tia moved to Northern California to a group home where they can finish high school. We text and stuff, and they want to come visit Staci and me next month. Lance has another big art show then, so we thought we would have a little party to celebrate. A Dunes reunion of sorts. And something to look forward to.

Speaking of reunions, it was so nice that your parents came to visit over the summer. They took Staci and me out almost every night for a week, and few times others came along. Yes, by "others" I mean Mitch. Mitch and I are close, but I wouldn't say we are romantic. I do know he was the first one I called when I got into Pepperdine, and his is the shoulder I cry on when I'm missing you an extra lot. Those things probably fall under a "significant other," description, but we aren't defining. We're pretty inseparable, though. Who do you think shuttles me back and forth to campus?

I leave for swim team in a few minutes, and after that, it's to the library and then early to bed. My life is pretty good now. I like my routines and obligations. Bad days aren't so bad anymore, and I don't feel guilty as much when I enjoy the good ones. Maybe it's the lessons learned or the time passage, hell, even the California sunshine, but I'm all right.

I just wish you were here to see it. You'd love the California sun, too. It hasn't rained in weeks.

Yeah, I think I'm on my way to "good."

I'll let you know when I get there.

Love,
Natalie

ALSO BY DANIELLA BLUE

Notes From The Deep End

Treading Water

ABOUT THE AUTHOR

Danielle LaBue has been a writer her whole life, penning her first story in purple crayon at the age of seven. When not at her computer, Danielle can be found on the golf course, tennis court, ski slope and occasionally the bowling alley. She is considering training for a triathlon. Other favorite activities include obsessing over classic 80's TV and getting her nails done. She lives in western New York with her three boys and two Dachshunds. Purple is still her favorite color.

www.ingramcontent.com/pod-product-compliance
Lightning Source LLC
Chambersburg PA
CBHW050306110726
47899CB00007B/2128